"I HATE YOU," SHE SAID QUIETLY. . . .

But the words were more for herself than for him, a final warning, a useless reminder.

He stepped toward her, stopping only when his hips were pressed against hers, through her heavy coat. Slowly, carefully, he pried her fingers loose from the blankets and let them fall in a soft rumple of sound to their feet. One by one he unfastened the buttons of her coat, and when they were all unfastened, his hands slipped inside, curving around her waist, pulling her closer still.

He lowered his head, his lips nearly brushing hers. She couldn't see his eyes, only the soft lashes resting on his cheeks.

"Ah, love," he breathed, and she heard the softness of self-mockery tainting his words. "I hate you too."

AFTER THE FROST

"URGENT AND ABSORBING . . . Ardently executed, this is a story deftly told."
—*Publishers Weekly*

"AN EMOTIONAL, BITTERSWEET LOVE STORY THAT IS AS HEARTRENDING AS IT IS TOUCHING . . . an impressive romance filled with heart-stopping emotion and a richly moving love story."—*Romantic Times*

"HAVE THE TISSUES READY, THIS IS A TEAR-JERKER. The characters are vital people with compelling problems. Great reading!"—*Rendezvous*

A CANDLE IN THE DARK
Winner of the Romance Writers of America RITA Award for Best First Novel

"A ROMANCE IN EVERY SENSE OF THE WORD. Bravo Ms. Chance for bringing us what we want in such an unusual and distinctive way."
—*Affaire de Coeur*

"AN EMOTIONALLY INTENSE, ABSORBING STORY THAT IMMEDIATELY GRIPS THE READER. The passion and power of the story lie in her ability to craft believable, vulnerable characters whose pain and rebirth will capture your attention."
—*Romantic Times*

"As heartwarming as it is unconventional. It is my kind of book, and I loved it!"
—Karen Robards, author of *Hunter's Moon*

Also by Megan Chance

AFTER THE FROST
A CANDLE IN THE DARK
THE PORTRAIT

A Heart Divided

Megan Chance

A Dell Book

Published by
Dell Publishing
a division of
Bantam Doubleday Dell Publishing Group, Inc.
1540 Broadway
New York, New York 10036

The trademark Dell® is registered in the U.S. Patent and Trademark
Office.

ISBN: 0-440-22081-5

Printed in the United States of America

Published simultaneously in Canada

July 1996

10   9   8   7   6   5   4   3   2   1

RAD

To Tonia,
for Scott and Veronica and Shane—

From the first to the last, they are always
for you.

And after all, what is a lie? Tis but
The truth in masquerade.

—*Don Juan*
GEORGE GORDON, LORD BYRON

Prologue

July 1877—Chicago

IT WAS A DARK NIGHT. CONOR ROARKE STRODE quickly past the shadowed alleys, hearing the soft echo of his own footsteps on the wet cobblestones. It was always dark in this part of town, in the immigrant slums of Chicago, but the rain had made it especially so tonight, just as it had cleansed the air and washed away the scents of smoke and grease and sickness—at least for a little while. The stink would be back with the sun tomorrow, Conor knew, and his heart squeezed a little at the thought.

It was very late, and he was tired. He'd spent the day in Pinkerton's offices, being briefed for his next assignment—an outlaw gang in Kansas this time. It meant leaving again, and it seemed he'd just got back. But there were too few operatives in the Chicago office, and he was the only one available, so he was being sent west for a time, even though he needed—deserved—a rest.

Conor shoved his hands into his pockets and lifted

his face to the steady breeze blowing down the narrow alleyways. His house was just ahead, a cramped, two-story brick with crumbling cornices, and at the sight of it he felt a surge of energy. He quickened his step and grabbed onto the rusted metal railing, swinging up the two short steps to the door.

It wasn't much, but it was his. Someplace to come home to, even though he spent far too little time here. He had come to appreciate its shoddy meanness, but never more than in the last two days. He stepped into the small hallway, closed the door behind him, and glanced up the darkened stairs. A light angled across the floorboards, illuminating the shadows. He heard a cough.

With a smile, Conor hurried up the stairs. He passed the small room that served as his office and went straight to the bedroom. The door was cracked open, the light that streamed out was warm and welcoming.

He knocked lightly on the door and pushed it open without waiting for an answer, frowning again immediately when he saw the man in the bed—or, more accurately, the man who was struggling to get out of bed.

"I thought I heard you," the man said, peering toward the doorway. He pushed back the bedcovers. "Good, lad. You can help me up."

Conor sighed and stepped into the room. "You should be asleep," he said.

"I was sleeping. But now you're here, and—"

"Get back in bed." Conor went to the bed and pushed his adoptive father gently back against the pillows. "They don't need you at the rectory. I stopped by on my way here. Sister Theresa says you're to rest."

"Nonsense." The older man struggled upright, pushing aside the blankets to reveal the nightshirt tangled around his body. His wiry red hair stood out around his head in a vibrant halo, but his skin was pale, his voice gravelly and thick with congestion. "The good sister doesn't know how to write a sermon, me boy. It's early yet—"

Conor loosened the blanket from his father's hand and smoothed it back over his chest. "It isn't early, Father. It's late. It's nearly eleven o'clock. They'll understand when you aren't there tomorrow." He sighed, admiring Sean Roarke's stubbornness even as it exhausted him. "It won't be the first time the good people of Saint Mary's have had to listen to Father Callahan."

Sean made to get out of bed again. "But—"

"Sit back," Conor commanded. "I'm not letting you up until Dr. Johnson has a look at you. He said at least a week of bed rest."

"A week . . ." Sean's body shook as he was seized with a fresh bout of coughing.

Conor was at his side instantly. He wrapped his arm around his father's shoulders. Sean's frail, emaciated body shuddered. The old man's bones rattled beneath his thin skin. "Did Anna keep a poultice on you today?"

"She's a . . . she's a bit . . . scattered, that lassie," Sean said, breathing audibly. "Now, at the rectory—"

"They're all sick there," Conor said impatiently.

"That's why you're here, remember? Damn that girl anyway. She needs a good talking to."

Sean waved his hands, shaking his head as he coughed helplessly.

"All right, all right. I won't yell at her," Conor said. "I'm going downstairs. I left that poultice recipe from Sister Mary in the kitchen."

His father's protestations floated in the air as Conor hurried down the dark stairs, not bothering to take a lamp to illuminate the familiar way to the kitchen. The light from a nearby streetlamp gave an eerie yellow-white glow to the room, and Conor spotted the recipe on the table and lifted it to the window, squinting to make out the words. Onions. Lots of onions. He wrinkled his nose at the thought, then heard the echoes of his father's coughing ringing down the narrow hallway.

It wasn't getting better. It was getting worse, and for the hundredth time Conor cursed himself for staying away so long. He'd always tried to keep his father from overworking, but for the last two years Conor had been assigned to the Pennsylvania coalfields, and while he'd been toiling to bring the Molly Maguires to justice, the nuns in the rectory had cheerfully given in to Sean's reassurances and let his father work himself into the ground. But things were different now that Conor was home again. This time he would make sure his father had a caretaker before he went off on a new assignment. This time he wouldn't stay away so long. And in the few weeks he had before he left for Kansas, he would be too busy caring for his father to think any more of the

Molly Maguires . . . Or of the guilt that still haunted him.

Conor took a deep breath, but almost the same moment that he told himself not to think of her, the vision of her face came into his mind. Dark hair and dark eyes that were always laughing. . . .

She didn't laugh anymore, he reminded himself. At least not for him.

Conor pushed the vision roughly away. Sari was in the past, and he wanted to leave her there. She had shown where her loyalty lay, and it wasn't with him, and there was no point in thinking about her or the Molly Maguires again. It took too much concentration, when what he should be concentrating on was his father and making sure he lived through this damned illness. Sean Roarke was all Conor had left. All he'd ever had.

Conor unlatched the basement door and went down the rickety steps. Cold dampness seeped over him. Cockroaches scurried over the dirt floor, crunching beneath his boots, but Conor crossed without hesitation to the root bins and dug through the straw until he had a pile of onions. Gathering the sprouting vegetables into his hands, he turned and took his first step up the stairs.

The explosion deafened him. The house rocked, the stairs crumbled beneath his feet. He fell to his knees and something hit him between his shoulder blades—the kitchen collapsing into the basement. Conor rolled to the wall and huddled there, shielding his body against the side of the onion bin while dust and cracking wood flew up around him, and the acrid scent of burning wood and oil singed his nostrils, mixing with flakes of ash.

It was over almost as soon as it began. The sound of the explosion died away, leaving only the noises of collapsing brick and wood, the crackling of fire. Warily Conor lifted his head from his arms and squinted into the smoke and dust fogging the air. Timbers and beams hung crazily—creating eerie shadows in the dust. Dust that filled his nostrils and his lungs. He struggled for breath, for comprehension. Christ, what had happened?

Conor blinked, forcing himself to think. He looked up through the hole in the floor, and suddenly the answer came to him. A bomb, he thought dazedly. It was a bomb.

He stared, confused, at the splintered floor, at the flames licking the timbers. He could see the collapsed timbers of the second story, the falling bricks. Christ, someone had set a bomb in his house. Didn't they know his father was sick in bed? Didn't they know his father—

His father . . .

Conor froze.

His father was upstairs.

CHAPTER 1

November 1877—Beaver Creek, Colorado

SARILYN TRAVERS WAS PLANTING DAHLIAS when she first saw the rider. He was only a silhouette at first, a shadow against the brown and withered plains, but even then there was something about him she recognized, a presence that made her stiffen.

No, it wasn't him. It *couldn't* be him. Sari gripped the tuber in her hand convulsively; her mouth went dry. She knew that stance—the arrogant confidence of it.

It was Jamie.

No, not Jamie; the newspapers had called him Conor Roarke, she remembered—his real name. Jamie O'Brien had been another fiction, just like everything else about him.

Sari closed her eyes. *Please, let me be wrong,* she prayed silently. *Don't let it be him.* There was no reason for him to come here. He had what he wanted. What more could he take from her?

The rider came closer, closer. He was advancing

rapidly. In the rarefied atmosphere of the high altitude, he could be a mile away or only yards—it was so hard to tell. The leather duster flapped against his legs; he sat the horse with broad-shouldered ease. There was no denying it. Conor Roarke. Back from hell, or wherever it was he'd gone.

Hastily she looked around for her uncle, but Charles was in his own small soddy behind the main sodhouse, probably immersed in one of the Grange journals he read by the dozens. She doubted he even heard the approaching horse. Desperately she willed him to feel her discomfort, to come to her. She concentrated so intently, she half expected her uncle to come rushing around the corner. But there was nothing. Nothing but the sound of the wind picking up speed over the plains. Nothing but the steady approach of the rider.

As he came into the yard, Sari lurched to her feet and leaned against the sun-warmed grass bricks of the soddy. She watched as he led the horse to the fence near the well and looped the reins around a post. His face was darkened by the wide-brimmed hat he wore. The shadows from the windmill blades crossed over his body in the fading sunset. Sari barely breathed as he stood there, surveying the house as if he had all the confidence in the world, and all the time.

She walked around the corner.

He did nothing for a moment, though she sensed she'd surprised him. Then he walked toward her, his head down against the wind, hands fisted to protect them from the chill. The cold blew against her, molding her skirt to her legs, spinning tendrils of her hair from her chignon.

His step seemed eager. Sari frowned. He should be hesitating, wary, ready to beg for forgiveness. Dammit, he should be *crawling*.

He stepped up to her, and Sari backed away as he looked at her from the thin opening between his hat and collar.

"Hello, love."

A shiver of shock ran through her at the familiar greeting. The voice was the same. Thin, raspy, quiet. But it was different too. The Irish brogue was gone, another fiction he'd discarded when his "job" was done.

Fury washed over her with such virulence, she was afraid she'd faint. She dug her fingernails into the palm of her hand. "Get the hell off my land."

"Sari—" He moved toward her, pausing when Sari recoiled sharply. "Dammit, Sari—wait—"

"Do you think I'm joking?" she managed. "Do I have to get a rifle to prove I'm not?"

She saw his sudden, whip-taut tension, but before she had the chance to feel any satisfaction, he leaned back on his heels, pushing his hat back on his head to reveal his eyes, to show the slow, charming smile curving his full lips. "It's good to see you haven't lost your spirit."

It was all an act. A horrible one. All the more horrible because, for a split second, she had started to respond to that familiar charm. Sari stiffened. "Get off my land."

"Not just yet." The smile died, she saw a flicker

of anger cross his face. "I haven't come all this way just to turn around."

"Oh? Why have you come, then? You should know you're not welcome."

"We have some things to talk about."

"We do?"

"Yes."

She took two short steps to the front door and grasped the handle. "Talk to yourself."

She wasn't quick enough. He was beside her in a moment, slamming his gloved hand against the door so hard it thudded against the sod, sending dirt pebbling from the walls.

Sari turned back to him. "What do you want from me, Jamie? What more could you possibly want?"

"My name's Conor."

"Conor?" She wanted to spit in his face. The name was a reminder of everything about him she wanted to forget. "Oh yes, the notorious Conor Roarke. For now, anyway. Tomorrow it will be a different name." She locked her eyes with his, letting her hatred shine in her glare. "Won't it?"

His jaw tensed. "It might." He bit off the words. "It's my job, Sari."

She crossed her arms over her chest, lifting her chin in challenge. "Every day a different name, a different betrayal. Tell me, how do you sleep at night?"

His eyes were inscrutable. "I don't doubt I deserve some of your anger. But that's not why I'm here. I need to talk to you."

Sari eyed him warily. "Talk, then."

"Not like this." He motioned to the doorway. "Ask me in."

"To ask you in implies that you're welcome here. Nothing could be farther from the truth."

"I won't misinterpret the words, then," he said with a smile. Too charming. Too familiar. Sari opened the door and nodded for him to enter. He ducked his head under the low doorway, stopping just inside, and she saw his surprise in the second before he could hide it.

For a moment she saw the small house as he saw it, and she felt a wave of embarrassment. The sod was all they had for house building on these plains, and she had done the best she could to make the makeshift dwelling a home. The dirt walls were plastered with the pinkish clay from the creek beds, and pages from magazines and newspapers were pasted edge to edge across them in a dismal attempt at wallpaper. The pages curled against the damp of the sod bricks, mold seeped through the words. The ceiling above her loft bedroom was covered with cotton to keep the dirt from falling from the roof, and the well-made, simply decorated pine furniture she'd brought from Tamaqua crowded the room. But none of her efforts disguised what it was. A dirt house, a house for someone who could not afford wood on these plains.

He was as responsible for that as she was. The thought added fuel to her anger. "What is it you want, Co——?" She stopped midword, unable to bring herself to say his name, the hard syllables stuck in her throat.

He glanced up at the darkened loft. "Where's Charles?"

"Leave him out of this."

"For Christ's sake, Sari—"

"He's borne enough because of you. I won't have him bothered."

Conor's eyes flashed. "This is important."

"Another matter of life or death?" She jeered. "Another lie? Damn you, I won't have him involved. Not this time."

"This is not a game."

"Oh no, it's never a game with you, is it?" Sari fought to keep her voice even. "It's always important, it never matters who gets—"

"Sari?"

She whipped her head around at the sound of her uncle's voice. Charles stood in the doorway, his gray hair blowing in the wind as he looked at the two of them, one thick brow lifted in surprise.

"Charles," Conor said slowly, as if uncertain of his welcome. "It's good to see you."

"O'Brien?" Charles stepped into the soddy, closing the door firmly behind him. His voice was harsh with a German accent. "It is you?"

"It's not his name anymore," Sari said bitterly.

"No, no, of course." Charles frowned. He extended his hand. "Welcome, Conor Roarke. Or perhaps I should not be so quick to greet you, *ja*?"

Conor threw a glance to Sari. "It seems that's the way of it."

"You must carry some of the blame for that," Charles observed quietly.

Conor said nothing, but his eyes shuttered—the same closing off of emotion Sari had seen the last time they'd spoken to each other. Years ago, it seemed. She took a deep breath. "Perhaps it's time to tell us why you're here."

"We've heard reports you've been blackmarked, Sari." His reply was as blunt as her question.

Sari felt the blood drain from her face. Blackmarked. She'd heard her husband use the word before. It was a term Evan—and the other Molly Maguires—had whispered in low and secret voices. She hadn't heard it in a year, but she wasn't likely to forget it. It meant someone was targeted for assassination. But now Evan was dead, hanged with the eighteen other men the Pinkerton agency—and Conor Roarke—had brought to trial.

"Blackmarked by who?" she asked quietly, bitterly. "Who's left?"

"There are a few," Conor said. "Michael, for one."

Michael. Sari swallowed.

He must have seen her shock; he attacked that quickly. "You've talked to him?" Conor asked. "He's contacted you?"

She hesitated. She wanted to laugh in his face, to tell him that her brother would never allow her to be blackmarked, that it was absurd. But she wasn't so confident. "He doesn't have to contact me. He knows where I am," she lied. "And if he didn't, you've undoubtedly led him right to me."

"We had to take some chances." Conor said. "We decided you needed protection. Immediately."

"We? Who is 'we'? Pinkerton?" When he didn't deny the accusation, she went on. "Once again you've pushed in where you don't belong. I don't need your protection. I don't want it."

Charles frowned. "*Liebling* . . . Perhaps you should listen to him—"

Sari turned to her uncle. "Listen to him? This man's never once told the truth—at least not to me. Why should I listen to him? Why should I believe him?"

"You can't really think I want you in danger." Conor's voice was so quiet, it cut the soul from her anger.

She stared at him. What did she think, really? What did she know of this man? For the first time since he'd arrived, she looked at him. He was Jamie O'Brien and yet he wasn't. The same brown hair curled against his collar, he had the same blue eyes, and in the soft illumination of the oil lamp on the table, Sari was once again struck by how ordinary he looked. Attractive, yes—she knew the shoulders beneath that duster were broad and well defined, knew his strength and the smooth warmth of his skin. But he didn't stand out in a crowd, didn't over-whelm a woman with his looks. He was the perfect man for Pinkerton—quiet, unobtrusive, unnoticeable. A man who could be anyone.

Sari stiffened. "I'm not a fool. What is it you really want? You're not here because you care about me."

"That's where you're wrong, Sari," he said, and the way his tongue eased over her name, the smooth molasses feel of it, brought a lump to her throat. As

if he sensed it, he went on, saying it again, warmly.
"Sari, it's important to us—to me—to keep you
safe."

She crossed her arms over her chest. "I don't want
you here. If the sleepers decide to kill me, they will,
whether you guard me or not. You know that's
true."

"*Liebling . . .*" Charles pleaded.

Conor cleared his throat. "I'm sorry you're angry.
God knows you have reason to be. But I want you
to know . . . I'm sorry about Evan."

Another lie. She flinched. "I can't imagine why
you think I'd want to hear that from you."

He met her gaze evenly. "Nevertheless I *am* sorry.
I never meant to hurt you."

The sudden, blank admission startled her, even
though she knew it was a lie. Oh, he was good. So
good, he could lie and almost believe it himself.
Without thinking she stared at him, feeling the full
power of his apology. And for a moment his eyes
captivated her. If his hair had been a few shades
darker, his eyes would have been startling in con-
trast. As it was, they were just blue. Plain blue. Too
well, she could remember how they warmed to tenderness or sparked with teasing. She remembered
how they darkened with passion.

And she remembered how expressionless they'd
been at Evan's trial. Sari shivered, not wanting to
think about any of this and yet unable to stop. It
angered her that he could rile her so easily, that he
could make her feel anything at all. She looked up
at him, steeling herself to look into his eyes. Plain

blue, indeed. The bastard, he knew just what to do, how to read her. She threw a pleading glance at her uncle.

Charles nodded. "I think you should leave, Roarke," he said.

Conor frowned. "You'd send me to the prairies in this weather?"

Sari smiled coldly. "I'd send you to hell if I thought you would stay there."

Sari pulled the quilt up around her shoulders, staring at the sod-and-cotton ceiling, listening to the wind screaming around the sturdy little house. This late at night there was no light in the loft; she could barely make out the bags of dried corn and meal and sacks of flour that lined her walls. The sweet smell of dried cakes of fruit and preserves mixed with the earthy must of dirt and spicy sausage.

Normally the smell of the loft comforted her. Tonight it was almost suffocating. The sound of the wind wouldn't let her sleep. She kept thinking of him, wondering if he was out there.

It didn't matter, she told herself. She didn't care. He could freeze. He could turn into a statue of wind-whipped ice for all she cared.

But there it was. She did care, and that alone bothered her.

She had spent the last months trying to forget him. Trying to forget Jamie O'Brien and his brash self-confidence and too-honest eyes. And now here he was again. The same Jamie, yet . . . not the same. More a stranger than he should be. She didn't know this man without the Irish brogue. Jamie O'Brien had been always smiling, always talking. Jamie O'Brien she'd trusted, even when it was a mistake to do so. But this man. . . .

Conor Roarke wasn't the man she'd known, but he wasn't that different either. She knew his charm too well, knew how it sneaked up on a woman and worked its magic before she had a chance to combat it.

Sari twisted on the bed. The corn-husk mattress whispered beneath her weight, *He's a con man, a liar. You can't forget that.*

You must not forgive.

Sari felt the pain again, as real as a fist thudding into her abdomen. She had been in love with him once. She had betrayed her marriage vows and her husband and had succumbed to Jamie O'Brien's flirtatious ways and tender words. They had been a balm to her spirit after so many years of Evan's neglect, and she had basked in it, had imagined shining futures full of hope . . .

Then it had all come crashing around her.

At the heart of it she blamed her husband—and her brother. Both had been members of the Molly Maguires—a secret miner's group formed to fight for miners' rights. It had been innocent enough at first— a few meetings and loud talk, nothing more. But then their methods had grown increasingly violent, their fanaticism hard to ignore.

It was after they'd bombed the railroad that the Pinkerton agency came in. Jamie O'Brien had been their spy, and he had infiltrated the group, pretended to be one of them, and brought them down. When his investigation was over, nineteen men were dead—including her husband.

Sari stared up at the darkness, living the nightmare over again in her mind, seeing those nineteen men walk to the gallows.

It was why she couldn't let Conor stay. If he was telling the truth about her being blackmarked, she would have to face her brother and his friends alone. She had always expected retribution for her betrayal—and if God meant for her to die that way, at least it would be quick.

It wouldn't leave her lingering with a heart that beat but didn't feel, a slow anguish that haunted her days and nights. Unlike Conor Roarke, the Mollies would only take her life.

Not her soul.

Damn, it was cold.

Conor huddled against the trunk of the lone cottonwood, pulling up the soft leather of his collar and burying his face in it. His horse stood nearby, head lowered, but the gelding was sorry shelter from the merciless buffeting of the wind and the icy fingers that reached into every unprotected slit of his clothing.

Conor eyed the ground, wishing he could burrow into the soil like the prairie dogs whose homes dotted the fields. How warm it would be with the dirt and grass blocking the wind. Like the soddy.

He cursed, shoving his freezing hands beneath his armpits. Damn her for her stubborn anger. The last thing he'd expected—the *very* last thing—was to be shoved out into the prairie night like some wandering cow. Hell, even the cows had a barn to protect them against this incessant wind. He glanced over his shoulder, seeing the shadow of the soddy in the clear darkness, imagining its warmth.

He'd made a mess of things. He'd let his emotions get the better of him, which was exactly what William Pinkerton had told him he'd do—and the reason why they'd taken Conor off the Kansas case and ordered him on a forced sabbatical. Conor had thought it would be so easy. He had hoped to simply walk in and charm her again, ask her to take him back, to pretend he wanted to make up for the mess in Tamaqua. She was a woman, after all. And not just any woman either. She'd already shared his bed; they had passion as common ground. She was angry, yes, but anger was easy enough to melt, passion easy enough to incite.

Or so he'd thought.

Conor leaned his head back against the tree and stared up at the dark, starlit sky. He hated these plains, their cold loneliness, the way they made him feel small and unimportant. The way William Pinkerton's admonitions seemed to echo in the voice of the wind. *"Look at yourself, Conor. You're no good to us this way. You can't be objective. What happened to your father was a tragedy . . ."* A tragedy.

His father's face hovered before him. Conor's throat closed with tears. After nearly two months he still couldn't believe the man who had changed his life was dead.

It had been twenty-one years ago that Father Roarke had taken him in, but Conor remembered it clearly. He'd been ill then, existing on the streets as well as a twelve-year-old boy could exist, living from one day to the next. Simply surviving had taken all the energy he had.

But Sean Roarke had changed everything, had given Conor food, a home, safety. It was more than he had ever expected from life. He owed the man so much, and how had he repaid it?

Conor thought of the regret etched on William's face, the sad heaviness of his words. *"We've traced it back to the Mollies, Conor. The man who set the bomb—we believe it was Michael Doyle. I'm sorry, my boy. So sorry. . . ."* As if sorry had been enough. As if anything but Michael Doyle's death would ever be enough.

Conor remembered how Sari's brother had been the first to line up when violence had been ordered. Doyle had been the triggerman for the Mollies, and the most dangerous of them. But unlike the nineteen Mollies who paid for their crimes with their lives, Michael had escaped punishment. Sari had seen to that.

Conor clenched his jaw. He remembered the way Doyle's eyes had lit with blood lust and anticipation just before a hit. Had the man had that look in his eyes before he bombed Conor's house? Before he killed Sean Roarke?

Anger churned in Conor's gut, forcing the guilt he felt over using Sari again below the surface. She didn't matter. She'd made her choice long ago, and so had he. What mattered was paying Michael Doyle and the others back for what they'd done to his father.

And if that meant he had to lie to her again, well, he was good at lying. He'd spent two and a half years living another identity, living and socializing with people he knew he would eventually have to betray. He remembered Sari's words to him the last time he'd seen her, saw her accusing eyes, heard her voice. *"You're a liar and a killer, Jamie O'Brien. That's all you'll ever be."*

She was right. It was what he was. A Pinkerton agent. A man trained to lie and cheat and steal. *The end justifies the means.* William Pinkerton believed it. Conor himself had always believed it.

The end justifies the means. There was a price for everything. This time it would be Sari who paid it.

Conor stared out at the prairie, at the shadows of drifting clouds trailing across the darkened grass. He had come all this way because he needed something from her—she'd been right about that. He needed Michael, and he would not leave this place without him. Conor owed his father that much. Michael would find his way to his sister eventually. He always did.

Conor's gaze turned hard and cold as the icy air. It was why he'd lied to her about the blackmark. He'd wanted to scare her into letting him stay. He needed to be close enough to know if Michael contacted her by letter or messenger.

Or in person. Conor had to make her believe his threats, false as they were.

He got to his feet, slapping his freezing hands on his thighs, startling the gelding. There was a telegraph at Fort Morgan, and a man in Greeley he had to talk to.

He had no time to lose.

CHAPTER 2

SARI GLANCED THROUGH THE TINY WIN-
dow, searching for Charles's familiar form. It was
growing dark, but she could still see him beyond the
yard, fighting with a bale of barbed wire. She saw
his shoulders strain and knot with the effort, the sur-
ety of his gloved hands on the tearing fence. He
seemed so strong, so vibrant, but Sari knew it was
only an illusion, habits born more from routine than
from strength. Charles never complained, but she
worried about the toll settling this land was taking
on him. It was a hard life, and he'd already done his
time when he'd settled the farm in Pennsylvania.

She pushed away the worry, as she did every day,
and rose wearily from the table. Neither of them had
anyone else, and she'd been glad when Charles had
said he needed a new challenge and insisted on joining her. It had been a kind lie. He'd been worried
about her going off into the world alone, she knew,

especially now that he was almost the only family
she had left. Almost.

Her brother's face flashed through her mind, and
Sari squeezed her eyes tightly, willing it away. But
Michael's image was as hard to banish as the man
himself. She saw his burning, zealot eyes, heard his
impassioned pleas, and once again her words of a
year ago came back to haunt her. *"This is the last
thing I'll ever give you, Michael, do you hear me?
You're dead to me now."*

A pot boiled over on the stove. Sari pushed away
from the window restlessly and opened the door.

"Onkle!" The echo of her voice bounced over the
windy plains. *"Onkle!* Supper!"

By the time Charles trudged through the front
door, bringing with him a gust of cold evening air
and the smell of leather, a platter of ham and dump-
lings was steaming in the center of the table. Charles
paused in the doorway, closing his eyes and
breathing deeply.

"Ah, *Liebling."* He smiled. "This smells good."

He pulled off his coat, sinking into a chair at the
table. Sari joined him, cradling her chin in her hands.
Her worries seemed groundless when she saw him
this way. She focused on his strong, unshaking
hands, on the smooth confidence of his blunt fingers
as he ladled food onto his plate and broke open a
biscuit. There was no reason to worry about the Mollies, but if there was, she had every confidence that
between the two of them she and Charles could handle any threat.

Damn Roarke for giving her one more thing to worry about.

Charles glanced up. "His visit still bothers you?"

Sari started. "His visit? You—"

"You are too quiet," he explained. "And it does not take a seer to know what you are thinking about."

"He was here ages ago, *Onkle.*"

Charles tried to hide his smile. "Two days. Not long."

Sari watched as he smeared a biscuit with butter and took a bite. "It's already forgotten," she said irritably. "There's no reason to remember it."

"Hmmm." Charles nodded sagely. "You do not think he is right about the blackmark?"

"I don't know." Sari took a deep breath. "Maybe he is, though Michael loves—"

"Michael loves only himself."

Sari nodded distractedly. "Perhaps. But he wouldn't hurt me. I know it."

"There are his friends to worry about. They all believed you betrayed them to Roarke."

Sari sighed. "Yes. His friends."

"You think he is strong enough to stop them if they want vengeance?"

"I don't know."

"*Ja.*" Charles paused. He stabbed a dumpling with his fork and stared thoughtfully at it. "I know you do not like to hear this, *Liebling,* but perhaps it is a good thing Roarke came. He can protect us, and you need a man like him. A man to give you back your spirit. You are more like yourself when you speak of him."

"It's not spirit, *Onkle,* it's anger."

"It is *something.* I have been worried, watching you waste away, never smiling, never eating. It is not good. It is not the Sari I know."

Sari studied her hands. "Perhaps it's a better one."

"No." The quietness of his answer underlined his conviction. "I cannot believe that. But I do know God has reasons for everything. Even for Conor Roarke to return."

Sari met her uncle's eyes. "A reason? Of course there's a reason. He never did anything without one. But protecting me isn't it."

"Are you sure?" he asked slowly. "Perhaps he tells the truth. I can see he cares for you, *Liebling.* It is in his eyes."

Sari turned away. "Eyes lie, *Onkle,* just as he does. He's not here to protect me from the sleepers. He wants something else."

"What has he to gain by lying to you about this?" Charles pursed his lips in concern. "I, too, have worried about the sleepers. I would rest easier if you were protected."

She leaned across the table, covering his hand with her own. "I *am* protected, *Onkle.*"

"I am too old, Sari. I am no match for those men."

"Don't say that."

"I am an old man." He patted her hand, smiling wryly. "I wish it was not true, but it is."

"You're all I need." Sari smiled gently. "Believe me, *Onkle,* I—"

The sharp whinnying of a horse cut her words dead. Sari dropped her uncle's hand in confusion. "Is Marta in the barn?"

"*Ja.*" Charles frowned and turned to the window. "I have . . ." He stiffened. "There is something out there. Get—"

The window cracked. Charles jerked, stumbling backward onto the floor, stopping Sari's scream half in her throat.

"My God, *Onkle*!" Sari scrambled to him. "*Onkle*!"

"Douse the lamp!" Charles gasped. "Douse it!"

She reached for it, but in her haste it slipped between her fingers, crashing against the table, spreading oil, fire, and glass over the surface. Sari lunged at the flames, batting at them with her sleeve.

A bullet sang past her. Sari wrenched back, struggling to see through the darkness. But there was nothing. Only the pounding of hooves.

"Get down!" Charles yelled.

She threw herself to the floor beside her uncle.

"It is the Mollies," he whispered harshly. "Roarke was right."

"It could be anyone."

"I feel Michael's hand in this," Charles said.

"How can you?" Sari asked, but almost in answer she heard the murmured voices outside, the sound of nervous horses. Her uncle was right. This was like Michael. A surprise visit, shots in the dark. But it couldn't be him. It wouldn't be. Surely he wouldn't hurt his own sister. . . .

But she hadn't thought he would kill a man either, and she'd been wrong about that. So wrong.

Charles motioned toward the loft, his hand a shadow in the darkness.

"No," Sari whispered, understanding him. "I won't leave you."

"Go!" The word forced out in a breath. "You must hide. They want you, not me."

"I won't leave you—"

"Go!"

Sari recoiled, the desperate tone in her uncle's voice unfamiliar and frightening. He was right, she knew it and yet she couldn't move from this spot, couldn't leave him.

There were footsteps now, and she felt Charles's panic. She felt his push; her own feet seemed numb as she stumbled toward the ladder.

She pulled herself up without conscious will, scrambling toward the back corner of the loft, behind the sacks of flour. The sound of the front door wrenching open had Sari pulling aside the heavy bags, her fingernails tearing on the burlap as she squeezed between them.

Her heart was pounding in her chest. Sari curled into a ball, burying her head, willing the intruders downstairs to go away, to leave them in peace.

Below she heard muffled noises. Sari resisted the urge to pull away from the bags. She knew Michael's friends, knew their desperation. If it *was* them and they suspected she was in the soddy, they wouldn't rest until they found her.

All the horrible stories Evan had told her spun

through her mind, mixing with one another until they were a single blood-red haze of brutal memory. Beatings, murders, bombings. . . . She remembered her husband's laughing, almost maniacal, pleasure in relating the events, as if he knew her distaste and reveled in it.

Thumping, loud and urgent, vibrated up through the floor, the high tension of voices arguing. Then there was sudden, horrible silence. Fear made her mouth dry, her throat tight. Sari strained, trying so hard to listen, she heard the very particles of the air. Nothing. No movement, no sound except for her own harsh breathing.

She hadn't heard the door close, could she have missed it? Slowly Sari uncurled, horror and tension still throbbing in her ears. She should wait, they couldn't be gone so soon, but the thought of her uncle lying dead or wounded was too much for her to bear.

She pushed at the flour sack, dislodging it enough to wedge past. The floor squeaked beneath her, and Sari stopped, catching her breath as she waited for the inevitable shout of discovery. None came.

"They're gone, *Liebling.*" Her uncle's voice came to her in a cracked whisper, and all thoughts of self-preservation fled. She ran across the short loft, flung herself down the ladder.

Charles lay sprawled on the floor, a lump mottling the darkness. She heard his labored breathing, and Sari moved quickly toward him, stumbling over the furniture.

"*Onkle, Onkle,* are you all right?" She knelt be-

side him, pushing aside the shattered glass and juice
of a broken jar of pears. The spicy aroma from the
crushed fruit nearly nauseated her. *"Onkle,* please—"

"I am . . . fine." His voice was weak and strained.
He struggled to sit up, falling back helplessly.
"Fine."

"You aren't fine." Sari fought to keep the panic
from her words. "What did they do to you? Oh,
God—"

"Ahhh—" Charles rose, grasping her arm tightly.
"A . . . few . . . bruises," he said as they took a few
steps. Then he slumped into a chair, gasping. "It
wasn't Michael . . . but . . . I think . . . his friends."

Sari fumbled in the darkness, feeling for the base
of the lamp. Glass stuck to her hands, needled her
fingers as she swept the tabletop. "They hurt you,"
she said harshly.

"Don't light it." Charles's voice was suddenly
strong. "No light yet. Not until we are sure."

"Oh *Onkle.*" Sari dropped into the other chair.
"I'm sorry. I'm so sorry."

"Not . . . your . . . fault."

"Yes, it is," she said miserably. "It is. You know
it's me they want. I—I thought it would be safe
here."

Charles said nothing. Sari stared at the broken
window. The moonlight shone and then disappeared as clouds moved through it. Shards of glass
littered the sill, sparkling like gemstones. Cold
whistled through the cracks, easing with the
wind.

"I can't stay here with you," she said finally.

"They didn't find me tonight, but there's tomorrow and the next night. Eventually they will." She took a deep breath. "I won't be responsible for your death, *Onkle*."

"That is my . . . risk to take."

His labored breathing made her own chest ache. "No," she protested. "I can't let you do that— please, *Onkle*. I just can't."

"Only one . . . other thing to do," he wheezed.

"One other thing?" She knew the answer to her question before she asked, and a strange sense of inevitability swept her, along with a helplessness that frightened and saddened her. Her voice was a mere whisper of sound. "What other thing?"

Charles raised his head, and even though Sari couldn't see his eyes, she felt his gaze gripping her, squeezing her.

"You must ask him to stay, *Liebling*," he said slowly. "I cannot protect you. We need Conor Roarke here." He reached for her hand, tightened his warm fingers around her freezing ones. "We have no other choice."

The moonlight dappled his skin as he rode, its touch frigid as the night air. Conor rode leisurely, in spite of the cold. There was plenty of time to get to the soddy. Probably morning would be soon enough, though Sari's anger was preferable to spending another night in the freezing, dilapidated stage station.

There was no reason to hurry. The men he'd hired were good. They were well paid to follow Conor's orders to the letter. He wanted Sari and Charles frightened. Not hurt, just scared enough to welcome him back with open arms. Just enough so that he could ride in a hero.

Conor set his jaw, banishing his distaste at the whole idea of forcing Sari and her uncle to let him stay on the homestead. It was *necessary* to frighten them. *The end justifies the means.* There wasn't any other way Sari would permit his presence, even for a few days—a week at most. The last report on Michael had him heading west, and Conor would bet Sari was Doyle's destination.

Conor frowned. He would have to guard himself every moment. If she even suspected he was lying in wait for Michael, if she found out he'd set up the raid on the farm . . . He didn't want to think about what she would do or how she would feel. He told himself it didn't matter. If Sari got hurt, it was her own fault. Revenge came first. It had to come first.

The clouds passed over the moon, drenching him in instant darkness, and Conor narrowed his eyes, searching the dark horizon for the soddy's shadow. He was close, he knew it. He smelled the faint traces of smoke in the clear, freezing air. It was too late for welcoming lights. Hoping for a hot cup of coffee probably wasn't a good idea either.

He saw it suddenly, rising out of the darkness as the moon peeked through again, its light glancing across the grass bricks. Conor urged the horse to a trot. It was then he saw the damage to the window, the wooden door hanging crookedly on its hinge.

"Sari!" He called, spurring the horse, suddenly

panicked as he strained to see some movement in the darkness. Damn, he'd told those thugs to scare them, not damage their property. The men weren't supposed to do more than circle the farm and fire a few shots into the air. Fury and guilt swept through Conor, and he pushed it away. He'd talk to them about it later, when he had time—

He heard the crack of a bullet before he saw the gun. The gelding reared, its high-pitched whinny deafening, its forelegs pawing the air.

Conor hit the ground so hard, the breath was knocked from him. Dazedly, relying solely on instinct, he rolled, trying to dodge the dancing hooves of the gelding, frantically fumbling through the twisted folds of his duster for the Colt revolver strapped to his hip.

Conor grasped the gun, wresting it from the holster, pushing aside his coat. He rolled onto his stomach, inching backward and raising the pistol.

"Don't move."

In the same moment he heard the voice he saw the silhouette of boots and skirt. And he felt the long nose of a rifle pressing into his back.

Relief washed over him. "Sari—"

The rifle stabbed him. "I said don't move. Drop your gun."

Conor let the Colt drop. Without lessening the pressure on his back, she kicked the weapon out of reach.

"Sari—who is it?" Charles called from the doorway of the soddy. "What is going on?"

"Stay there, *Onkle*!" Sari answered.

"It's me, Conor Roarke!" Conor said, ignoring the sudden, quick pain of the pressing rifle. "Call her off, will you?"

"My God, Sari, it is Roarke!"

"I know who it is," she said calmly.

Conor heard the ice in her voice. It sent a chill over his skin.

"And he's finally where he belongs, crawling on his belly through the mud." She poked the rifle into his ribs. "See any other snakes down there, *love*?"

CHAPTER 3

"GODDAMMIT!" CONOR ROLLED FROM BE-
neath the rifle and scrambled to his feet. "What the
hell do you think you're doing? You could have
killed me!"

"I wasn't sure who it was," Sari returned. "And
I'm still not sure shooting you wouldn't be the best
idea."

He shoved the revolver back in its holster. "Then
do it now, goddammit." Conor's eyes glinted with
anger. "But I thought you were smarter than that.
I'm here to *protect* you, goddammit, not hurt you."

She regarded him stonily. "If it weren't for you, I
wouldn't be in danger."

"Sari?" Charles's gruff voice cut the darkness.
The old man sagged against the doorway, clutching
his stomach. The lamplight shone around him, lighting his thin gray hair and making him seem frailer
than ever.

Conor frowned. "What's wrong with him?"

"They hurt him," she said harshly, glaring.

"What do you mean?"

"What do you think?" She turned on her heel. "They came in, trying to find me, and they found him instead."

Conor strode toward the soddy, following Sari quickly as she slid Charles's arm over her shoulders and helped him from the doorway into the warmth of the little house.

Conor shut the door tightly behind them, ignoring Sari's frown. She helped her uncle into a chair, then she straightened, folding her arms over her chest. Conor took in her formidable stance calmly, noting the ragged patches on her faded skirt, the long rip in her coarse linen apron.

Fighting to keep his guilt under control, he said harshly, "I warned you."

Charles glanced up. He coughed, his thin shoulders convulsing. Sari knelt beside him immediately. "Are you all right?" She asked. "*Onkle—*"

The coughing eased, Charles slumped back in the chair, waving her away. His shrewd, pale eyes met Conor's. "Did you see them when you rode in, Roarke? Three men?"

Conor shook his head slowly. "No." He glanced away, focusing on the burning lamp on the table. "I saw no one."

"You see what I mean, then, Sari?" Charles insisted. "You are not safe."

"I'm not worried about my safety," she said. "It's you I'm concerned about."

Conor snorted. "There's no need to be a martyr, Sari. They'll hurt you, too."

She didn't look at him. "So what do you suggest I do? Hide forever?"

"Let me protect you, Sari," he said quietly. "It's why I'm here."

"Is it?" The cold bitterness in her voice sent chills over his skin. "Or is there another reason? Where did those men come from tonight?"

Conor kept his gaze steady. "What are you saying?"

"Only that this attack seems awfully well timed. It happened right after you left, and now here you are, on the heels of it."

"Sari," Charles gasped. "Think about what you are saying."

She threw her uncle a look Conor couldn't interpret. "Believe me, I know exactly what I'm saying."

Conor spoke carefully. "I had nothing to do with this."

"Of course not," Charles agreed, frowning at Sari. "Conor is not like Michael. He is not an evil man."

Evil. The word was unexpectedly brutal. There was too much at stake to let it bother him now. Conor forced a calm, reasonable tone into his voice. "Even if you don't believe me, Sari," he said. "Are you so certain it wasn't Michael's doing that you're willing to bet your life on it? Your uncle's life?"

They were the right words, he knew it instantly. She paled; her lips set tightly.

"Sari," he said, "I never took you for a fool."

"Then perhaps we both made errors in judgment," she said. "Because I never took you for a liar."

Her words cut straight to the bone; it was all Conor could do to keep from flinching at the pain he heard in them. *Remember,* he told himself. *Remember.*

"I know this is hard for you," he said slowly. "But I'm asking you to trust me."

She laughed shortly. "That is not a mistake I'll repeat twice."

The anger in her words was so intense, Conor had to restrain the urge to step back. Pinkerton had been right. There was too much between them. It was going to be next to impossible to fight her anger, to get her to trust him.

But he couldn't give up. The memory of Sean Roarke's bloody face filled Conor's mind.

"I have had enough of this," Charles said, rubbing his face with his hands. "Enough of both of you. I am making the decision, Sari. Roarke is staying. To protect you. To protect me, if he can. If Roarke can do that . . ." He smiled, a weak, tired smile. "Perhaps the two of you will learn to like each other again."

"You ask too much, *Onkle*," Sari said, her voice toneless. She turned her eyes to Conor—they were as expressionless as her voice. "Stay if you will, then, but I won't have you in my house." She lifted a wool blanket from a chair and dropped it into Conor's hands. "You can sleep in the barn. If the cows can stand you."

Conor bent beneath the low ceiling of the barn loft, shuffling through the hay and sweet-smelling alfalfa. He glanced at the tiny, barely inhabitable space and then looked over the side of the unsteady platform.

And onto the backs of two cows, four oxen, and two horses.

The animals shifted; their big, wet, snotty noses pushing through the hay in the feed bins; ugly, white-rimmed eyes rolling as one pushed too close to another. Their hooves clomped on the hard-packed earth. Low moos and nickering filled the silence.

Conor clutched the blanket Sari had given him more tightly against his chest. If the rest of the Chicago office could see him now, the jokes would never cease. Conor Roarke, one of the top Pinkerton agents, was living among cows. Ugly, stupid cows. God, he hated farming.

At least their bodies kept the damn place warm. It was a good thing, too, since there was no other source of heat in the makeshift sod barn. Conor set the blanket aside on the ground and glanced through the near darkness before he pulled the saddlebags off his shoulder. He wouldn't be staying here long, anyway. With any luck Michael would show up soon, and Conor could get back to Chicago, away from these empty plains that made him feel lost and alone.

He swallowed, pushing aside the maudlin thought

as he knelt on a pile of straw. He was tired. Too tired to unpack. His fingers stumbled over the leather ties of his bags as he unknotted them and rummaged through the contents. Luckily he traveled light—always. A man's wardrobe revealed a great deal about him, and because of that, Conor kept little more than two changes of clothing, both unexceptional. If anyone went through his saddlebags, they would find his shaving kit, another pair of boots, spare bullets, food, and a water bag. All calculated to tell an average man nothing about the owner.

Conor's lips tightened as he felt the small bulge in an inside pocket. There was only one thing he carried that was strictly against Pinkerton's best advice. A small photograph of Sean Roarke. It was almost the only thing he owned to remind him of his father, something even the threat of death couldn't have forced him to sacrifice.

He lifted it out, opening the worn leather case to look at it. The photograph had been taken four years ago, before Conor was assigned to the jobs that took him away from Chicago for months on end. In the photograph Sean's green-blue eyes looked pale—almost white—but they twinkled at some private joke that didn't touch his lips. His thinning, flyaway red hair stood out from his skull as though it, too, were laughing.

Conor's throat tightened; he closed his eyes briefly against the pain squeezing his heart, squeezing him. He could almost hear his father's voice, admonishing him for his curses. *"Swearing allows the devil in, lad, don't forget that. Satan looks for signs of weak-*

ness." And Conor remembered how he'd filled the hallways of the rectory with his curses—as if to prove to his father that he was brave enough to take on the devil himself.

Well, he had, in a way, and tempting Satan had left him with nothing but a burning desire to wipe the earth clean of the Molly Maguires and everything they stood for. Once, he'd understood their motives. Once, he'd felt sympathy for their cause. No more. They'd managed to erase any lingering understanding. There was nothing but hatred left inside him now.

Conor let the anger boil, closing the small portfolio to hide the suddenly condemning eyes of his father. Sean Roarke would never approve of what he was doing. He'd said more than once that revenge was a petty emotion, that it was the shortest road to hell. But Conor was sure his father had never felt it for himself. How could Sean know the way the need for vengeance ate up everything inside until there was nothing left to do but go after it?

Conor shoved the portrait back into his saddlebags and pushed them against the wall. He had no time for those memories. There were other things to think about now. Plans to make. Revenge took all his concentration.

He sat back against the damp sod, resting his arms on his knees, leaning his head back to stare at the makeshift grass ceiling. He thought about Sari. The evening had not gone anything like he'd planned.

The fact was that he had underestimated her. His memories of Sari in Tamaqua were colored by the reasons he'd been there to begin with. It had been different then. He'd been sent to infiltrate, to become one of them, to form an alliance. Sari had been that alliance. She'd been lonely and unhappy, but when he'd noticed how easily she laughed and talked with him . . . Well, it had been easy to start a friendship. To start more than that.

In spite of that he had underestimated her. Underestimated and forgotten.

The words she'd thrown at him—*"I never took you for a liar"*—stayed with him. It was disturbing, how much they stung. Disturbing that when he looked at her, his actions seemed irritatingly profane.

Conor swore to himself and sat back on his heels. She had been one of them in the end, and he couldn't forget that. At the time, he'd thought she was innocent. He remembered how she'd talked about Michael in Tamaqua. The way she'd spat his name and hated his politics and his friends. She'd talked as if she didn't know Michael's true role with the Mollies—he was their best executioner. But now he wondered—again—if it had all been an act. Was she as good a liar as he was? And if she hadn't been lying, had she realized, when she warned her brother away, that Michael was the man assigned to kill her lover?

Undoubtedly she had. Conor closed his eyes. He suspected she had guessed he was the traitor long before the others did. It had been his biggest miscalculation. He'd thought she was loyal to him. He'd thought—he would have sworn—she was in love with him.

Conor snorted softly. What did he know of love anyway? Except for his father, he had no experience with it.

But he knew about wooing. He knew how to kiss a woman and seduce her with words. He knew the touches that made a body burn. The touches that had made Sari burn. And if he had to utilize them again, so be it. . . .

Conor smiled. He would find Michael Doyle this time. He would bring him to justice—*his* justice. No matter what it took.

CHAPTER 4

IT WAS DINNERTIME, AND SARI HUMMED AS she took the lid off the pot of boiling potatoes and sniffed their earthy, mealy scent. They were almost ready. Sari lifted the bowl beside her and quickly mixed the crumbly dough of the noodlelike rivels, dropping the tiny pellets into the boiling water to cook along with the potatoes.

Wiping her floury fingers on her apron, Sari glanced at her uncle, huddled in a chair by the bookshelves. He was sound asleep, the knitted afghan falling from around his shoulders, his head angled back against the seat. His soft snores filled the soddy, and Sari felt a quick wave of relief. Sleep was what he needed now, and she hoped he was having pleasant dreams.

Which was more than she'd had herself. Sari frowned, remembering last night. Remembering Conor's easy assumption that he belonged here.

Irritation stabbed her, along with a twinge of fear.

She had spent the morning trying to reconcile herself to the fact that he was staying, but she still didn't believe that protecting her was the only reason he was in Beaver Creek. He had walked away from her more than a year ago, had disappeared without a word. She had been convinced then that he would come back, sure that he was just hiding from the assassins. After all, she had been the one who told him the other Mollies suspected him of betrayal. *She* had been the one to warn him.

Sari clenched the fabric of her apron, letting anger bury the anguish that was as real today as it had ever been. Had she known then what she knew now, she would have let Michael and his men have Conor Roarke.

But she hadn't known. Instead she'd waited for him, anxiously checking the mails, living for a message that never came. It wasn't until just before Evan was arrested that she knew for certain what she had suspected for some time. Jamie O'Brien *was* the traitor. It was then she realized that he was never coming back.

Sari took a deep breath. There was no reason to think he was any different now. But at least Conor had taught her something. Now she expected treachery. He hadn't changed, she knew. He was already lying to her. Why would he want to protect her from the Mollies? He'd shown no such compulsion back in Pennsylvania, when she'd been in much greater danger. Her betrayal of Evan was common knowledge. There was more reason to kill her then, and more opportunity. Perhaps Conor was here to make sure they *did* get her. Sari smiled thinly at the thought. Now, *that* made sense.

She glanced out the window, catching sight of him as he crossed the yard to the house. The cotton shirt he wore stretched across his shoulders, the tails of a dark bandanna flapped against his throat. He wore no hat and no coat, though she knew the day was cold, and the wind fluttered back his brown hair.

The sight sent a wave through her of almost forgotten longing. She spun away quickly, suppressing it. Her hands shook as she lifted the lid on the pot of soup again, and clanked it back down when the steam scalded her face.

The leather hinges of the door creaked open; cold air cut the warmth of the room as Conor walked in.

Sari turned, catching his glance. The unexpected touch of his blue eyes threw her. But only for a moment. "You missed breakfast," she said coldly. "I was hoping you planned to keep your own company."

Conor lifted a brow. "Sorry to disappoint you. I think it's best if I stay around the house as much as possible."

She pulled open the iron door of the stove and took a handful of flat, dry buffalo chips from the fuelbox beside it. "How conscientious of you." She threw them in and wiped her hands on her apron. "What kept you from your duties this morning?"

"Sleep." Conor smiled as Charles yawned and stretched awake. "I'm not used to farmers' hours, I'm afraid."

"You will learn." Charles's voice was hoarse, but

amusement touched it even just out of sleep. "It will not take long, I promise you. A few mornings of listening to the cows . . ." He shrugged, smiling. "We will make a farmer of you yet."

"No threats, please," Conor said. He went to the stove and grabbed the pot of coffee simmering there, bending close to Sari. She smelled the astringent scent of bay rum, the faint, musty odor of straw. It was absurd, how seductive the scents seemed, how alluring.

Sari backed into the corner, trying not to touch him as he took two cups from the shelf and poured coffee into each. He crossed the room, handing a cup to Charles before he sat at the kitchen table.

Nervously Sari grabbed thick pottery bowls from the shelf above the stove and piled crumbly corn bread onto a plate. Her hands trembled as she ladled soup into the bowls, the pottery clattered as she set them on the table. Soup sloshed onto the stained oilcloth. She glanced carefully at Conor. "What's Pinkerton's opinion on how long you'll be here? Will this go on as long as your last investigation did? Do I have to house you for two years?"

That wounded him, she noted with satisfaction. His eyes hardened, she caught the tensing of his jaw.

"I'm here to do a job, Sari," he said quietly, his raspy voice grating against her nerves. "When it's over, I'll leave."

"Just like last time," she said bitterly. "And in the meantime?"

"In the meantime we'll both have to make the best of things."

She lifted her brows in mock admiration. "How noble you are for making such a sacrifice. It's horrible that you had to put your own life aside to travel here—to protect *me*, no less. How painful that must be."

"Sari—" Charles warned.

Sari ignored him. "Or wait—I forget. How could there be pain when you never cared in the first place?"

Conor looked away. "You don't know anything about it."

"Obviously."

"I can't help the past. It was a job—"

"And I was part of it. I know. I was there." She turned to her uncle, who seemed to sink into the chair under the heat of her stare. "Tell him, *Onkle*, tell him what happened when he left." When Charles didn't respond, she swiveled to Conor. "Tell him how they all looked at me as if they couldn't bear the sight of me. As if I were responsible."

Conor straightened. "I never meant for that to happen."

"Didn't you?" She laughed shortly. "What did you think would happen? Did you expect them to excuse me? They *knew*. They knew about us, they suspected I'd given you information. Evan knew I'd warned you."

"I couldn't help that," Conor said quietly, just as emotionless as he'd been since he'd walked into the soddy this morning. "Life isn't fair, Sari."

"Fair? Is that what you call it? Well, then, it doesn't seem *fair* to me, Jamie—" she caught her breath as the name slipped out. "It doesn't seem fair that you caused it all, and yet I don't see any guilt in your eyes. There's nothing for me to do except think that you don't feel any. Tell me I'm wrong. Tell me you feel guilty for everything you did."

He hesitated, and when he looked away again, Sari felt a sinking inside that had nothing to do with anger. "You don't," she whispered. "You don't feel guilty at all, do you?"

She heard the barest pause before he answered. "I'm sorry for what I put you through," he said, his voice so soft, she had to strain to hear it. "But guilt is a luxury I can't afford right now."

Sari squeezed her eyes tight, willing him away. She couldn't stand this, not the torture of seeing him every day nor the constant reminder of her own guilt and humiliation. "How wonderful for you that you can dismiss it so easily."

"You're wrong," he said softly, dangerously so. "You're wrong. I don't dismiss it. But I can't think about it. The sleepers could be outside right now, watching the house, waiting for you to step outside. Waiting for me. I can't afford distractions."

She stared at him—at the tightness of his face, the hardness of his eyes. He was a stranger this way, a man she didn't understand, a man she didn't know. And she felt the aura of danger hovering around him. It seemed to fill the air between them.

Charles cleared his throat, the chair creaked as he rose. He walked slowly to the table, rubbing the back of his neck. "The two of you are enough to make me lose my appetite," he said lightly. "Come, Roarke, sit down. Let us eat, and then you can come with me to the fields. I would like your opinion on something."

Conor nodded, not taking his eyes off Sari, who stood motionless by the stove. "Can I see the soddy from there?" he asked.

"*Ja.*" Charles nodded. "It is not far. Sari will be safe enough."

Conor hesitated. "I'm not sure how much I can help you," he said finally, moving to take his place at the table. He sat heavily in the chair, picking up the spoon and drawing it through the soup. The earthy, buttery smell of potatoes wafted hot and aromatic in the air, but his appetite was gone.

He barely heard Charles as the old man began talking, outlining plans for the rest of the afternoon. Conor watched Sari from the corner of his eye, noting how stiffly she stood, how jerky her movements were. She seemed oblivious to them both, but he knew that was only a facade. The tension stretched between them until he felt as if a thin, taut wire held them together. One false move, and they would both snap.

She took a pie from the sideboard and set it on the table with such force, the top of the smooth custard cracked. Charles jumped.

Conor glanced at it doubtfully. "What's that?"

"Sugar pie." Sari slid the knife through the custard as if it were his heart she were slitting instead. She lifted out a piece and set it, quivering and collapsing slightly, on a plate. She shoved it in front of him.

"Sugar pie." Conor eyed the dark cream souping delicately in a golden crust. The smell of molasses greeted his nose. "I don't think I like sugar pie, thank you anyway."

"G'schenkte gaul, gook net ins maul."

You don't look a gift horse in the mouth. Conor recognized the phrase, he'd heard her say it a hundred times before. She spoke the archaic German with gentle gutturals and softly rounded vowels, the way she'd learned it from her uncle. The husky burr struck him in the stomach with force, and with it came the memory, quick and burning, of the German love words she'd whispered in his ear, the way her warm, moist breath shivered at the hair curling at his neck. The way her silky tresses had swept his chest, and her slender fingers had stroked him.

He swallowed quickly, then saw by the quick flush staining her cheeks that she was remembering it too. He opened his mouth to say something, anything, but she turned away.

"You'd best eat, *Onkle,*" she said softly, "before it gets cold."

"What do you think?" Charles straightened, his gaze sweeping the land before him with pleasure and pride.

Conor took in the view, the purple-hued mountains that broke the prairie, the snowy rock face of Pike's Peak rising jagged against the rest. And below it the plains covered with brown and withered buffalo grass and sage—even the few cottonwoods lining the banks of Beaver Creek looked beaten and gnarled, punished by the harsh wind.

He chose his words carefully. "I think there is a lot to do."

Charles smiled. "*Ja*. There is much work." He pointed to the long brown scar of a half-dug ditch. "The canal is the most of it. The ground is frozen now, but in the spring we will dig again."

"For water." Conor eyed it skeptically. "Enough to water crops?"

"Enough." Charles nodded. "I have seen the canals they dig in Greeley. Enough to water fifty farms." A small grin curved his lips. "Ours will not be that big. Can you see it?"

Conor buried his chin in his upright collar, wishing like hell that Charles had let him sit by the fire in peace. He looked longingly back to the soddy, where smoke rose from the stovepipe chimney poking through the roof. "I'm no farmer, Charles."

Charles eyed him soberly. "No, you are not."

Conor turned away from Charles's suddenly harsh eyes, not for the first time feeling pressured and tense. The icy wind cut through his clothes; his hands were so cold, he couldn't feel his fingers. Damn, it was desolate here. In more ways than one. He hated the brown, empty land that matched the hollowness inside him; he hated Charles's kindness because it was so undeserved. But mostly he hated the rage that blew through him whenever he looked at Sari, and the way her lonely, hurting eyes made him want to forget that rage.

Revenge. It was all that was important. He closed his eyes briefly, forcing himself to remember that Sari was as much an enemy as her brother had been.

"This is not why I have asked you to walk with me."

Charles's strong, clear voice pierced Conor's thoughts. He looked at the old man curiously. "No?"

"I am wanting to talk to you about Sari." Charles walked slowly, looking straight ahead, hands clasped behind his back. He lapsed into silence for a moment, as if weighing his words, and Conor followed, saying nothing. Charles finally stopped, staring distractedly into the distance. His heavy gray brows furrowed together.

"I do not approve of what you did to her," he said finally, rubbing his jaw.

Conor took a deep breath. "No, I didn't imagine you would."

"Did you not wonder why I took your side?"

Conor shrugged. "I supposed you understood that she needed to be protected."

"*Ja,*" Charles nodded. "It was that, and more than that. Sarilyn has not been herself."

"I'm not surprised." Conor tried to keep his voice even. "It must have been hard for her when Evan was arrested."

Charles threw him a sideways glance. "Perhaps in ways you do not know, *mein Freund.*"

They were even, then, Conor thought bitterly. And then, because he couldn't help it, he said the words he'd been aching to say. "And Michael? What of him?"

"It was hard for her, losing a brother and a husband at the same time," Charles answered obliquely. "And in such a way."

Conor was startled. "In what way? Michael's still alive, isn't he?"

"*Ja. Ja,* he is alive. But he is gone as if he were dead."

But not dead. Not yet, anyway. Conor took a deep breath. "I did what I was supposed to do, Charles. I can't make excuses for it. I'm a Pinkerton agent. It's my job."

"And it is you who must live with that." The old man shoved his hands deep into the pockets of his trousers. "It is not my place to help you do that, Roarke. My only concern is for Sari."

"I'm here to protect her," Conor said gruffly, speaking the lie easily. "You can rest assured I'll do my best."

"She has lived with fear and anger for months." Charles went on as if Conor hadn't spoken. "I would have it end. I would have her happy."

Conor said nothing. The request was too big. It wasn't something he could do for Sari, not even something he wanted to do. Her happiness was not important, not in light of what he needed.

"She was happy with you once."

"It was all a lie then, Charles."

"Was it?" A tiny half smile curved Charles's lips. "Are you so sure of that?"

Was he so sure? Conor tried to think, to remember the emotions that had chased through him when he'd kissed her, when he'd held her. She had been a friend when he needed one, and at the time, he'd thought maybe he even loved her. But today he couldn't remember how that love had felt, how true it had been. It was in the past, a role he'd played, and if it had been more than acting—well, it was over now. It wasn't real and never had been. It was just a job.

The thought was unsettling. Until he remembered the ceiling crashing in around him, the clouds of dust and cracked timber, the acrid scent of burning oil and his father's cry.

That was real, he reminded himself bitterly. And nothing else meant a damn.

CHAPTER 5

CHARLES'S WORDS FILLED CONOR WITH A sense of urgency. He had intended to wait a day or two, to see if he could find out with judicious questions what Sari knew about her brother's whereabouts. But she was too angry and too suspicious. It would be better to start searching the soddy for letters or pictures—something to tell him where Michael was now, or when he might show up here.

The next morning Conor was up early, but not early enough. Sari and Charles were already in the soddy, eating breakfast. It wasn't until after the noon meal that he had the chance to search. When Sari went out to dig potatoes and Charles announced he was going to take a short nap, Conor nearly leaped from his chair with anticipation. It was all he could do to wait until they both left the room.

It was his chance, and Conor forced himself to go slowly, to utilize his training. He surveyed the room first, looking for clues, for good places to hide a receipt or a letter.

There were too many possibilities. Three trunks were pushed against the newspaper-covered walls, their curved lids firmly shut against the dampness. Shelves laden with books and papers held places of honor next to two threadbare chairs, and a stack of boxes in the corner hid who knew what. Clutter filled every corner of the room. The thought of pawing through it all exhausted him.

Conor shifted in his chair, knocking his leg against a long, low trunk shoved beneath the table. It would take him forever just to search the main room—and that was if he could get Sari to disappear long enough for him to look. His eyes strayed to the ladder leading to the loft. Sari's bedroom.

He glanced out the window. He couldn't see Sari, and that was dangerous. If he couldn't see her, he couldn't tell what she was doing, wouldn't know when she was readying to come inside. Damn, he had so little time. If she caught him up there, it would be impossible to explain, and it would only convince her that her intuition was right, that he was lying about why he came.

The loft would have to wait for another time. He pushed aside his coffee and got to his feet. Stacks of books were piled on the floor, overflowing two double- and tripled-loaded shelves that were jammed against the wall. It was the most obvious place to start, the best place to hide something was in plain view. He'd been taught that lesson well enough.

The books were musty from the damp sod, some

of them had mold growing along waterlogged pages that had dried curled and warped. All of them had a moldy, dusty smell. Conor wrinkled his nose as his gaze swept over the first layer of books. Nothing. There were anthologies, tomes on farming techniques, novels, Grange journals, and poetry. It was a large and varied collection, but he saw no loose papers. Of course it could be inside, hidden in the pages. With a sigh Conor grabbed a book and riffled through it—

"What are you doing?"

Her voice cut through the room in the same moment he heard the door swing open. Conor froze, his hands gripping the binding of a volume.

Sari closed the door behind her carefully, her expression as stiff as her spine. "What are you looking for?"

Conor forced himself to turn casually. He turned the book in his hands over as if searching for the title, then lifted his eyes in mock innocence. "You sound angry. I'm sorry, I didn't realize your books were forbidden to me."

Uncertainty flitted through her eyes. She relaxed marginally, though the fingers that gripped her full apron were white. "They aren't," she said carefully. "Of course they aren't. It's just—it seemed as if you were looking for something in particular."

"I was." He shoved the book back onto the shelf. "I thought there might be something here about fencing. I'd like to at least try to be of help to your uncle."

"There isn't much time to read here," she scolded

gently. "*Onkle* will tell you what he needs you to know." Unceremoniously she dumped the potatoes bundled in her apron into a bucket, then reached for the butternut sunbonnet she wore. The yellow was the only color in her otherwise colorless outfit and she lifted it from her head and laid it aside almost reverently. Strands of smooth brown hair strayed across her face, grabbing at the corner of her mouth. Impatiently she swept them away. "*Onkle*'s in his soddy now," she said. "I'm sure he can find something for you to do."

He heard the spite in her words, and couldn't keep from smiling. "I'll go find him, then, love."

Her brown eyes were cold. "Stop calling me love."

"Old habits are hard to break."

"Not so hard." Her smile was small and icy. "I used to trust you. I unlearned that quickly enough."

Conor hesitated, tensing with the will to reply in kind. And then he saw her hands when she picked up a potato, saw the way she attacked the brown-gray skin as if she were trying to scrub it off. He watched her thoughtfully: the strands of hair tumbling into her face, the tight line of her lips, the shaking of her fingers.

He was getting to her. It was more than anger that made her react in such a way, he knew. There was something else in her movements, a nervousness, an uncertainty.

He spoke carefully. "Sari, we don't need to be such enemies."

She stopped as if stung. "No?" She asked softly. "What should we be, then?"

"What if we call a truce? Forget the past?"

Her eyes narrowed suspiciously. "Why would I want to do that?"

He shrugged with deliberate casualness. "Maybe to make things more comfortable. I'll probably be here awhile. There's no point in making it miserable for both of us."

"Perhaps they should have sent someone else, then."

"Would you have allowed anyone else to stay?"

"I'm still not sure having *anyone* here is necessary."

"I see," he said stiffly. "You'd rather take the risk."

She bit her lip, turning to stare out the window. Conor saw the quick worry in her eyes, the flush of memory.

"I still don't know that they'd harm me," she said finally.

"You think Michael could prevent it?"

He saw the harsh, bitter pain in her eyes when she whipped around, the wild uncertainty. It startled him, but not as much as her next words.

"Don't mention his name to me."

"Why not? He's your brother. You can't deny blood."

Her eyes burned. "I will not discuss him. Not with you." She dropped a potato into the bucket with a thud. Her hands shook. "Stop pretending you care—about me or my brother. You would have hung him without a thought, even though he was your friend. Your *friend*, like Evan was." She took a deep breath, her jaw clenched. "I know you too well. None of us matter to you. You'd do anything to get what you want. I've seen what you'll do. I haven't forgotten what you are. You're lying to me now."

"Sari—"

She lifted her chin defiantly. "I don't want you here, and that won't change—believe me. So make it easy on both of us, Jam—Conor." Her voice lowered, he heard the hatred in her tone. "Protect me if you want, but leave me alone. Just leave me alone."

The memory burned, quick and lethal, piercing the fog of his dream until it became a nightmare. Over and over he saw it, saw the white faces of the men who had become his friends, the disbelief in their eyes when he walked into the eerily silent courtroom and took a seat on the witness stand. The bow tie tightened against his throat, constricting him, but his voice was strong and sure, even when the defense lawyers ripped into him.

He'd given the information without a pause, had looked into the eyes of his friends and seen their fear.

He could not forget that. Even though those left had killed his father, Conor could not forget the terrible hopelessness he'd seen on their faces. Could not forget that he had betrayed them.

The dream gripped him, the bodies of the men he'd sent to the gallows growing formless before his eyes, their mouths dark holes yawning in misty spirits. *I should have let them kill you when I had the chance.* Evan Travers's voice was the loudest of all. *I trusted you, Jamie O'Brien. I called you friend.*

Conor sat straight up, his body drenched in sweat. It took him a moment to realize that the rustling of hay and the movements of the animals were not part of his dream. He was not in Pottsville, not in the courthouse. He was in a dark, damp soddy barn, and he could hear the wind shrieking outside.

He took a deep breath, raking back his hair and staring into the darkness. It had been months since he'd had that dream. With his father's death the memories of his disquieting feelings about the Molly Maguires had faded into the background. He'd thought they'd disappeared forever.

They should have. God knew, he was about as far from feeling any sympathy for the Mollies as a man could be. There had been days when he'd questioned his involvement, when he'd wondered if the lies and violence that were part of his job were necessary, but he thought he'd long resolved that.

He'd come to terms with that betrayal, had realized that the two and a half years of living among them, being one of them, had been too long. Hell, he'd almost started to believe he was a Molly. For a while, he'd believed in their causes. That had never happened to him on any other job, never before had he questioned his role as a Pinkerton agent.

It had only been a temporary feeling. His uncertainties had disappeared when Michael Doyle planted the bomb that destroyed his house and his life. It was absurd that he should be feeling anything like it now.

But Sari's reaction today had him confused. Conor

lay back, crossing his arms beneath his head and staring up at the dirt ceiling. She had been furious when he mentioned Michael to her, and he had not imagined her bitterness or the way her mouth went white with tension. *"Don't mention his name to me,"* she'd said, and then there'd been Charles's words of yesterday: *"He is gone as if he were dead."* Conor wondered why. Was it because Michael had done something so brutal, Sari could no longer condone it? Was her anger with her brother real? Or was she lying for Conor's benefit?

He thought back, remembering Sari's relationship with her brother. She'd never agreed with Michael about anything. They had been as different as a brother and sister could be. Doyle was a fanatic, a man burning with conviction that bordered on madness. He had been the perfect Molly assassin—a man convinced that murder was acceptable if it gained them an edge. Jack Kehoe, the bodymaster of the Girardville Mollies, and one of the most ruthless men Conor had ever known, had trusted Doyle with their most sensitive assassinations. By the time Conor infiltrated the gang, Michael was one of their most valuable members.

And Sari was one of their biggest liabilities.

Conor closed his eyes, remembering Evan's careful warnings about his wife. *"She don't like this stuff, my friend. Keep her out of it."* It was a vast understatement. Sari had despised her husband's friends, had blamed them for her brother's violence. But in the end she never stopped loving Michael.

Or so Conor had thought.

"He is gone as if he were dead." Maybe. Or maybe it was a lie, something calculated to put Conor off Michael's trail. That seemed more likely. Sari had denied Michael, yes, but in almost the same breath she'd accused Conor of betraying him. It made Conor wonder—for the hundredth time since he'd known her—just how far her devotion to her brother went. Was she Michael's enemy or—more likely—his ally?

There was only one way to find out. When Conor left her before, he'd thought she was innocent, had been consumed with guilt for the way he used her, dismayed and disgusted with himself over the hurt he caused her.

Those days were long over, and there was no point in thinking about them again. But Sari Travers had reminded him of a lesson learned long before: Misplaced trust was a dangerous thing.

He knew the hazards now, the sweetness of her body and her warm words, the fire of passion that burned between them. This time he could protect himself from them even as he seduced her into trusting him again, into giving him the only thing he wanted: Michael.

Conor closed his eyes against the darkness. This time he wouldn't forget. This time there would be no guilt when he walked away. Not this time.

CHAPTER 6

SHE HEARD THE WAGON THROUGH THE wind. For a moment her heart raced; she remembered the raid of the other night and felt a surge of unrelieved panic. Sari forced herself to turn casually from the potatoes she was digging up, and she saw Conor rushing from the barn. He stood in the doorway, watching the wagon approach, and even from where she was, yards away, Sari saw his alert tension.

Just then the wagon cleared the barn and came into view, and Sari's panic fled in relief and pure happiness. It wasn't the Mollies, not Michael at all. It was John and Miriam Graham, their closest neighbors. Sari smiled and put aside the trowel, wiping her hands on her apron. It had been a long time since they'd visited, forever since she'd talked with another woman.

Then she saw Conor again.

How was she going to explain his presence? The

thought brought her panic crashing back. She had
the sudden wish that the Grahams would turn their
wagon around again, leave without even saying
hello. But even as she had the thought, John reined
in the horses and Miriam was jumping down from
the buckboard, hurrying toward her with an excited
smile and bubbling words.

"We were just heading into town, and we decided
to stop and see if you needed anything," Miriam said
breathlessly, her blue eyes sparkling. "And I wanted
to say hello—Lord, don't you look busy!"

Sari gave her a smile and got to her feet. "Not that
busy," she said. "You and John can stay for some
coffee, can't you? And dinner's nearly ready."

"I don't—" Miriam threw a glance back at her
husband, who was talking with Charles, and then
she laughed. "Well, yes. I'd love to. It's been so long
since we've talked. And I brought those *Godey's Lady's Book*s for you to look at."

It was hard to be fearful in the light of Miriam's
obvious pleasure. Sari's smile broadened. "I'm not
sure I even want to look at them," she said. "No
doubt I'll see something I want."

"I know." Miriam nodded. "I've probably ear-
marked twenty pages for myself—all for the Christmas dance." She chuckled, then stopped short, her
expression sharp with curiosity. "Goodness, who's
that?"

Sari's heart dropped in her chest as she followed
Miriam's gaze to Conor. He strode over to the wagon
with a confidence that made Sari clench her fist.

Charles was already at the wagon, talking to John, and Conor hadn't been there more than twenty seconds before the two of them laughed in response to something he'd said.

Sari frowned. That effortless charm, that facile talk. She knew how easily he could win John over, how quick he would be to feign friendliness. And it was all an act. Just a stupid, meaningless act.

"Are you all right, Sari?"

She looked up to see Miriam staring at her. Sari forced a smile. "I'm fine."

"Who *is* that?"

Sari slowed her step. "Conor Roarke," she said evenly. "He's a . . . an old friend."

"An old friend?" Miriam eyed Sari speculatively.

"He was a friend of Evan's," Sari said forcefully. "I barely know him."

"You barely know him?" Miriam asked. "And he came out all the way from Pennsylvania?"

They were nearly to the wagon. Sari shook her head quickly. "I'll tell you everything later," she said in a low voice.

The promise hushed Miriam's questions, if only for the moment. But Sari would worry about that later. Now it took all her concentration to keep from frowning her disapproval at Conor, to keep from hating his smile and easy manner.

"Hello, Sari!" John called as they approached. He lifted a bundle of magazines tied with string from the back of the wagon. "Miriam's brought practically her whole collection for you to see."

"Oh, John." Miriam laughed.

John grinned at her. He glanced at Conor. "Conor, this is my wife, Miriam. Miriam, this is Conor Roarke."

"Mr. Roarke," Miriam said prettily. "Sari was just telling me you've come all the way from Pennsylvania."

"All the way," he admitted, smiling. He glanced at Sari with a warmth that was horribly disconcerting. "But I think it was worth the trip."

She wanted to strangle him. Especially when Miriam gave her an oblique glance.

"You can stay for dinner, *ja*?" Charles asked. "Or at least coffee?"

"We're going into town," John said, "but I think we can spare a few minutes."

"Longer than that, I hope," Charles said, slapping John lightly on the back. "And I would like your advice, John, about the fence."

They went into the soddy, Miriam chattering the entire time, keeping up a constant dialogue that Sari was too distracted to hear. She was too aware of Conor walking behind her, too dismayed by that warm and far too intimate look in the yard. She would never be able to dissuade Miriam from her suspicions now, and she hated that he'd put her in this position, hated that he was interfering in her life—again.

She poured coffee and chatted with the others, but Conor's presence agitated her. She was constantly aware of him and the way he stood beside her the entire time, reaching around her for the coffee, keep-

ing Miriam and John laughing as he refilled cups.
When he and John and Charles finally went outside
to talk about the fence, Sari nearly sagged with relief.

"Now—" Miriam turned from the stove, her
black-and-brown print calico skirt waving around
her ankles with her quick, bustling step. Her blue
eyes were alight with curiosity, but she sat gracefully
and deliberately, pulling her skirts around her,
smoothing back tendrils of her pale blond hair.
"Now, you did promise to tell me everything."

"There isn't much to tell."

"Fiddle!" Miriam leaned over the table and pulled
aside the fading blue gingham curtain, and Sari felt a
quick stab of relief that Conor had already fixed the
shattered glass. That relief faded the minute she saw
how Miriam's pretty, fragile features tightened as she
scrutinized Conor, who was standing in the yard with
John and Charles. "There's a mysterious man staying
with you and your uncle, and you tell me he's not important. I don't believe you." Miriam frowned and let
the curtain drop back into place. "And not just any
man, Sari. Why, he's so handsome—almost as handsome as my John—and he came all the way to Colorado to check on his friend's wife," Miriam said. She
peeked again out the window. "I think he came out
here to sweep you off your feet."

"I don't think so," Sari said drily.

Miriam's small smile was secretive. "Perhaps he
has and you don't know it yet. What did you say he
does?"

Sari's hands tightened around her cup. The smell
of coffee made her head ache. There was nothing

about Conor that Sari wanted her best friend to know. Colorado was her chance to start over, the last thing she wanted was for anyone to know about her past. She had not told Miriam much about her life, preferring the lie of silence to bald dishonesty, preferring the simple illusion that she was a widow who had been deeply in love with her husband. She wanted people to think she was what she wanted to be.

Sari let her gaze wander again to the window. Conor and Charles stood in the yard, beneath the flanges of the windmill, deep in conversation with Miriam's husband. Though John Graham was a vibrant, darkly handsome man, Sari was sharply aware of how Conor, though not as tall or as broad as John, seemed to dominate him. Then Conor laughed. Sari's heart tightened at the sight of it, at the way his face crinkled in genuine mirth, at the long creases of dimples forming on either side of his face. He used to laugh often and irresistibly, she remembered, but it seemed as if she hadn't seen that side of him in a very long time.

She tamped down the longing that welled up at the thought and turned away, forcing herself to remember that he was a brutal, uncompromising man. But there was something about his eyes, something that brought back those vibrant memories, that pulled at her even through her anger.

"You're too quiet," Miriam said suddenly. "You're trying to decide how much to tell me, I can feel it. Well, it won't work. You must tell me everything."

Sari forced a smile. "I have told you everything, Miri. He used to work for the railroads, that's all I know." That at least wasn't a lie. After all, it *had* been the president of the Reading Railroad who'd hired Pinkerton to quash the Mollies. "I told you he and Evan were friends."

Miriam looked down at the table; Sari watched suspiciously as her friend traced the patterns of the stains marring the tablecloth with a slender, callused finger. "How long is he staying?"

Sari sighed. "Not long, Miri. Don't get any ideas—I can see you matchmaking already."

Miriam's head flew up. "Well, of course I am! You've been here nearly a year, and you haven't shown the slightest interest in anyone. I can't believe you mean to stay alone. Why, without John, I'd surely die of loneliness."

"I've got *Onkle*." Sari protested. "I'm not alone."

"That's not what I mean and you know it," Miriam persisted. "You wouldn't look twice at Michael Dunn at the Grange harvest festival. Sari, you wouldn't even dance with anyone but John and old Will Schmacher. Two married men—"

"I prefer things the way they are."

"That's nonsense," Miriam said sharply.

Sari closed her eyes briefly. "I had a husband, Miri. I don't want another one."

There was a long silence. Sari squirmed beneath Miriam's thoughtful glance. "Because you're still grieving?" she asked.

The question surprised Sari. Grieving was so far from her mind, she'd forgotten it was a normal way

of feeling. Grief over Evan—the idea was ludicrous.
But she bent her head and lowered her eyes in what
she hoped was an expression of quiet agreement.

Miriam sighed. "Oh dear. I'm sorry. How insen-
sitive of me to mention it. You must have loved him
very much. As much as I love John, probably. I
would be devastated if something happened to him."

Sari winced. She felt like the worst hypocrite. She
wanted to tell Miriam that Evan's death left guilt and
sorrow, but no grief. She wanted to pour out the
entire story to a sympathetic ear. But she knew that
if she did, Miriam's understanding would turn to re-
vulsion. Sari didn't want to see that look in another
person's eyes, couldn't stand seeing it. God knew,
she'd had her fill of it the last year.

So she let Miriam think what she would, and hated
herself for it.

"I'm sorry," Miri said again, covering Sari's hand
with her own. "I didn't mean to remind you."

"Stop, please, it's not important." Sari pulled her
hand away, biting her lip. "I've grown used to it."

The soddy door swung open. John stuck his curly
head into the opening. "Sari," he said breathlessly,
"is there any more coffee?"

"Of course." Sari nodded. "And dinner is almost
ready."

"We'll be in shortly." John grinned and blew Miriam a quick kiss, pulling the door shut behind him.

It sent a stab of envy through Sari. What would it
be like, she wondered for the hundredth time, to
have a man love you like that? She thought she'd
known once.

She swallowed as Conor turned slightly toward the window, and followed the line of his jaw with her gaze, the slightly bumpy nose. Not handsome, she reminded herself, staring at him. Not unlike a hundred other men . . .

His eyes caught and held hers for just a moment, and Sari felt her heart jump, her pulse race. Then he smiled that slow, easy smile that transformed his face.

She felt her own lips curve in involuntary response, and Sari looked down quickly, embarrassed and humiliated that he had caught her staring at him. She hated him, she told herself. He would not get the best of her. He would not.

She reminded herself of it all the way through dinner.

The smells of supper still lingered in the kitchen as Sari washed the last dish and wiped her hands on a cotton towel. It was so quiet tonight, so peaceful. Charles had gone to his own soddy for the night, and thankfully Conor was seeing to the animals. She had a few blissful moments all to herself.

Sari sank into a chair at the table, throwing the towel to the side. The day had been long, and fighting Miriam's questions along with her own anxiety over what Conor would do or say next had been wearying. Dinner had been interminable; she was on edge and too anxious to eat.

It felt so good to finally be alone. Really alone, without the worry of what he would say or do next.

Alone, with the night free and the morning still far away.

She caught sight of one of the *Godey's Lady's Books* that Miriam had lent her and pulled it across the table. The magazine was nearly a year old, but she'd practically memorized her own scant collection.

She opened the magazine and thumbed through the pages, staring longingly at women clad in delicately flowered silks and taffetas, jewel-toned velvets and exquisite laces. In Tamaqua she'd never seen anything so fine, though some of the ladies in Philadelphia had been dressed in such fashions. She and Evan had gone into the city for their honeymoon, and she remembered how he had laughed at her wide-eyed astonishment. He'd promised her dresses of equal beauty then, gowns with fine pleated bodices and stiff silk bows, bustles and godets, ruched skirts and long trains of Brussels lace.

Sari fingered the thick pages absently, hearing Evan's vows of riches and fine things reverberate in her ears. *"Feathers, Sari—big ostrich feathers on a hat even Mrs. Townshend would envy. Nothing's too good for the mother of my son."*

She swallowed hard. They'd been happy then, in the first year of their marriage, before she'd miscarried the baby and failed at conceiving another—

"I like that one." Conor's voice, deep and raspy, startled her. Sari jumped. Cold air from the open door brushed her back. She slammed the magazine shut.

"I—you scared me."

Conor shut the door and moved over to her, seemingly oblivious of her discomfort. He pulled the magazine gently from her fingers and studied the cover. "*Godey's Lady's Book*? Thinking of making a new dress?"

"No," she answered curtly.

He strode casually to the stove and grabbed a piece of leftover corn bread, the fashion magazine still clutched between his fingers. "Charles tells me there's a Christmas dance coming up. You should have something pretty to wear to it. Something that isn't brown."

"I like brown."

"I don't." He bit into the bread. Crumbs scattered over the floor, but he ignored the mess as he set the magazine on the table and flipped open to a well-marked page. "Ah, that," he nodded. "That's pretty."

His casual friendliness confused her even as it drew her. "Why should I care what you think? I'm not dressing for—"

"No, look," he insisted. "This one."

She followed his finger to an evening gown with small puffed sleeves and a square collar edged in lace. "Yes, it is pretty. But—"

He pulled out a chair, sitting down beside her. Sari felt the warmth of his body, the slight press of his trouser-covered thigh before he settled. He was so close, she heard him swallow. She smelled his scent, of outdoors and muskiness edged with the pungent sharpness of bay. Sari's fingers tightened. This mood, this light teasing, made her uncomfortable. It was too much like before.

Her throat tightened. "What are you doing?"

"Helping you choose. I've been told I have excellent taste in women's gowns."

Sari snorted. "That doesn't surprise me."

"And I like imagining you in something besides homespun."

"You can keep on imagining. It's all you'll ever see me in. There's no room for fripperies here."

"Fripperies," he mocked gently. "Such a funny word. Perhaps there should be more *fripperies* here."

Her discomfort grew. It was the one thing she couldn't fight, this sudden, intimate side of him that had been so much a part of Jamie. She squeezed her eyes shut in an attempt to block out the memories. "Where's *Onkle*?"

"In his soddy." Conor pulled the magazine toward him and began lifting the pages. "Now, come on, Sari, concentrate. Find something completely frivolous, meant for Christmas parties and dances and picnics." His mouth curved in a grin. "Of course, I'm not sure you're capable of picking something so useless, but this is your chance to show me I'm wrong."

His smile was seductive, but the glint in his eyes was too familiar. Too painful. She swallowed and grabbed the magazine back. "I'm not in the mood for tests."

"A game then." He suggested. "It's early yet, don't send me out to the cows."

She paused. For a moment Sari saw another time, another place, when Evan had gone into Girardville for the day and Jamie—the man she knew, not this man, this Conor—sat on the porch swing on her uncle's farm, one hand outstretched across the back, the other reaching for her. *"Come here, love. Come and sit with me awhile. 'Tis early yet."* And she'd gone, tumbling into his lap while he wrapped his arms around her.

In the grip of memory she relented. "Oh, very well. It *is* still early."

"Good." He smiled broadly. "We'll find a dress I like, and you can tell me whether it's simple enough for a Colorado seamstress."

"There won't be a dress like that." She thought for a moment. "Well, maybe for a seamstress in Denver." She flipped the pages nervously. "Or maybe—"

"Wait! Stop there. That one." His square hand stopped her ceaseless turning of the pages.

Sari glanced at the illustration. "Velvet trim? A bustle?" She shook her head firmly. "No."

"Then this one." Conor said. "I like those silk rosettes."

She smiled. "Do you like them enough to spend hours making them? Because you might have to."

The laughter in his blue eyes was hard to resist. "Ah, I'm a farmer now, Sari. I haven't got time for foolish pursuits. Or so your uncle tells me."

"Then no rosettes."

He reached over her and flipped the page. His voice lowered, vibrated with seductive tension as he pointed to the illustration. "No arguing with me on this one, I mean it. This dress. There must be someone who can make this dress."

Sari caught her breath. The gown was beautiful, with tiny off-the-shoulder puffed sleeves that were edged with lace and silk flowers. Ruched trim followed the lines of the bodice to a polonaise caught at the side with wide bows. Yes, the gown was beautiful. It would look perfect on her, there was no doubt in her mind. She knew it because she'd been wearing one almost exactly like it the first night she met Jamie O'Brien.

"No." Her voice was strangled. "Not that dress."

The laughter was gone from his eyes, but they burned bright and intense as he turned to look at her. "I'll never forget how you looked that night. You lit up the room."

"I was with Evan."

"I remember thinking how lucky he was. There wasn't a woman in Tamaqua who could hold a candle to you that night."

"Are those just words? Or did you really think that?" She forced the question from a throat that felt too tight to breathe. The lamplight played on his hair, sending golden highlights where before it had been just brown.

"I really thought that." He smiled softly. The truth of it was in his voice. "Don't you remember? I asked you to dance, and you refused me."

"You were a murderer. Evan said you'd killed someone in Buffalo." It had been hard to believe. He'd seemed too gentle, too quick to smile and laugh to be a killer. She remembered how he'd looked, polished and clean, standing across the room with his dark hair waving over his forehead. He'd been telling stories in a broad Irish brogue to a group of laughing men, and the evidence of his easy charm compelled her even as it made her instantly wary. Almost as if she'd known, somehow sensed, that he was dangerous to her. She swallowed. "I've been wondering about your brother. Is he still in jail?"

"My brother?" He looked confused for a moment, his blue eyes clouded.

A strange distress started in her heart. "Your brother. The one you killed that man for."

"Oh." He paused—a long time. Then he said gently, "Sari, I have no brother."

"No brother."

"No."

"But—" she struggled against her own sudden understanding. "But you said—you said you killed that man because he hurt your brother—what was his name?—Aaron, wasn't it? Wasn't it Aaron?"

He said nothing.

Sari rushed on. "You said you left Buffalo to keep your parents from suffering."

His gaze was inscrutable. "That wasn't me. It was Jamie."

The words lodged against her heart like a stone. For a moment Sari couldn't breathe. She'd known Jamie O'Brien was only a role he'd played, but for some reason she hadn't thought that everything had been a lie. Not everything. All those secrets they'd shared while twined in each other's arms. All the stories about his poverty-stricken family, his suffering mother, and the brother who'd gone to jail for a crime he didn't commit.

How easily he'd told those stories. She remembered listening with tears in her eyes, remembered aching with the poignancy of his pain. She had fallen in love with that man. With that man's life.

But that life was only a sham, a script written and performed for her benefit. Even though Jamie O'Brien hadn't turned out to be the man she thought he was, she hadn't expected this depth of deceit. Now, suddenly, she realized she didn't know Conor Roarke at all.

"Was any of it real?" Her voice was thin and whispery. She saw the quick tightening of his lips, but he didn't turn away.

"No," he said softly.

"Not even—"

"What do you want me to say, Sari?" he asked, and she heard a strange urgency in his voice, as though he'd justified these things to himself many times. "I was what I needed to be, I've told you that."

"It was all a lie."

He looked away then, taking a deep breath. "Is anything real? Anyone? Things are never what they seem, you should know that. Yes, I lied to you. I had to." He hesitated, and when he spoke again, his voice was so low, she had to struggle to hear it. "But I wish to God you'd trust me now."

"Trust you?" She laughed bitterly. "Why? How?"

His gaze was so intense Sari felt burned. "I'm just

Conor Roarke now, Sari. Just myself. No lies. I'm here to protect you. I'm here because I want you again."

Sari rose, nearly falling over the chair in her haste. She was trembling as she went to the stove, unable to look at him. The words wrapped around her, curled in her stomach. *"I want you again. I want you. . . ."*

The memories crashed over her so strongly, she felt heated: She saw his face bent over hers, heard the sweetness of his laughter, felt the soft, wiry feel of the hair on his chest.

She caught her breath, closed her eyes, but the memories wouldn't fade. She remembered the way his touch rendered her helpless, the way his smile weakened her. It was an attraction that hadn't gone away. Even his betrayal couldn't kill it, and she hated that about him, hated that he was still so hard to resist. She wanted to forget what they'd been to each other, but even if he wasn't Jamie O'Brien any longer, that charm was still there, the memory of passion was still there—

His hands touched her hips. Sari jumped, cracking her elbow against the coffeepot so that it splashed coffee down her bodice and onto the packed dirt floor. She spun away from him, batting his hands away, backing against the sideboard. "Damn you," she swore softly, wiping at her dress. "Look what you've done!"

"What I've done?" A slow smile slid over his face. "Why are you so afraid of me, love?"

Sari's heart was pounding; it was hard to catch her breath. "I'm not afraid of you."

"No? Then why did you jump?" He took a step toward her.

Sari tried to back away, but she was trapped against the sideboard. "You—you surprised me."

"Surprised you?" He moved until he was nearly touching her. "I see. Then you won't be surprised this time."

He reached out, cupping her chin. The touch was electric. Desperately, Sari jerked away. It was too close, too much like before. She dodged around Conor, so frantic to avoid him that she backed against the stove. The handle of the door jabbed her leg, and Sari flailed for balance, slamming her hand down on the stove, then yanking it away again as the hot metal seared her skin.

She jerked back against the sideboard. "Damn!"

"Hell." Conor pulled her to her feet. "What did you do? Let me see." He reached for her hand.

Sari grabbed it back again. "You've done quite enough."

"Dammit, Sari, let me see." He wrenched her hand from her side, turning it over to see the reddened swell of a burn rising on her palm. "Where's the grease?"

Sari nodded toward the can sitting on a shelf. She blinked rapidly, trying to dispel tears. Conor held her wrist as he reached for the can, scooping up a handful of the soft, gray-white mess and spreading it over the burn until her palm shone in the lamplight.

"There," he said with satisfaction. "Where's a rag?"

"You don't need to wrap it."

"Don't tell me what I need to do. Where's a rag?"

"In the bucket there," she said quietly, pointing to her makeshift sewing basket in the corner of the soddy.

He left her for a moment to grab the bucket, and Sari's hand felt suddenly cold where his fingers released her. She grasped her wrist, watching him fumble through the pile of old clothing until he came up with a shirt stained yellow from use, with a ragged tear across the back.

Conor ripped off a strip of fabric. "Come here. Sit down."

Sari's palm was beginning to burn in earnest, and she did as he instructed without protest. He pulled up a chair beside her, resting her hand on his thigh as he expertly wound the bandage around her palm.

There it was again, that tenderness. Her stomach cramped suddenly; the warm room was stifling. Sari took a deep breath, feeling a curious languor come over her as Conor wrapped the linen strip once, twice, three times over her palm and wrist. She glanced up, away from the sight of her hand nestled in his, hoping a view of the ceiling would help her control her unsteady breathing. But her gaze caught, locking onto the buttons of his collarless shirt. They'd come loose as he moved, revealing the jutting of his collarbone, the fine, dark hair that started at the base of his throat.

She tried to pull her hand away, but he held it firmly, finally looking up as he knotted the ends of the bandage. His eyes were caressing, serious now as he studied her expression.

"There," he said gently. Was it her imagination, or did his voice seem deeper? Hoarser? "You should be fine now."

"Thank you." It took all her will to force the words out.

"Does it still hurt?"

"Yes."

He leaned closer. "Is there anything I can do to make it feel better?"

Yes. Oh yes, there was. Sari felt her eyes closing despite herself, felt herself moving forward, caught in that heady spell of desire and yearning. Just one more inch. One inch would be all it would take to send her crashing into his arms—

She jerked back, her eyes flying open. She dragged her wounded hand back into her lap. "No." She said, stumbling over the word in her haste, getting to her feet. "No."

She heard the scrape of his chair, his slow, heavy footsteps as he moved across the floor. She'd thought he was heading toward the door, but suddenly there he was, his hands gripping her shoulders gently, turning her around. She stiffened as he drew her close.

"Trust me, love," he whispered. She felt his light kiss on her forehead, the warm brush of his lips across her cheek. "Sleep well."

His hands dropped. Sari sagged against the wall.

She watched his broad shoulders, the clean, spare movement of his hips as he crossed the floor.

And she felt the cold rush of air as he disappeared into the prairie night.

It was working. Conor crossed his arms beneath his head and laid back against his saddlebags, closing his eyes against the darkness and the night rustlings of the animals. He told himself that her responses tonight were exactly what he wanted. He'd seen her hesitation, had seen vulnerability in those dark brown eyes, heard it in her voice. He'd known, at that last moment, that he could have kissed her and she would have let him. She was starting—if not to trust him again, then at least to accept him. Everything was going the way he'd planned.

He told himself he should be satisfied.

But there was a churning in his gut and a nagging reminder in his head, the reminder that Sari wasn't the only one affected by tonight. Much as he wanted to, Conor couldn't deny that when she had smiled, he'd felt it clear into his soul, and when he'd seen that hesitant vulnerability in her face, it had done something to his heart he still didn't quite understand.

Despite himself, those things had brought back memories. Memories of sitting with Sari on her porch swing, talking while her husband and the other boys played cards inside. Memories of teasing her into laughter as they walked down the street, of dancing with her at a miner's dance and seeing the becoming flush in her cheeks, the sparkle in her eyes.

Memories of snatched conversations and fumbling, hurried kisses.

He had missed those things, he realized. In spite of everything, he had missed them. The knowledge made him uncomfortable. He thought he had put all that behind him, thought it had been buried in brick dust and splintered wood. But then, she had been in his life for two years. She had been the only person he trusted. He supposed those things were hard to simply put aside. It was natural to miss her. It was natural to regret those days were gone.

And now that he'd admitted that, he could get on with his plans.

Conor winced at the brutality of the thought, but it was true and he couldn't deny it. Missing Sari had nothing to do with now. Wanting her still only made his job easier. He had to keep himself from being drawn in, had to treat her as a means to an end and nothing more. When she looked at him with vulnerability in her eyes, he had to be sure it didn't bring back memories of those days in Tamaqua. When she smiled at him, it would be best to forget those other smiles. He was using her, and he couldn't forget that. Not even for a moment.

He could not care about her. He didn't want to care. And so he wouldn't. It was that easy.

That easy.

He ignored the chill the words cast around his heart.

CHAPTER 7

SARI BENT OVER HER MENDING, CONCEN-
trating on the flash of her needle in the dim lamplight, her lips pursed as she worked to make the
stitches small and neat. It was a difficult thing to
achieve tonight, her hands were trembling so.

"'Alas, they had been friends in youth; but whispering tongues can poison truth.'"

His voice moved over her skin like honey, the
whiskey-rough sound of it shaping Coleridge's
words into secret meanings and subtle seductions.
Her burned palm throbbed in time to his cadence.

He should be an actor, she thought, marveling at
the ease with which he formed the words and
worked the rhythms. But then, he *was* an actor, she
reminded herself. Strangely the grim thought didn't
help distance her from his words. It had been a horrible idea to let him read. She blamed her uncle for
suggesting it, though she had agreed readily enough.
But how could she have known Conor would pick

Coleridge—why should she suspect that he would even know the most romantic of the poet's stories?

Christabel. It had been her favorite as a young, romantic girl. A foolish girl, she amended quickly.

The thread snagged, and Sari yanked it free impatiently, too preoccupied to care whether she snagged the worn fabric. She stopped for a moment, trying to calm her emotions, but that voice of his wrapped around her nerves. The harder she struggled against him, the harder it was to escape. He tore down all her fences before she even had time to erect them.

It was becoming harder every day to remind herself of what Conor Roarke had been, what he had done to her. He'd said it was only a job, that it had only been an act. In a way that was what she wanted to hear. She wanted to know that he'd callously set out to break her, to use her.

Then there was last night.

The memory rose easily in her mind. *Trust me, love.* Those words, and his admission of deceit, affected her strangely, filling her with an odd desire to ask him questions, to learn about him all over again, to know what kind of man Conor Roarke was and how he felt. Was it honesty she sensed now, or was it simply that crushed gravel voice that lulled her, that made her yearn to trust him all over again?

He finished the poem. The sudden silence seemed to fill the very corners of the small room.

"You read very well." Charles's quiet voice was startling.

"Thank you." Conor said.

Sari felt his gaze on her, and reluctantly she met his eyes. "You do read well," she conceded.

"Sari should know." Charles grinned. "It is her favorite poem."

"*Christabel*?"

Sari nodded. Her throat felt tight and swollen. "I used to love it."

"Used to?" Conor prompted.

She glanced away, trying to control the butterflies chasing through her stomach. "There are more important things now than poems that are so—"

"Romantic?"

"I wouldn't have used that word."

"No, of course you wouldn't." He smiled, flipping through the warped, water-stained pages. "Shall I read another?"

Charles grinned. "No more poetry tonight, *ja*? Let us just talk. It has been long enough since we have done that."

"Talk?" Conor closed the book with a mild thump, his eyes shining with challenge.

"Perhaps that's not stimulating enough for our guest, *Onkle*," Sari said. "Our company must be dull after the excitement of Chicago."

"Chicago has a certain drama," Conor agreed, his lips quirking in a half smile. "But I find Colorado stimulating enough."

Sari swallowed. It was useless. She didn't have the concentration to watch every word she said. She balled the half-mended shirt in her lap and stuffed it back into her sewing bucket.

She looked to her uncle, but Charles was ignoring

them both, either not understanding Conor's double entendre or choosing not to comment on it. Charles rose from his chair; the rocker creaked back and knocked against the wall. He stretched as he went to the window. "It is a cold night out there," Charles mused softly. "It is very different from home."

Sari caught his wistfulness. "Tamaqua was freezing," she said.

"Not like here. The wind does not bite in Tamaqua as sharply as it does here."

"Do you miss it?" Conor's voice was warm.

Charles glanced over his shoulder. His face seemed more lined than usual, and she saw the memories in his eyes. "*Nein.*" He sighed. "*Nein,* I do not miss it. This place has its own beauty. I wish Bernice could see it."

"She was a fine woman," Conor said softly. "I was sorry I couldn't make it to the funeral."

"I know, Roarke." Charles focused on the clear, starlit sky beyond the soddy. "The telegram you sent was enough."

Sari said nothing, too saddened by Charles's memories and her own to trust herself. She was surprised by the genuine grief in Conor's voice. Her aunt Bernice had liked Conor when he was Jamie O'Brien. "*He is a good man,*" she'd said the first time she met him.

The sadness of loss welled in Sari's heart. A good man. Bernice had never had such kind words for Evan. She had never been comfortable around Sari's husband. But it was different with the Pinkerton spy. Sari remembered her aunt's laughter as she traded sallies with Conor, her flushed face when he told her one of his ribald jokes.

Yes, her aunt had felt a definite affection for Conor, and it had been easy to see that he returned the sentiment. It was easy to see now.

"They told me she'd caught a fever."

"Like the one that killed her sister, Mabel—Sari's mother." Charles sighed. "The family is mostly gone now." He turned, focusing on Conor with bright eyes. "Have you brothers and sisters, Roarke?"

"No."

The word speared through Sari, reminding her of last night.

"You were an only child." Charles nodded thoughtfully. "I have always thought an only child would be lonely."

"You don't miss what you never had." Conor looked down at the book in his hands.

His bleakness was like a shield. For a moment Sari felt the palpable cloak of his desolation as intently as anything she'd ever felt. And with it came that longing again, the yearning to know who he was, how he felt.

"Surely there were other children to play with," she prompted.

The bleakness was gone—so suddenly, she wondered if she'd imagined it. Conor looked up, his eyes as inscrutable as ever. "My childhood was the same as anyone else's," he said—a well-rehearsed answer, a lie she recognized.

"I see." She licked her lips. "I think I understand.

Does William Pinkerton caution all his operatives against telling their secrets?"

His glance was guarded. "It's a good habit to get into when you never know who your friends are."

Sari caught her breath. "At least we know where we stand, then."

He closed his eyes for a moment, then got to his feet, setting the large book down on a crate table. "I think it's time to say good night," he said heavily, swiping a hand through his hair, spiking it. "It's getting late."

Sari rose as well, taking a step forward. "I see you're not willing to take your own advice."

His eyes were sharp. "I don't know what you mean."

"You wanted me to trust you, you wanted to be friends. But friends don't hide themselves from one another."

Across the room Charles motioned for her to be silent. "Leave the man be, *Liebling*. He is tired to-night, and I would welcome a little peace."

"As you wish, *Onkle*." Sari stepped back, turning to the stove. "Good night, then."

"Good night."

She waited until she heard Conor's footsteps cross the floor, until the door was shoved tight again against the elements, before she turned back to face her uncle.

"You keep defending him, *Onkle*," she said softly. "Why is that?"

Charles shook his head. "You do not understand."

"No, I don't," she agreed. "I don't understand.

You know how I feel about him, you know what he did to me, to Evan. And yet you act as if it doesn't matter to you."

"That is not true," Charles said wearily. He walked to the table and sagged into a chair. "He is our best hope, Sarilyn. He can protect us against them."

"So that's it?" Sari asked carefully. "You're afraid of the sleepers? Of Michael?"

Charles nodded. "*Ja.*"

She laughed shortly. "*Onkle,* you are a poor liar. Why don't you just admit that you think I'm wrong? You think I should forgive him, that I should take him back into my life as though he never did anything wrong."

"*Nein,* I do not think that!" Charles shook his head vehemently. "Roarke was wrong to hurt you so. I do not deny this. But you are wrong to think he cannot change. You are like—" He struggled for the words. "He cannot make you happy because you will not let him."

"I can't help it, *Onkle.* I don't trust him."

"Then let him prove he can be trusted. Do not refuse to let him try." Charles smiled gently. "You loved him once, *Liebling.* Sometimes love hurts, eh? You do not think your *Tante* and I did not have bad times?" He shook his head sadly. "There were times when I hurt her as badly as Roarke hurt you. Times I will always regret."

Sari took a deep breath. "I don't know if I even have it in me to try," she said. "Sometimes the memories are so strong . . ."

"I doubt you are the only one who feels that way."

"You think *he* feels sorry?" She asked bitterly. "I don't believe it."

"And because you will not believe it, you make it so." Charles sighed in exhaustion. "Give him the chance to show you he is not the same man. Show him the woman he fell in love with."

"Fell in love with? He has never loved me."

"He did in Tamaqua." Charles disagreed. "He does now."

"He's told you this?"

"I am not blind. Not yet."

"Then your eyesight is fading quickly. Conor Roarke used me. I was a way to avert suspicion."

"In the beginning, *ja*."

"That poem turned your brain to scrapple, *Onkle*," she shook her head. "If I wasn't listening to you myself, I wouldn't believe you've said these things."

"The day will come." He waggled a finger at her. "The day will come when you will see I am right."

"You've missed your calling," she softened. "You'd be better suited as a *Wahrsager*, telling fortunes for a nickel."

"You are hard-hearted, *Liebling*." Charles rose, the smile in his eyes belying his harsh words. "You are little better than a fishwife, but I bless the day you came to us."

"So do I, *Onkle*." Sari smiled. "So do I."

Her uncle's words spun in her mind, a ceaseless rhythm Sari could not ignore or deny. *"He cannot make you happy because you will not let him. . . ."*

She no longer knew what to think. What if her uncle was right? She'd been telling herself for months that she wanted an apology, wanted Conor to regret what he'd done—what he'd forced her to do. Well, he'd apologized, and try as she might, she saw no lies in his eyes. What else did she want? Why couldn't she just accept that he was a fallible man who'd been caught in a bad situation? Why couldn't she believe that he'd returned to make amends, to protect her? Why couldn't she let her anger die?

Because it was safer to keep it alive. Sari stared at the ceiling, at the cotton muslin that swayed in the air wafting beneath the eaves. Forgiving was not the same as forgetting, and she couldn't forget the things she'd done for Jamie O'Brien. The things she *hadn't* done.

She knew too well her weaknesses when it came to this one man. In Tamaqua she'd wanted him so badly, she'd deceived herself. She hadn't seen the signs, though they hadn't been hidden. She'd told herself that she and Jamie had a future, that he was simply trying to work out what to do about Evan. She'd even told herself that he loved her, though he'd never said the words, never even alluded to them.

Everything between them had been a lie. Sari closed her eyes against the sudden onslaught of pain. It had been a lie, and deep inside she'd known it all the time. She'd fought the truth then, had refused to look at herself. She'd just fallen deeper and deeper under his spell.

Just as she found herself falling now. Little by little he was chipping away at her anger, replacing it with memories of kisses and caresses, of heady passion and unbearable joy.

She didn't want to feel those things. She wanted to remember the anger, to remember how she'd felt when she realized he was the traitor, when she'd had only days to make a decision that had meant the lives of her husband, her brother, her friends.

The night was hushed. Even the wind had died away. It was snowing; she could tell by the muffled quiet, the peace that seemed to settle around her. She wondered what Conor was doing. Was he awake, listening as she was? In the dead of night did he ever think about the past? Did he regret anything at all?

Sari squeezed her eyes shut, wishing she could read his mind, needing the reassurance of certainty. She wanted to know if Conor Roarke was a man worth trusting, worth sacrificing for. Jamie O'Brien had not been.

But Charles seemed to think Conor was. He'd never liked Evan. Her quick-tempered Irish husband had been too arrogant—more like a spoiled child than a man. And if nothing else, Conor was a man. In spite of everything, there was a sense of solidity about him, of security. In the last few days Sari had felt the change in her uncle, a lessening of tension over having another man about to keep the farm— and her—safe.

She had to admit that she felt more secure as well.

For some reason she felt able to depend on Conor, though she had no idea why it might be so. She had more cause to distrust him than to feel safe around him.

Sari turned her face into the pillow. Maybe her uncle was right. Maybe it was time to stop the torment. She had suffered enough for Evan Travers, for Michael. Surely it was time to pick up the pieces, to start healing. After all, it was why she'd moved to Colorado, why she'd left everything she knew and loved.

And perhaps, just perhaps, it was time to give Conor Roarke a chance.

CHAPTER 8

CONOR SAT AT THE TABLE IN THE SODDY listening to the sounds of morning: the coffee percolating, the crackling spit of the fire. Nothing else, no human sounds. He was alone. Finally.

He glanced over his shoulder, knowing the moment was too fleeting to last. Sari was milking the cows, and Charles was repairing a harness. Either one could step in at any moment. But still he sat there, thinking of yesterday, of Sari's sad eyes just before he'd stepped out into the cold. Such sad eyes . . .

The image made him feel guilty for what he was about to do, and Conor fought the feeling and lumbered to his feet with a sigh. He told himself that Sari's sadness was well deserved. He could not afford to feel compassion. He couldn't afford to feel anything.

The thought renewed his purpose; without hesi-

tation Conor went to one of the trunks against the
wall and lifted the heavy curved lid.

It was filled with books. Conor's heart sank in
frustration, but he lifted them quickly, his fingers
growing dusty as he flipped through volumes about
farming, religion, mythology. How the hell did Sari
find so much time to read? He frowned, hastily leaf-
ing through each one and dropping it to the side.
More important, why had she and Charles hauled so
many of them cross-country? Had she expected to
spend the rest of her life in well-read isolation?

The thought depressed him, primarily because he
knew it was probably true. Sari was a private person,
a woman who preferred her own company. If no one
stopped her, Conor knew she would lock herself
away from the world, never knowing pain or regret
or happiness.

He jammed shut the lid and turned to the other
trunk, not bothering to analyze the anger that assailed him at the thought.

"Damn!" He swore quietly, fumbling through the
layers of wool blankets that filled the second trunk.
There were no letters there, and time was passing
quickly. She would be back soon, or Charles
would—

The door opened. Conor leaped to his feet, wincing as the trunk lid slammed shut. He grabbed a
book from the bookshelf, pretending to study it avidly while he struggled to calm himself. He turned
slowly, as if preoccupied with his study, to see Sari
close the door with her hip.

"Oh, hello," she said breathlessly, depositing a

pail of fresh milk on the table. "I wondered why I didn't hear you in the barn this morning."

"I was up early," he explained. "I decided to take a walk."

She offered him a tentative smile. "I always love the first snow. It makes me feel so—so good. As if all the ugly things in the world are covered up."

There was something different about her this morning. Her face was red and shiny from the frigid air, her eyes sparkled with good humor. He tried to remember the last time he'd seen the quick spontaneity of her smile, heard her ready laughter. It occurred to him that he'd seen far too little of it. When was the last time he'd seen her happy?

It was discomforting how much he wanted to keep the expression on her face now. "It just feels cold to me," he said, pushing the book back into place. "When I woke up this morning, my clothes were standing by themselves—hell, my lips were frozen to the blanket. Right now I'm doing everything I can to pretend I'm in Mexico."

Sari's answering chuckle made him warmer than any fire. She lifted off her bonnet to reveal her mussed chignon and shrugged out of the too-large wool coat. Unconsciously she rubbed the bandage covering her hand.

"How's your hand?"

"Better." She shrugged.

"Better? Who milked the cows this morning? You or Charles?"

A strange expression lit her deep brown eyes. "I did, of course."

"You shouldn't have," he scolded, startled at how the thought of her struggling with the injured hand bothered him. "You should have asked me to do it."

Her eyes lit with surprise—or was it pleasure? "Can you milk a cow?"

"Of course."

She laughed. "I'll bet you've never even tried."

"How hard can it be?"

"Not hard at all," she teased. "Until Elsa senses you've never touched a cow in your life. Then I'm sure she'll protest."

"Elsa," he repeated slowly. "I suppose that's the cow's name."

Her brows rose in mock surprise. "You mean you don't know? After all those nights sleeping with them, you never bothered to learn their names?"

"I didn't know cows cared if they had names."

"And I thought you didn't know anything about livestock. Or is that some other secret you've kept from me all this time?" She took a step toward him until they were both standing by the stove. She smelled like cold prairie air and warm milk. Her cheeks and the tip of her nose were red, and Conor had a sudden, fierce desire to take her in his arms and kiss away the color.

"Well?" she prompted, her eyes sparkling.

"I had to spend the night with a bunch of cows in a boxcar once. Will that do?"

"You did?"

"Yeah." He leaned back against the wall, saw the way her breath caught at his movement. That soft catch sank into his stomach. He swallowed. "We were pursuing rustlers at the time."

"For Pinkerton?"

He nodded. "We infiltrated the gang—I played cattle rustler for a few months."

"You must have been a very bad one."

He laughed. "Very bad."

The door opened again, bringing a rush of cold wind and Charles. Conor stepped back almost guiltily. He felt a swift disappointment, and his gut clenched when he saw Sari's quick reserve. The joking was over, the brief interlude was ended. He was irritated to realize how much he'd wanted it to go on.

"*Guten Tag,* Roarke." Charles smiled. "*Liebling,* the wagon is ready. Are you?"

Conor frowned. "Wait a minute. The wagon's ready—for what?"

"We're going into town," Sari said, brushing past him. "I've butter ready to be shipped to Denver. We go in every two weeks to sell it."

"Butter?" Conor asked, confused. "Why the hell didn't you tell me about this little trip?" He directed his glare at Charles, who frowned.

"Did you not tell him, Sarilyn?"

She glanced over her shoulder, reaching again for her wool coat. "I must have forgotten."

"Surely you can't mean to go without me?" Conor asked.

"Would you let us?"

"No."

"We would not have gone alone," Charles assured him. The old man threw a chastising look at his niece.

"Of course not," Sari said, opening the door. Her full lips curved in a slight smile. "I go nowhere without my knight in shining armor."

She disappeared outside, leaving Conor to stare after her. For a moment the morning floated before him like a strange illusion. Things had changed somehow, but it was a welcome change, better than her sadness or her accusations. For a moment she was like the old Sari again, the woman who had laughed and smiled with him, who had welcomed his arms and his kisses, and he found himself wanting to play along. It was a relief to be rid of the tension, he told himself, and that was all he let himself think as he grabbed his coat and followed Charles out of the soddy.

Sari jumped down from the wagon, her boots exploding the powdery snow into puffy clouds where she walked. She tugged at the deep collar buttoned against her lips. Her breath had frosted the wool, but she ignored the discomfort, too enchanted by the newly white-covered world to care.

She glanced back at the two men climbing down from the seats; their talk was quiet and deep as they took care of the horses. Conor was hunched against the wind, his hat low over his face, his collar fastened high. As if he felt her scrutiny, he looked up, and though she couldn't see his mouth, she knew he was smiling.

The thought brought a strange, giddy tingle into her stomach and Sari turned away quickly, feeling the hot flush of awareness creep up her cheeks. She stiffened instinctively, then forced herself to relax. Last night she'd made the decision to be honest about what she felt for him, to put aside her anger long enough to give him the benefit of the doubt.

Today's snow had made it easy to be benevolent, but Sari wondered how much of that feeling was due to the day—and how much was due to the sheer magnetism of Conor Roarke. God knew it was difficult to keep fighting him. Difficult to continue to ignore the gentleness in the way he handed Charles a cup of coffee after a long day, or in the way he'd doctored her burn and asked after it as though her health were somehow important to him.

"Where do we go now?" Conor spoke from behind her, and Sari jumped slightly as his voice invaded her thoughts. She turned to see him hefting two trays of molded butter from the wagon bed.

"To Clancy's," she said, pointing ahead to the row of buildings that made up the tiny town. Their blistered gray sides lined a street that was nothing more than ruts cut into the mud. "Right there."

He squinted in the direction of her finger. "Clancy's?"

"The store." Charles nodded, shoving his hands into his pockets. "There is one, trust me."

"If you say so."

Charles laughed at the doubt in Conor's voice. "It does not look like much, but there is a Grange hall as well. It is enough for us."

"It's nothing like Chicago," Sari teased. "No dance hall girls, no fancy shops—"

"Why, Sari, I'm surprised you know about dance hall girls," Conor said with a smile.

She grinned back at him. "I'm a coal miner's wife. I'd have to be blind not to know about them."

"As you say." He brushed by her, carrying the trays of butter without effort, and his voice was low as he bent close. "But you're not a coal miner's wife. Not anymore."

He was past her before she had time to react, but his words hovered around her ear; she felt the warmth of his breath against her skin, the heat of his quick annoyance. He'd only gone a few feet when he turned around and stopped, watching her, waiting for her as the wind whipped his duster around his legs.

Her uncle's chuckle surprised her as he walked to her side. "You had best go after him, *Liebling,* before he gets lost."

"As if he could get lost in Woodrow."

"Go on," he said, giving her a slight push. "I am going to the saloon. Mrs. Landers has some stories to tell me today."

"But—"

"I will meet you back here, *Liebling.*"

He started off, his cheerful whistling piercing the cold air, his breath a frozen cloud. Throwing one last glance at her disappearing uncle, Sari lifted her skirts and hurried toward Conor.

Woodrow was quiet today; the crunching of a few wagon wheels and cheerful hellos were the only sounds that floated on the dry, frigid air. Sari shielded her eyes, needing more than the protection of her bonnet to keep from squinting. The bright but ineffectual sun glittered on the snow until it sparkled like crushed diamonds.

"So," he said when she grew nearer. "Where is this 'Clancy's' anyway? And where did Charles go?"

"He's off to visit his friend Mrs. Landers." Sari fell into step beside him. "Every time we come into town, he has to pay her a visit. She's a terrible gossip."

Conor's eyebrows rose. "I didn't know Charles listened to gossip."

"He says he doesn't." She smiled. "He *says* he only goes because she's lonely and it makes her happy when he visits." Her voice lowered conspiratorially. "But I think he likes to hear her talk, though he wouldn't be caught dead passing it on. Besides, she sometimes has cherry pie. It's his favorite."

"Cherry pie," he mused, shuffling the trays in his hands. "I've forgotten what that tastes like. The last time I had it was—" He stopped abruptly.

Sari felt the wall go up, his expression shuttered. She glanced at him curiously. "The last time you had it—?" she prompted.

He gave her a smile; it seemed oddly forced. "Your aunt Bernice," he said. "I ate it with her last." But though the words were easy and casual, Sari sensed a lie. She tensed in sudden wariness. It was there again, this hiding, this *something* he didn't want her to know. What was it?

Sari turned away. She hurried her step until she reached Clancy's General Store. There, on the torn planking of the narrow porch, she paused. She swiveled on one foot to face Conor. She wanted to forget, she wanted to be able to believe him, to forgive him. "It's such a beautiful day," she said evenly. "Do you think we could be kind to each other?"

His gaze was inscrutable, his ice-blue eyes nearly froze her with their emptiness. But his voice was warm, vibrating with a tension that pierced her heart. "I want nothing more than to be kind to you, Sari," he said softly. "It's the reason I came here." He stepped onto the porch and walked past her to grab the door. It swung wide, and a string of bells jangled.

Sari took a deep breath and went through the door. She paused to breathe in the mélange of odors—dried fish and smoked meats; the rich, mellow aroma of tobacco and coffee; the dusty smell of spice. Conor went up to the counter and set down her trays of butter. Almost proudly, she thought, the sight dispelling her tension. Almost as if he had a right to be proud.

Then she noticed the curious glances of the other people in the large room. The three men huddled around the stove in the corner had stopped talking; the women comparing fabric turned to stare. Sari's heart beat rapidly, her pulse fluttered as she dodged the barrels lining the floor and hurried to the counter. She felt Conor's eyes on her as she gripped the edge of the scarred board and leaned over it.

"Mr. Clancy!" she called, feeling the edge of

panic, even though she knew it was absurd. It was too familiar—all these staring eyes. Too much like Tamaqua, though it was innocent curiosity here. Nothing more. Not those rigid, condemning expressions or the stares that called her a traitor—

Conor's hand curled around hers. The touch was warm and comforting. He squeezed her rigid knuckles gently, and Sari stared up at him.

"It's all right, love," he whispered, his voice like molasses over her frayed nerves. "Relax."

He understood. The knowledge was too frightening to believe. Sari tore her hand from his, trying to still the rapid-fire beating of her heart, trying to pretend he hadn't known, that her terror was still her secret. She scanned the room. "Where is Mr. Clancy?"

"He's around back." One of the women near the bolts of fabric spoke quietly, but her dark eyes were bright with curiosity. Sari's heart fell. Thelma Abbott. The woman was a bigger gossip than Audra Landers.

Sari couldn't help the thinning of her lips. "Hello, Thelma."

"It's nice to see you, Sari. You haven't been in town lately." Thelma's nearsighted squint lit on Conor. Sari could almost see the wheels turning in the woman's head.

She introduced them, then stifled a smile when Conor dropped Thelma's proffered hand as quickly as politely possible.

"I'd heard there was someone staying at your farm, Sari," Thelma twittered, fidgeting at the wide bow of her sunbonnet. "No one told me it was—are you a relative, Mr. Roarke?"

"I'm an old friend of the family."

"Oh?" Thelma's smile was brittle with curiosity. "From—where was it, Sari?—Pennsylvania, wasn't it? I imagine the rest of the family is quite worried about our Sari, out here in the wilderness. I'm not surprised they sent you out to check on her."

Sari jumped in quickly, before Conor could answer. "Mr. Roarke was out this way, on business."

Conor went on smoothly. "I thought I'd stop and see how Mrs. Travers and her uncle were getting on."

Thelma arched her brows. Already Sari could imagine Thelma's gossipy words. *"Sari Travers is keeping company with a man—he's living at her farm. Why, it's hardly proper. . . ."* Despite herself Sari's cheeks felt heated.

"Will you be staying in Woodrow long, Mr. Roarke?"

Conor was saved from answering by the rustling of the calico curtains behind the counter. A short, balding man with a thick gray beard pushed aside the material. His arms were filled with bolts of cloth.

"Here you are, Mrs. Abbott," he puffed good-naturedly, plunking the heavy fabrics onto the counter and wiping his shining forehead with the back of his hand. "Like I told you, I've got no yellows in, but I'm expecting a shipment soon from Julesburg. If you find nothing you like today—"

Thelma sighed dramatically. She wrinkled her

nose at the selection before her. "It looks like I'll have to go into Denver after all."

"Mr. Clancy." Sari interrupted Thelma's posturings impatiently. "When you have a moment . . ."

Clancy smiled. "I've got a moment right now, Sari." He glanced quickly at Thelma. "Since it looks like Mrs. Abbott's going into Denver."

Thelma lifted her chin haughtily. "Well, I may *not* go."

"Ah, now, don't let me talk you into doing something you don't want to do," Mr. Clancy said amiably. "I won't have any of my customers saying I forced them into buying something."

"But I—"

"Now, now, Mrs. Abbott," Clancy shook his head. "I'll just go ahead and wait on Sari here, and when I'm done, if you're still interested, you just call me over."

Sari looked at the counter, trying to hide her grin as Thelma huffed and flounced off to the stove to corral her husband.

"Thank the Lord," Clancy murmured. He leaned forward, his beefy hands resting on the rough wood. "You're a pretty sight today, Sari. What can I do for you?"

Sari smiled. "Mr. Clancy, this is Conor Roarke."

"I'm a friend of the family," Conor said with an ease that made Sari's heart jump. "Just checking up on Sari."

"Well, I don't mind telling you it makes me feel better to see another man at that place." Clancy nodded approvingly. "No telling what trouble's way out there." He pulled the trays of butter toward him, lifting the cheesecloth off the firm, molded cakes. "Looks lovely as usual, Sari. I've got some money for you—"

"Apply it to our account," Sari interrupted. "There are some things I need as well."

"I don't suppose one of those things would be a new dress, would it?" Clancy asked hopefully.

She hesitated. "I don't think so."

Clancy pushed the trays aside and leaned over the counter persuasively. "I'm telling you, girl, I got in some fabric yesterday that made me think of you. I kept it aside just in case you'd be interested. A lovely color, cream with dark green stripes." He pursed his lips appreciatively. "It would look beautiful on you."

"Stripes?" Sari laughed, trying to hide the fact that she was tempted. It had been a long time since she'd had anything pretty, and the evening she'd spent with Conor poring over the *Godey's Lady's Book* had only made her wish for things she couldn't have, such as silk gowns and ribbons and a man who wanted to wrap her in them.

She sighed, trying unsuccessfully to keep wistfulness from her voice. "It sounds far too fancy for me, Mr. Clancy."

"Now, girl, I know it isn't practical, but Christmas is coming. Thought you might want a nice silk dress."

"For what? Imagine how silly I'd look parading around the soddy in something like that."

"Mr. Roarke, help me persuade her," Clancy

pleaded, spreading his big hands. "Tell this pretty lady that she needs a fine dress for the Christmas dance this year."

One corner of Conor's mouth lifted. "Sari's not much for *fripperies*," he said. His eyes twinkled, and Sari was struck with the brief, insane wish that he might care whether she wore silks and satins, that it might matter to him how she looked.

"It would be nice to touch the smoothness of silk again, eh?" Clancy pushed away from the counter. "Wait here, wait here. Let me show it to you, you won't be able to resist it."

He disappeared behind the curtains, and Sari bit her lip, staring at the counter. "A silk dress," she said quietly. "It's such a luxury."

"He's right, you know, you deserve it." Conor's voice was soft, caressing.

"In the middle of the plains?"

"There's that Christmas dance to consider."

"It's so impractical."

"It would add some color," he teased. "Something besides brown."

His finger touched her sleeve. Even through the thick wool of her coat, she felt the heat of it, the sure, gentle pressure as he ran his finger down her arm to her elbow. She swallowed, unable to look at him.

"You'd look beautiful in it, Sari," he whispered. "Let me see you in silk."

Please, she thought, *don't be so kind.* She couldn't bear such tender kindness. She pulled away, leaned back just enough so that his hand fell from her sleeve. It was too much like her dreams, the dreams she had once before—first with Evan and then with Conor—and she knew how they ended. They never came true. "I can't buy such a thing."

"Can't?" he murmured, his eyes hooded. "Or won't? Why are you so afraid of being pretty, Sari?"

"I'm not afraid," she lied. Her heart felt heavy— lonely and yearning suddenly. She wished she could see the expression in his eyes.

His jaw tightened, he looked away. "Christ, I could have killed Evan for what he did to you."

"It wasn't just Evan," she said slowly. The words felt wrenched from her heart, her fingers curled inside the warmth of her gloves. "It wasn't just Evan."

Her words fell on silence so big, she couldn't breathe for the tension of it.

"Here we go." Clancy's voice was loud and startling as he returned, his arms filled with a bolt of rich cream fabric shot with gold thread. The green stripes shone nearly black and lustrous in the light. He laid it on the counter proudly. "What did I tell you, Sari? Beautiful, eh?"

Sari tried to blink away the glaze of tears covering her eyes, tried to garner a weak smile. "Yes," she said dully, not even able to touch the soft, shimmering fabric, hating the sight of it because of what it meant. Because of what she would never have. "But someone else will have to buy it, Mr. Clancy. I can't."

"But I can."

Unbelievingly she heard Conor's voice. She looked at him, stiffening, unable to speak or stop him as he laid his money on the counter. It was too calculated, and his smile was too stiff. Instead of gratitude or happiness, she felt a dull disbelief, a painful swelling around her heart. Because she knew why he was buying it, and it had nothing to do with caring about her or wanting her to have fine things. It was blood money, payment for services rendered, a way of assuaging his guilt.

And she wanted no part of it.

Sari moved away, walking to the door of the general store with her tears forming a lump in her throat, suddenly knowing that the past was too strong to fight, that she would never be able to forget what he'd done to her—and wishing with all her heart that it was different.

CHAPTER 9

CONOR CURSED AS THE TRAP'S SLIDING door collapsed once again beneath his fingers. He glanced up at the gray snow clouds racing across the sky, covering the sun. Not that the sun would help the cold, he thought drily. He doubted there was a warmth strong enough to ease the wind that beat at his back, stinging through the leather of his coat, dragging at the brim of his hat. It carried ice particles that burned his cheeks whenever he turned his head. His knee was soaking wet where he knelt in the snow.

He switched knees and tried the trap once again. This time it took only seconds to tangle into a useless mess. Conor's fingers caught in the wooden sticks rigging the sliding door. Angrily he tossed them aside. Damn the stupid trap. What the hell had he been doing, promising to catch a rabbit this week for dinner?

He got to his feet, shoving back his hat. He'd

promised because the suggestion had made her smile. And he'd felt the need to atone after bungling their foray into town so badly.

He winced at the thought of it. He'd been so caught up in her laughter and teasing that it had been easy to stick to his plan, to seduce her into a false sense of trust, to make her believe in him. It had been too easy. He had forgotten how much he'd truly enjoyed her company in Tamaqua, how the friendship between them—a friendship that had its genesis in lies—had become something more. It was so easy to be with her, so tempting to sit back and tease her, to watch her eyes light in laughter and trust.

That was what had made him buy the silk—the stupid need to see her smile at him. It had been a huge mistake, he'd known it almost instantly. The act was too intimate, too selfish and shortsighted. But he couldn't seem to think straight around her. The sight of her wide eyes, dark with a sad longing for something as meaningless as a bolt of cloth, had moved him.

Damn, he wished he hadn't seen the loneliness in her eyes. For a second he understood her, knew why she had betrayed him to save her brother. In the store he'd seen a hint of what life had been like for her in Tamaqua, the life he'd left her with, and he'd been ashamed.

Now he knew why she'd run away as far as she could. The hell of it was, he didn't want to understand. It was easier just to see her as the enemy, to manipulate her without worrying about her feelings.

She was a means to an end, why couldn't he remember that?

Conor grimaced. He knew why. It was the constant exposure to those deep brown eyes, that winsome smile, the swaying grace of her slender body. He was more affected by his seduction than Sari was. Yes, it was deliberate. Yes, he wanted her to trust him. But he was tormented by his own manipulations. And what made it worse was his memories—memories of the way it felt to make love to her, the way she twisted beneath him and whispered his name in that deep, honeyed voice.

He closed his eyes briefly, for a moment letting the fire burn painfully inside him. She was only a woman. A woman he'd needed to do a job. He was not alone in that. She had betrayed him as well. They had used each other. It would be best if he remembered that.

Conor took a deep, calming breath. He glanced back at the mess of a rabbit trap lying on the thin cover of snow. At least there was one thing he could count on. There'd be no rabbit tomorrow—or any other day this week. At least not due to his efforts. He picked up the loose strings and sticks, shoving them into the deep pockets of his duster, and lodged the box under his arm.

From this short distance the house looked friendly and comfortable. Smoke rose from the stovepipe poking through the gently sloping roof. Late-afternoon shadows slanted against the walls, blending Charles's smaller soddy into the darkening grass bricks, making the blades of the windmill rising behind seem stern and forbidding.

This was a bleak place. Conor glanced at the purplish-gray mountains edging the horizon like a huge wall. He felt tired and depressed; even anger and revenge seemed an effort. The cold wind tore at him, flapping his coat at his knees, biting the exposed parts of his face. Conor speeded his step; his boots crunched and slid on the quickly evaporating layer of snow. Frozen buffalo grass already peeked through the ice; lumpy hillocks had been exposed since yesterday. As he rounded the corner of the soddy, he saw the lamplight slanting from the window.

He walked past quickly, not daring to look inside, knowing that he'd see Sari and Charles talking animatedly, without the tension that constrained them when he was around. It was a homey, warm place, and the thought filled him with a sudden wistfulness, the quick and unfamiliar wish that he were simply a normal man with a normal life—and not a man ruled by lies and roles. What would it be like to have a job that didn't require hurting innocent people?

Or watching loved ones die?

The thought startled him. He was what he was, and he'd known for a long time that the Pinkerton agency suited him well. He had relatively few talents, but one of them was his ability to mimic accents, to absorb a personality. His childhood had taught him quick thinking and stealthy movement—one did not survive as an orphan on the streets of Chicago without those talents. Violence and lying had been a part of him since he was a child, and he'd never lived without them. Even under Sean Roarke's tender ministrations, Conor had always felt unworthy of the priest's affections, had always known that deep inside he was too filled with demons to let heaven in.

For a while with his adoptive father Conor had allowed himself to envision a different life. For a time he'd wondered if he was capable of honesty and peace. But those speculations had been short-lived. When he met William Pinkerton, he realized he was born to be a Pinkerton agent. And if there were times now when he wondered if there was something else worth doing, well, they were few and far between. All he had to do was remember his ceiling crashing in around him, the ash floating over his father. *That* was why he was here, *that* was reason enough to go on. And as for living a normal life . . .

That was for other people, not for him. It would never be for him.

Sari squinted out the window, trying to focus on the figures moving over the hill to the farm. She wiped her hands on her apron, frowning when she realized what she was looking at.

"My God," she said slowly. "*Onkle,* look who's come."

Charles glanced up. "Michael?"

Sari shook her head impatiently as he moved beside her. "No. The neighbors. Oh, Lord, Miri's done it. She's brought them all."

"A party?" Charles smiled. "Do not worry, *Liebling,* it is only for fun. You could use such a thing."

"A party." Sari repeated the words, her heart sinking. What had Miriam been thinking? The last thing Sari wanted was a group of neighbors congregating at their house for two days, asking questions, drawing conclusions. "I can't allow it. I can't. There will be so much talk."

"You cannot send them away. And you worry too much. There is nothing to fear. You think Roarke will reveal something? He has as much to lose as you."

He was right, she knew. Conor would say nothing. Hadn't he proven that with Miriam? He wouldn't mention Michael or the Mollies, would mention Evan only in passing. She could trust him that far.

The thought was comforting even as it frightened her. She had made the decision to trust him, to let him prove to her that he was worth trusting. It was absurd that she was afraid of the speed with which he was proving it.

She took a deep breath, braving a weak smile. "Well, then," she said briskly. "They'll be here shortly. Where is he?"

"Roarke? He is in the barn."

"The barn." Sari threw another glance to the line of wagons moving slowly into view. "Will you get him, *Onkle*? There's a lot to do."

She waited until Charles had left the soddy before she scurried around, looking with quiet desperation at the cluttered house. The books that usually comforted her with their closeness now looked dusty, ill kept, crowded. The lovingly made pine rocking chair took up too much room. How was she going to make the space for a party?

She rushed around, pushing piles of books onto the shelves, trying to shove chairs against the walls. Their legs dragged on the cowhide covering the floor and caught, and Sari was suddenly filled with frustration and depression so strong, she couldn't fight it. Images of other parties filled her mind, parties with dancing and laughter and silly games. Stories and glowing fires and warmth that fought the wet chill of the Tamaqua winters. Then, there'd been no reason to pretend. Nothing to hide. She'd laughed and talked, happy for company. The tables had groaned under the weight of all the food.

Sari froze. Food. Oh, God, was there enough food? Her uncle's Dutch custom was always to be sure to have seven sweets and seven sours on the table. Less than that was bad luck. Just what she needed. More bad luck. Sari knelt at the pie safe, searching the rows of canned goods on the bottom shelf. Was there any rhubarb jam left? Cherry relish? Had Charles eaten the few jars of pickles she'd brought?

The door opened. Sari twisted to see Charles and Conor come inside, rubbing their gloved hands against the cold.

"What are you doing?" Conor asked.

Sari looked at her uncle. "There isn't enough, *Onkle*. Not for seven of each."

Charles grinned. "I think we do not need to worry about that tonight."

Conor frowned. "What the hell are you talking about?"

His bewilderment made her smile, and Sari sat back on her heels, relaxing. "Seven sweets and seven sours," she explained. "For company. Or it's bad luck."

He threw a glance at Charles. "Undoubtedly some strange German custom," he said. "I don't think they'll care. Or even notice. Besides, I'm here to keep bad luck away."

Sari got to her feet, closing the sideboard doors just as she heard the creaking stop of wagon wheels in the front yard.

"Then I'll let that be your job," she said. "But I warn you, the curses of my family are nothing to ignore."

His brows lifted. "I'm familiar with them, believe me."

There was no time to wonder about his words.

"Help me! Help me!" The shrieks of ten-year old Becky Schmacher played havoc with Sari's already frayed nerves. The little girl scrambled across the floor, dodging between Sari and Miriam.

Miriam frowned. "Whatever—"

"Aaaaah! I don't have it!" Becky nearly knocked Miriam over in her efforts to elude her pursuing brother. She twisted around Sari, grabbing her skirts to hide behind. "I don't have it!"

Samuel Schmacher skidded to a halt just before he crashed into Miriam. "You do too! Give it back!"

"I don't!" Becky buried her face in Sari's hip.

"Tell him to go away and leave me alone, Mizz Travers!"

"Becky! Samuel!" Miriam scolded. She stepped back, grasping Samuel's arm to keep him from flailing upon his sister. "Goodness, you two are causing a ruckus." She knelt down until she was at Samuel's level. "What does she have, Samuel?"

"I don't have it!" Becky objected. Her fingers dug into Sari's hip, her wide eyes peaked from the edge of the fabric.

Miriam threw her a quick look. "Now, Becky, it's not nice to tease your brother. Where's your ma?"

"In the barn."

"Why don't you go and get her, Samuel? Perhaps she can help Becky find what you're looking for."

Becky dropped Sari's skirts. "No—don't tell Ma." She held out her hand, uncoiling chubby fingers to reveal a well-worn stone. She turned earnest eyes to Sari. "It's Sammy's lucky rock."

Miriam checked Samuel's hasty grab. "Take it nicely, Samuel. There, that's right. Now, do I have your promise there'll be no more of this screaming?"

Samuel eyed the ground reluctantly. "Yes, ma'am."

"Becky?"

"I didn't—"

"Becky."

"Yes, ma'am. Me too."

"Good." Miriam stood, Sari could almost see her wipe her hands of the Schmacher children. "Go off and play now. Mrs. Travers and I are talking."

Samuel threw a scathing glance at his sister before

he ran back to the other children. Becky came from behind Sari's skirts reluctantly.

"Do I have to go?"

The little girl's plaintive tone tugged at Sari's heart. She laid a hand on Becky's light brown curls, smoothing them back. "Why don't you want to go back, Becky?"

"Sammy'll be mad."

"You gave back his rock."

"He'll still be mad. I'd rather stay with you."

Sari smiled gently. "Mrs. Graham and I will be talking about boring things, Becky. I'll tell you what: Go and play with the others. If Samuel's still mad, you can come back and sit with us for a while. All right?"

Becky hesitated. "Well—all right."

Sari watched as the little girl weaved reluctantly across the floor. Within moments she was happily chatting with the other children. Sari glanced up to see a smile caressing Miriam's mouth.

"You'll be a good mother, Sari."

Sari frowned slightly. "Maybe. I expect I'll never know."

"Never know?" Miriam looked scandalized. "Surely you aren't intending to hide away forever? Why, I thought you and Conor—"

"Miri." Sari warned.

"Well, I can't help it. He's perfect! And I haven't missed the way he looks at you."

Sari couldn't help asking. "What way is that?"

"Like he wants to—" Miri paused, blushing furiously, then went on eagerly. "Like he wants to drink up your very soul." She sighed. "It's so romantic."

Drink her soul. Sari smiled grimly. The words were apt—Miriam didn't realize how much so. Conor had never been content with just her body.

Sari looked out the window again, searching for him despite herself. It was becoming easy—too easy—to forget that he was the same man who had used her to gain his own ends.

"What *do* you keep looking for?" Miriam peered around her. "Is Isabel making a fool of herself again?"

"No. I'm just looking." Sari fidgeted with the pies gathered on the sideboard, pushing a dried apple one here, a custard one there.

"Oh, leave those be. They're fine." Miri edged closer, her blue eyes sparkling. She lowered her voice. "Did I tell you Adelaide Pierce is expecting again? That's why she's not here tonight—she was afraid the drive would hurt the baby, though she's not even due for another seven months. Goodness knows where these city women get their ideas! Why, I'll bet she's lying abed right now, making Edward do all the chores."

Sari laughed. Miriam's chatter was infectious. "The drive *is* long, Miri."

"Long? Why, it's hardly more than ten miles from their place!" Miriam lowered her voice. "Look at Mary Anderson over there—seven months along if she's a day. *She* was more excited than anyone to get out here."

Sari slanted a glance at the obviously pregnant woman sitting in the rocker. Mary Anderson fanned her flushed face with a magazine, punctuating her conversation with emphatic pulses of the makeshift fan.

Miriam rushed on. "She was dying to see the infamous Conor Roarke."

Sari looked up sharply. "What do you mean?"

"You're the talk of Woodrow, Sari," Miriam said guilelessly. "Surely you knew that."

Miriam's news sent a shaft of unease through Sari, though it wasn't as if she hadn't expected gossip. She frowned.

"I told you," Miriam said. "Didn't I tell you everyone would be wondering?"

Sari rolled her eyes. "*You* were the one wondering, Miri."

"And I'm still wondering." She sent a sly glance through the crowded, noisy room. "Where is he, anyway? I thought I saw him when we came in."

"He's probably in the barn, hiding from all this commotion."

"In fact, where's John?"

Berthe Schmacher came through the door just in time to answer. "He's out talking with Mr. Roarke." Her plump face lit. "My, my, he's a handsome one, Sari. Wherever did you find him?"

Sari focused on the sideboard, on the golden crumb topping of what smelled like a shoofly pie. The scent of molasses churned her stomach. "He was a friend of my husband's."

"How long is he planning to stay?"

Miriam frowned. "Heavens, Berthe, you're as bad as Thelma Abbott."

"At least I ask Sari straight out instead of hinting around," Berthe said haughtily. She pulled her scarf from her head, shoving loosened hairpins back into her graying hair. "The whole town was talking about Thelma's nasty suspicions. Can you imagine?" A sharp shriek cut the room, and her gaze automatically followed. "Becky! Samuel! You two children behave!" She turned back to Sari. "You actually talked to her?"

Sari nodded. "She saw us in Clancy's."

"No doubt she was looking for a silk party dress." Berthe's full lips pursed. Another scream, this time from a different corner. Berthe sighed heavily. "Good Lord—excuse me, won't you?"

Sari tried to fight the exhaustion steadily creeping up on her. It would be a long night if she had to fight off questions about Conor for most of it. She sighed, glancing at the groaning sideboard, remembering his promise of protection. She could use his support now; he was so much better at fending off unwelcome questions.

Sari's tension only increased as the night wore on. By the time the potluck dinner had been eaten and the children were cheerfully playing games in the corner, she was ready to scream. She glanced toward Conor, feeling an unfamiliar tightening in her throat as she saw how readily he smiled and teased Isabel— and how easily the woman responded. One would almost think she was a young girl flushed with first love rather than a twenty-five-year old woman with two young children—and a husband standing less than a yard away.

For a moment Sari wished heartily that Tom Johnson would develop a sudden jealous fury. She could almost picture the big man striding over, pulling his slender, meekly pretty wife aside and landing a stiff uppercut to Conor's jaw.

Isabel's high-pitched twitter cut the buzz of conversation, and Sari winced. She knew the way his eyes focused on Isabel as though she were the only woman in the room, and Sari knew exactly what kind of effect that look was having. God knew she'd found herself caught in that heady, sensual gaze more than once.

Sari resisted the urge to crush her cup. Conor Roarke could flirt and talk with Isabel Johnson—or any other woman in the room—as long as he wanted. She didn't care.

"Everyone, everyone!" Miriam stood, clapping her hands to gain attention. "Come over here now, it's time to sing! Will, did you bring your fork?"

Will Schmacher nodded, a broad grin spreading across his face. "Why, Miri, it's the whole reason I'm here!"

Everyone laughed, and Miriam placed her hands on her pink-swathed hips. "Now, come *on,* everyone. Sari—get over here. Help me organize!"

Miriam smiled. "Very well. Now, I'm going to break everyone up into couples, and we'll take turns."

Sari groaned inwardly. Couples. She suddenly knew without a doubt what Miri was planning. She tried to back away, but almost as if she sensed Sari's withdrawal, Miriam reached out and grabbed her hand firmly.

"Now." Miriam was in her element. She waited expectantly until everyone was watching her. "Berthe, since your husband will be leading, you're without a partner. Charles—" Laughter filled the room as Charles started in surprise, slopping coffee on the floor. "Charles, you will partner Berthe."

Charles bowed slightly. "I will be delighted."

"You'd best watch your wife, Will." Tom chuckled.

The naming of partners went on. Slowly. Agonizingly slowly. One by one, they were all paired off. Sari threw an anxious glance at her friend as they began running out of names, but Miriam ignored her.

"And Isabel with John." Miriam put a finger to her chin, her eyes narrowing in thought. "Now, is that everyone? Oh, wait! Conor!" Miriam sighed in mock exasperation. "Oh dear, I'd thought to split you and Sari up, but I guess I forgot." She threw a dimpled glance at Sari, who felt an immediate and overwhelming urge to strangle her friend. "Conor and Sari. Now the fun can begin!"

CHAPTER 10

"READY TO DANCE?"

Conor's voice was soft in her ear, and Sari started, surprised to feel his warmth at her side, the sudden, intimate touch of his hand resting lightly against her elbow.

"This is ridiculous," she whispered, shrugging away from both his touch and the evocative sensations it aroused. "It's getting late. Long past time for games."

"Coward."

Sari's chin snapped up. She glared at him challengingly. "I am *not* a coward."

"No? Then what would you call it?" His smile was even and warm. "Why are you so afraid, Sari? Believe me, even I wouldn't ravish you in front of ten other people."

No, not physically, Sari thought. That at least was true. *But emotionally . . .* She took a deep breath. There was no help for it now. The other couples were already shoving back the chairs, making room for the silly dances. Breathless laughter and joking filled the room.

"Shall we sit down?" he murmured. Then, as if she hadn't just pulled away from him, he took her hand, tucking it in the crook of his arm. Sari caught her breath at the contact. His broad fingers were warm; the touch sent tingles through her. He seemed oblivious to her reaction as he led her to a nearby chair. She sat numbly, her heart making a queer little jump when he sat on the arm of the chair and his thigh brushed her arm.

"Okay, okay." Miriam clapped her hands, surveying the seated couples with satisfaction. "Who will start?"

Will hit the tuning fork against his knee. Its pure, clean hum rose above the chatter.

Berthe and Charles stood up. " 'Old Dan Tucker,' please," Berthe requested. She dimpled. "It's the only dance I know, since Will's always sitting out."

The tuning fork rang out again, joining the companionable laughter. Sari leaned forward, smiling at her uncle's obvious delight in the game. Charles had always loved to dance, to laugh. She focused on him, on his lighthearted enjoyment, and tried to forget how close Conor sat.

> Old Dan Tucker was a mighty man
> Washed his face in a frying pan
> Combed his hair with a wagon wheel
> Died with a toothache in his heel

The tune was familiar, the singing filled with choking laughter as Berthe and Charles promenaded to the silly words, the strained harmonies. They bowed to each other, hooked arms, and spun around in a caricature of a dance. The sprigged skirt of Berthe's simple wrapper swirled around her legs, and she lifted it with both hands, revealing her lace-edged drawers, sending a sly wink to the crowd.

Sari laughed at Charles's feigned shock. Her uncle had missed his calling. He should have been an actor, the way he postured and gestured like a preacher at a revival show. She clapped her hands in time to the music, stamped her feet on the hard-packed floor along with the others, and raised her voice to belt out the final chorus:

> Get out the way for Old Dan Tucker,
> He's too late to get his supper
> Supper's over and breakfast's cookin'
> Old Dan Tucker just stands there lookin'.

"The two of you should join a troupe!" Tom suggested when the song was over, and Charles and Berthe sank exhausted into their chairs.

"A troupe?" Charles sputtered breathlessly. "*Ach*, Johnson, I am too old for such a thing."

Sari smiled and glanced over her shoulder, expecting to hear Conor's answering chuckle. But there was no smile on his face.

Sari's laughter died in her throat. His eyes glowed as he looked at her. She saw desire in his burning glance, the stiffness of his jaw. The touch of his thigh against her arm was suddenly burning hot. She felt the flush of her face, felt dizzy at the quick racing of her heart.

The singing started again. Sari was dimly aware that Isabel and John were now dancing. Isabel's dark green skirt flashed at the edge of Sari's vision.

Conor's glance never wavered. Sari swallowed. "Please—" she whispered.

He bent forward. His hair fell into his face at the movement, his shoulders flexed. "Please?" he repeated. "Please what, Sari? *Please* what?"

"Please don't."

He leaned back again. "Please don't?"

"Don't look at me that way."

His smile was enigmatic. "What way is that, love?"

The pounding of dancing feet seemed to reverberate into her brain. Was it that, or was it the way his mouth curved in a funny half smile that made her feel dizzy? She paused. "When you look at me that way, there are no secrets in your eyes. Not like . . . other times."

"What does that mean?"

"Other times," she said softly, "it's like there's a wall behind your eyes." She caught his gaze, holding it steadily. "But I suppose you know that. It would be safer for you that way."

He said nothing. Isabel's laugh pealed, sharp and strident, over the singing. The children were giggling now, their high voices competing with the singing.

Sari pressed on. "I would think a man who takes on different roles has to be able to keep secrets."

He opened his mouth to answer, but before he could, the singing stopped, and Miriam squealed, "Sari, Conor, it's your turn!"

The moment fled, the uncertainty she'd glimpsed disappeared. Sari turned to her friend, pasting on a smile. "Isn't there someone else who'd like to go?"

"Come on, Sari," Miriam grabbed her hand, pulling Sari to her feet. "Conor, please. Don't tell me they don't dance in Chicago. Will, start the song!"

Sari tensed. She felt as if Miriam had kept her from finding out something important, something that mattered, and disappointment made her heart heavy. She glanced at Conor. He was watching her, a slight smile on his face, his eyes glittering.

Will hit the tuning fork. Her neighbors started singing. Conor held out his hand.

There was something in his face that made the gesture more than a simple request to dance. As if he'd said, *"Give me your hand. Give me your trust and we can start over."* She wondered if that was what she wanted. To start over. She'd told herself to give him a chance, but in the face of his desire tonight—and her own—she wondered suddenly if she'd been wise. He wanted her, she knew, and she'd never stopped wanting him. But was she ready for such intimacy again? Could she trust him?

Eighteen pounds of meat a week
Whiskey here to sell—

Sari put her hand in his, curtsying in response to his bow. His fingers curled around hers, holding tightly. She felt the heat of his gaze brushing over her flushed face.

The singing was off-key, discordant, but it rang with humor. Whistles and shouts emphasized the silly words. She tried to concentrate on the steps, tried not to think about how broad and strong Conor's shoulders were when she do-si-do'd past him and their bodies brushed. She tried not to see how tousled and vulnerable he looked with his brown hair falling into his eyes.

> How can the boys stay at home
> When the girls all look so well—
> When the girls all look so well.

Sari stood back as Conor did the intricate steps of the first lines, laughing in spite of herself.

"How's this?" He shouted above the singing, looking at Miriam. "This is what you get for that crack about Chicago."

Miriam laughed and shook her head, continuing her light soprano. Conor turned back to Sari, motioning for her to join him again, and she tiptoed in, swinging her brown calico skirts. The room was warm, and thin trickles of perspiration gathered between her breasts. Her hair loosened, trailing across her cheeks, and Sari brushed it aside, ignoring it for the moment while she joined Conor's antics.

"Oh, Conor, no!"

"That's it, Sari, you tell him!"

Amid the cheers and the jests, she pointed her toe, dragging up her skirt to show off her calves clad in black stockings, smiling with mock coquettishness at Conor, then pretending horror at the words.

> If I had a scolding wife
> I'd whip her sure as she's born—

Sari stumbled backward, shaking with laughter at Conor's wagging finger. It felt good to laugh, good to feel the sweet enjoyment of simple fun. How long it had been.

She had to admit it had been Conor who brought it to her. The last man in the world she could have believed could make her smile. Until the last few days, until this minute, she would have denied he any longer had the power to make her feel so good.

She twined her arm in Conor's, swirling around him, her skirt catching on her legs. Her chignon slid to the side. He caught her at her waist, swinging her around in the dance. The touch of his hands on her body made her giddy.

He leaned close. "I'd forgotten this."

His whisper trembled through her, his breath fanned the loose tendrils of hair at her throat. Sari raised her head, staring at him, seeing the passion in his blue eyes. His hand curled at her waist, the touch shockingly intimate even though there was nothing overtly seductive in it, and in his eyes she saw a memory. The memory of that dance so long ago, when they'd first met. There had been desire then, before they'd even talked to each other. Yes, there had always been desire.

The song ended, wild clapping followed. Conor's eyes and mouth crinkled in a smile, he made an exaggerated bow. "Thank you, thank you. But don't waste all your applause on me." He grabbed Sari's hand, pulling her against his side. "Don't forget to cheer my partner. She doesn't contribute much, I know—"

Sari pulled away, playfully slapping his chest. Her hair was falling into her face and she wiped it away, along with the fine film of perspiration on her forehead.

"You don't even look out of breath, Roarke!"

Conor shrugged. "Charles's been making sure I'm not lazy."

He grasped Sari's hand, linking his fingers through hers, and led her back to the chair as if nothing had happened.

But she knew it had. As the other couples danced, Sari was overwhelmingly aware of how close Conor sat to her. She tried to ignore him, but the air between them was charged and heavy.

She knew she was as guilty as he for letting it happen. God help her, but she wanted him badly. Even though she told herself she shouldn't, even as she tried to warn herself to beware, the sheer headiness of his presence made those warnings impossible to heed.

She refused to look at him, even when he tapped her on the shoulder or tried to get her attention with a slight press of his leg. She kept her eyes firmly trained on the party in front of her, singing as loudly as she could—as though sheer volume could make the longing go away.

But by the time Miriam and Tom Johnson collapsed in a giggling heap on the floor, Sari was a bundle of nerves. The moment the singing stopped, she was on her feet, moving to the still uneaten pies on the sideboard.

She pulled plates down from the shelf above the stove, busying herself with starting a pot of coffee and cutting wedges of pie. The children huddled around the table. Their high, tuneful voices were comforting—an oasis of innocence that helped ease the confusion of Conor's sexual aura. The voices of the other adults rose and fell behind her.

"I haven't heard singing like that since I left Ohio," Tom Johnson joked. "Haven't missed it either."

"Ohio?" Charles's voice was sharp with interest. "You are from there, then?"

Sari turned in time to see Tom sit back in the rocking chair and light his pipe. "Sure am," he nodded. "From Youngstown."

"Youngstown?" Charles leaned forward. Sari heard the interest in his voice with a touch of foreboding. "Sarilyn and I come from Pennsylvania."

"Really?" Isabel's winged brows rose delightedly. "Why, then, we were practically neighbors. Where in Pennsylvania? I've been to Pittsburgh a few times."

Sari's tension increased. She threw a glance at her

uncle, silently begging him not to say anything, vainly telling herself there was nothing to fear. Perhaps the Molly Maguires weren't news outside of Pennsylvania. But if they were . . . She didn't want to take the chance. *Please, Onkle,* she pleaded silently. *Please say Philadelphia—*

"From the Blue Mountains," Charles said vaguely. "Near Reading."

"Really?" Tom puffed, a cloud of smoke rose around his head. "Not the mining country?"

Sari's heart fell. She felt her uncle's trepidation as clearly as her own. She could not bring herself to look at Conor.

Charles nodded slowly. *"Ja."*

"Oh, my goodness," Isabel put a hand to her mouth in mock concern. "Don't tell me you were there during that awful railroad scandal! Weren't they killing railroad men?" She frowned, looking to her husband. "What was the name of that group, Tom? The Milly something—"

"The Molly Maguires." Tom filled in easily. His brown eyes lit with curiosity. "I suppose, coming from there, you knew all about it?"

"Such a terrible job, working in a dark mine all day," Isabel commented quickly, rearranging her skirts as if she hadn't a care in the world. Her gaze was sharp with interest as she met Sari's eyes. "Didn't someone say your husband was a miner, Sari?"

"He—he was—" Sari cleared her throat, but her voice still sounded stiff and harsh.

"Oh, that's right!" Miriam piped up. "You worked for the railroads in Pennsylvania, didn't you, Conor? Why, you must have all kinds of stories to tell."

Sari froze. She couldn't breathe, couldn't bear to glance to Charles or Conor. Here it was. All her careful lies were about to be revealed, and it was so easy. Just one innocent question, and the life she'd worked so hard to build was going to fall apart.

"I'm afraid that all happened long after I left."

His voice, sure and deep, surprised her. Sari's gaze jerked to his. His eyes swept her face; she saw soft reassurance, soothing comfort. Her fear eased, the constriction in her chest loosened.

"You missed the most exciting time, then," John smiled. "What about you, Charles? Did you see any of it? Was your whole family there?"

"*Ja.*" Charles said gently. "*Ja*, we were there. It was a terrible time. A time I do not like to remember."

Sari felt her uncle's sadness, mixing with her own bleak memories. But still there was relief—so intense, it made her breathing harsh. It was only a brief respite, she knew. The questions never ended. Someone would get too close, and the speculation would begin again. Sooner or later someone would find out the truth.

And she would see those condemning eyes again.

She closed her eyes, turning her back to the crowd. Conor could so easily have told them. The horror of that realization made her swallow hard. He could make her life a living hell if he wanted to. A few choice words, and her newfound friends would ostracize her as surely as they had in Tamaqua.

And yet he hadn't done it. Why hadn't he done it?

The questions bombarded her, dizzying in their intensity. She'd told herself she'd try to trust him. But she knew that deep inside, she still expected his betrayal. She had not expected this support from him, this subtle care.

She felt suffocated suddenly. The voices were too loud, crowding her, the laughter and shouting of the children pounded in her head. She had to get out, had to breathe, had to think.

She glanced at her neighbors. They were talking animatedly. No one would notice if she slipped out for just a moment. There were blankets in Miriam's wagon, and they'd need them soon. She could go out just long enough to get them, long enough to get a breath of fresh air, to clear her mind.

Sari eased to the door, grabbing her coat from the peg. Quickly she slid out into the frigid night air.

She closed the door behind her and leaned against the sod wall, breathing deeply of the darkness. It felt so good here. Quiet and cold—a chill that seared her lungs and froze her nose. She tilted her head to stare at the sky. Here on the prairie, on the edge of the world, the night seemed close enough to touch. Sari felt as if she could reach up and snag one of the millions of stars that littered the dark sapphire blue like glitterdust—so thickly it was as if a fine film of them covered the sky. There were no snow clouds tonight. Only clouds of stars.

Sari smiled slightly, but the beauty of the night was painful somehow. It tore at her heart, pulling at a void inside her. Even filling the emptiness with stars didn't ease that loneliness.

She pulled her collar more closely about her. The feeling had been with her most of her life. She should be used to it by now. She *was* used to it. It was just that Conor's unexpected support had startled her. Now, suddenly, she was beginning to want things again. Things that only Conor had ever been able to give her. Laughter, friendship, desire . . .

But she remembered how quick he'd been to take them away before.

Sari blinked back tears as she made her way to the Grahams' wagon. Her boots clomped on the frozen ground, alerting the animals corralled against the wall of the barn. There was no room inside for them, but their closeness would help keep them warm through the cold night. Two horses raised their heads to nicker a soft greeting as she approached.

"Hello, boys," she murmured. She pressed against the buckboard, fumbling inside for the blankets. Their ears pricked as they watched her. "How're you doing? It's a pretty night, isn't it?" She felt for the blankets and found them, pulling them out, clutching them to her chest. "Yes, a pretty night," she breathed, turning back to the house.

Crashing right into Conor's chest.

His arms went around her, his fingers tightened on her forearms. "You're right, it *is* a pretty night," he said softly, his eyes glittering like the stars in the darkness. "How do you think we should celebrate it?"

CHAPTER 11

SARI'S HEART THUNDERED IN HER EARS. "What—what are you doing out here?"

"I saw you leave," he said. "I didn't want you out here alone."

Sari pulled away, her arms tightening around the blankets as if they were armor. His arms fell limply to his sides. "I imagine I'm safer alone than with you."

"Probably."

Sari swallowed. "I suppose I should thank you for what you did inside—for not telling them the truth."

His slight smile was lit by the moonlight. "You're welcome."

Sari licked her lips nervously. His stillness made her anxious. "I'm not sure why you did it, but I— I'm grateful to you."

"You didn't answer my question," he said.

Sari frowned in confusion. "Question?"

He gestured to the sky. "How should we celebrate?"

"I've nothing to celebrate," she said brusquely, stepping around him. "I should go back inside before they wonder what happened to me." She began walking, unexpectedly frightened of herself. Of him. Of what it meant to be alone with him in the frigid, beautiful night.

He caught up to her easily, and she stopped. There was nowhere to run, nowhere she wanted to go. And suddenly she knew this moment was inevitable, as certain as day and night.

Slowly she turned to face him, fighting the urge to shiver as she met his eyes. They were shadowed and dark in the moonlight, his face cast in planes of light and darkness. The breeze ruffled through his hair, pulling it back from his face to sculpt his jaw, the line of his nose, the full lower lip. He'd stepped after her so quickly, he'd left his coat behind. The wind billowed under the edge of his collarless shirt; she saw the shadowed darkness of the hair that began just above his collar bones.

"Don't do this to me," she whispered.

He said nothing. Simply reached out and took the hairpins from her chignon. Her hair fell in heavy strands, tumbling over her shoulders.

"Sari," he said slowly. "My name is Conor Roarke. I'm not Jamie O'Brien, I'm not a cattle rustler. I'm not a Pinkerton man." He took a deep breath. "I'm just a man. A man who wants to kiss you."

She stared at him, unable to move, unable to say

anything. The raspiness of his voice made her feel like liquid inside. Sari was suddenly sure that her knees would not be able to hold her another second. She fought for enough breath to speak.

"I—there's too much—" She couldn't finish the sentence, couldn't even finish it in her mind. Because when she looked at him, she no longer saw Jamie O'Brien. She no longer saw pain and blood and sacrifice. She saw a different man, a man who cared enough to reassure her on a bitter winter's night. She could no longer even think of him as Jamie O'Brien, and the longing she felt had nothing to do with the past, but only with the man who stood waiting in front of her. Only with Conor Roarke.

Sari retreated, but two steps brought her up against the wall of the barn. Her breath caught in her throat.

He stepped toward her, stopping only when his hips were pressed against hers, through her heavy coat. Slowly, carefully, he pried her fingers loose from the blankets and let them fall in a soft rumple of sound to their feet. One by one he unfastened the buttons of her coat, and when they were all unfastened, his hands slipped inside, curving around her waist, pulling her closer still.

"I hate you," she said quietly, but the words were more for herself than for him, a final warning, a useless reminder.

He lowered his head, his lips nearly brushing hers. She couldn't see his eyes, only the soft, short lashes resting on his cheeks.

"Ah, love," he whispered, and she heard the soft-

ness of self-mockery tainting his words. "I hate you
too."

She told herself to struggle. Just a little bit. But she
couldn't. Her bones were without strength as she
melted against him. His leg pressed between hers
and she felt his hipbone against her stomach; his
strong hands sent shivers of pleasure over her skin.
She had no power to resist him, there was nothing
else but the feel of his body, the warm, compelling
need.

Sari was lost, falling into the chasm of Conor's
eyes and mouth, giving way to his hands. Oh, she
had been right to be afraid. Because now she knew
there was nothing she wouldn't give him, nothing
that wasn't his for the asking.

The stars were blanketing them. Sari imagined she
saw them touching his hair, lighting his cheeks. Her
skin felt raw, her breath rasped in her throat. There
was nothing but the feel of him, the press of his body
against hers, the taste of him, of coffee and salt, the
bay-rum taste of his lips.

He pressed her farther into the sod bricks of the
barn. His heartbeat pounded against her breasts, his
hands tightened on her waist. She felt the press of
his tongue against her lips, urging them farther
apart, stealing inside, stroking, caressing as his
hands moved up her body, his fingers fumbling with
the fastenings of her bodice—

She twisted away, her hands came up against his
shoulders. "No," she breathed. "Conor . . . no."

He stiffened against her. She felt his withdrawal

even though he didn't move away, caught the glitter of his eyes in the starlight.

"Sari—" he said.

"I . . . can't do this," she said, looking away, past him. "Not yet. Not . . . now."

He sighed. His hands left her, he stepped back. Her body, the air around her, was suddenly freezing.

"Is it Jamie?" he asked in a low voice. "Has he come between us?"

She laughed sadly. "He's always been between us." She hugged herself tightly. "But that's not it. Not tonight. I just . . . I want to trust you, Conor. I do. I'm trying. I just need . . . more time."

"More time," he repeated thoughtfully. Then he nodded. "I can give you that," he said. He looked at her, and she saw something in the darkness of his eyes—concern, caring, a tenderness that made her warm again, that filled the hollow places in her heart.

"I've missed you, love," he whispered.

Sari touched his cheek. "I've missed you too."

Sari tried not to look at him for the rest of the evening, but it was impossible. He was everywhere—his voice, his laughter, his smell. Oh, especially his smell. She was sure everyone knew that she and Conor had been kissing. Her skin smelled of his inimitable scent of bay rum and musk, she felt burned on her throat where his stubbly jaw had scraped her. How could they *not* know?

But they didn't seem to. Her guests laughed and talked and played a game of charades that kept getting interrupted by arguments and jokes. It was almost as if her and Conor's absence hadn't even been noticed. Except by Charles. Sari avoided her uncle's thoughtful gaze almost as studiously as she avoided Conor's.

Sari shifted in her seat. It was all she could do to keep from climbing to the loft and burying herself beneath a mound of quilts and darkness. She needed time to be alone, to think. Her mind whirled with images, with feelings she couldn't separate long enough to identify.

"Oh, I could just sit here all night." Mary Anderson said with a tired sigh. "It's so nice to be around other people. Sometimes the cows seem to be the only friends I have."

"I know what you mean." Berthe smiled and tapped her husband's hand. "Just the cows and Will here."

"You calling me no better than a cow?"

"You're almost beginning to look like one," Berthe teased. "Not like Mr. Roarke over there. I declare, you're a sight for sore eyes, Conor. You haven't got that beaten look about you. Not yet."

Conor smiled slightly. The expression caused butterflies to dance in Sari's stomach. "You don't strike me as 'beaten.' "

Berthe chuckled. "You must have been a regular flatterer in the big city."

"Yeah, be quiet, Roarke." John Graham leaned back in his chair, putting an arm around a sleepy Miriam and pulling her close. "You're making us all look bad."

"It's good for you," Miriam provided softly.

John smiled down at her. "I suppose it is."

Sari felt strangled by their intimacy. Hastily she rose. "Would anyone like coffee?"

There was a murmur of refusal. Sari went to the stove. "I'll start some anyway. Maybe later—"

"Sit down, Sari," Conor said gently. His voice was like warm oil sliding down her spine. "The night's about drawn out."

She looked over her shoulder, catching his gaze despite herself. He was staring at her as if he could devour her face; his eyes almost burned her with their intensity.

She turned away again, remembering not their kiss but the quiet walk back to the soddy. She remembered how he paused at the door, buttoning her coat with sure fingers, gathering the loose strands of her hair into a chignon and anchoring it with the few hairpins they'd been able to find. She'd been nervous and edgy; his quick squeeze of her hand had been warm and reassuring.

"You are beautiful, Sari," he'd whispered, his breath stroking her jaw. "Don't let anyone make you forget that."

For those few moments after she stepped through the door to face her friends' welcoming glances, she'd felt that way. Beautiful, cherished.

But it had vanished as soon as she'd seen her uncle's gaze. He knew, and embarrassment enveloped Sari when she remembered her adamant denials of the other night. It was humiliating to have to admit that her uncle was right, that her hatred for Conor had been a lie. Her protests had been a shell of a defense. How could she explain that she had no control when it came to Conor? How could she explain what she didn't even understand herself?

Her pleas for more time tonight—those had been the words of a frightened girl, a girl afraid of her own emotions, of what one man did to them. More time, she'd asked for, but there would never be enough time. She had never had any control when it came to Conor, and it was useless to pretend otherwise.

"Look at the children," Miriam said softly. "Peter's asleep already."

Sari glanced at the six children huddled around the kitchen table. Their voices had become whispers, and then faded altogether in the last half hour.

"Well, well," Berthe was on her feet instantly. "Up with you now—all of you. Out to the barn."

"But Mama—" Becky Schmacher was instantly wide awake. "But Mama, we don't wanta go to sleep!"

Everyone was rising, readying to go to bed. Conor rose with them, and when Sari caught his thoughtful gaze, her heart dropped. He would want to talk about tonight, and she wasn't ready. Nervously she stepped forward.

"Perhaps Mr. Roarke will tell you a story once you're ready for bed," she said hesitantly.

"Me?" Conor asked, surprise coloring his voice. "Why me?"

"The children are staying in the barn tonight," she

said. "Since that's where you sleep, it seemed only natural that you should look after them."

His hand dragged through his hair. "But—"

"If it's too much trouble, Roarke . . ." Will Schmacher got to his feet.

"I'm sure it's no trouble at all," Sari interrupted before Conor could say a word. "Mr. Roarke loves children. He's told me so often."

Conor smiled wryly. "Of course. I'd forgotten."

"If you're sure—"

Conor shrugged. "How much trouble can they be?"

"Obviously you haven't spent much time with children." Miriam giggled.

Conor stood. He tossed a mock-threatening look to the children. "But these are such well-behaved ones." He held out his arms for the blankets Berthe and Mary handed him. He walked to the door, throwing Samuel Schmacher a blanket and shoving the rest under his arm. He grabbed Becky's little hand in his big one.

"But I don't wanna go out there!" Becky wailed.

Conor paused. The smile that lit his face when he spoke to Becky made Sari melt inside. "Why, you should be feeling sorry for your poor mama, Becky, since she has to stay in here."

Becky looked at him uncertainly.

His smile broadened. "We'll be having so much fun in the barn, she'll be sorry to miss it. But if you'd rather stay here and take care of her . . ."

Becky tightened her fingers around his. "I'd rather go with you."

The cold winter air rushed into the room as the group went outside, Conor flanked by Samuel and Becky, Peter Johnson stumbling sleepily beside. The other three children ran after them, suddenly revitalized by the excitement of their new adventure and the man who was there to lead them.

Conor walked toward the barn, one hand wrapped around Becky's, the blankets held loosely in the other. The sight made Sari's insides tighten; she couldn't look away. He walked slowly, matching his steps to the little girl's, now and then cocking his head to listen to her nonstop chatter. The other children trailed behind him as though he were some latter-day Pied Piper leading them to some precious storybook land.

CHAPTER 12

CONOR'S THOUGHTS WERE JUMBLED AS HE
herded the children to the barn. He tried not to think
of how uncertain Sari had looked when he left the
house, as if she couldn't decide whether she wanted
him to stay or go. He tried not to remember the way
she'd twisted her hands together or the way she'd
leaped at the chance to banish him to the barn.

He wasn't sure what it was he'd wanted to see in
her eyes. Longing, maybe? Desire? Devotion? Or
maybe just simple need. God knew, he felt it. The
need for her was burning him up inside; the hasty
interlude against the barn wall had only left him aching for more. He wanted to spend the night in her
bed, with her warm body pressed against his, his
hands in her hair.

"I can't get it open, Mr. Roarke!" Samuel
Schmacher's voice carried, thin and reedy, over the
wind. The boy pulled at the barn door.

"Push it." Conor struggled to shove away the image of Sari. If he had to spend the night with a bunch of children, he was damn sure not going to be thinking about her.

He pulled Becky along beside him and quickened his step. Samuel was slamming his narrow shoulders against the unrelenting door while Ida and John Johnson looked on. Conor dropped Becky's hand and pushed above Samuel's tousled red head. The door opened; Samuel went tumbling to the floor.

Becky burst into peals of laughter. She was still laughing when Samuel climbed to his feet, brushing bits of straw from his clothing.

"Stop it, Becky!" he demanded crossly. He advanced, small fists clenched at his sides. "I said stop it!"

"You—you looked so silly," she said, giggling. "Fallin' on the floor like that—"

"Stop it!"

"Ah, it's okay, Sammy." John brushed by his friend, shrugging. "She's just a dumb girl."

"I am not a dumb girl!" Becky's laughter abruptly turned to indignation. "You take that back right now, Johnny. Sammy's the dumb one. He's the one who fell."

Conor only half heard the exchange as he went farther into the barn. He looked around wearily. How much comfort did six small children need, anyway? Was the floor soft enough? He glanced up to the loft, his bastion of quiet. Would he have to bring them up there? The question brought a quick frown. He couldn't watch them all the time; who knew what kind of mischief they'd get into with all his possessions shoved haphazardly against the wall—

"Aaaaaaaah!" Becky's drawn-out scream split his skull.

Conor spun on his heel, dropping the blankets where he stood. The children were gathered in a circle, avidly watching as Samuel pummeled his little sister.

Conor surged forward. "Stop!" Then, as his cry went unheeded, he pushed through Peter and Ida. "Dammit, I said stop." He grabbed Samuel's collar, hauling him off the sobbing girl. The boy's feet slid out from underneath him and he plopped to the ground with a whoosh of air.

Conor paid little heed to Samuel as he knelt beside Becky and helped her to her feet. Her eyes were red-rimmed. Tears streamed over her cheeks to mix with her runny, snuffling nose. She wiped a pudgy hand across her face. "He—he hit me."

Conor looked over his shoulder to Samuel. "There's no excuse for hitting a girl. Especially your sister. Even if she *did* deserve it."

"She was laughing at me." Samuel said sullenly.

"Better get used to it." Conor got to his feet and reached into his pocket for a handkerchief. He wiped at Becky's face with unthinking roughness before she grabbed the cloth away from him.

John spoke up, his freckled face wrinkled in confusion. "Why should we get used to it?"

"Because boys are silly, that's why," Ida said haughtily.

Conor sighed. Ida Johnson was going to be a tough

one when she grew up. She was already tossing those brown curls like a debutante. "I'm afraid Ida's right," he informed the boys dourly.

"Silly?" Samuel sputtered. "We are not! Girls are the silly ones. They—"

"Sammy," Conor said patiently. "What has your mother taught you about girls?"

"Uh—mostly not to hit 'em. But then Becky sticks out her tongue—"

"That's the whole problem," Conor said drily. "Girls have tongues. And they know how to use them. As long as they can speak, you'll never win."

"But that's not fair!" Little Peter pulled his thumb from his mouth long enough to complain.

"It is too fair," Ida said.

"So what does a guy do, then, Mr. Roarke?" John wondered.

Conor leaned close. "Learn how to lose gracefully, Johnny. It's an old trick. Works every time."

"I don't get it."

"You will someday." Conor raked his hand through his hair. "Sammy, Johnny, why don't you two help me lay out the blankets?"

"Do we hafta sleep with the cows?" Becky eyed the animals skeptically, still wiping at her runny nose with his handkerchief.

Conor sighed. He looked up at the loft. His private sanctuary was about to be invaded.

"We'll all sleep up there," he said. "Can everyone climb the ladder?"

Before they could answer, Conor grabbed the blankets and stepped up the ladder, motioning for the others to follow him. When they were secure in the loft, he busied the boys with laying out the make-shift beds while he tried his best to push his belongings into dark corners.

It didn't take long to get the children settled. The excitement of the day was wearing off, and the cold night made them grateful to climb beneath the heavy wool blankets. Conor felt as if every muscle in his body was stretched to the limit as he crawled between his own covers. Sleep would come easily to him tonight.

But it didn't. It eluded him nimbly, and he lay there listening to the soft breathing of the children as he stared at the ceiling only a few feet above his head.

His muscles ached, but there was a subtle energy sneaking along his spine, a feeling that things weren't quite finished. He couldn't chase the images of Sari from his mind. Over and over again he saw the eerily blue-white coloring of her skin in the moonlight, the almost black passion in her eyes, her lips swollen from his rough kiss.

Sari Travers was no ordinary woman. She was an addiction. His addiction. How had he ever thought he could get her out of his blood?

For a moment he toyed with the idea of sneaking from the loft to the soddy. The women would be sleeping on the floor—all the men were with Charles. He could sneak around them, silently climb the ladder to where she was sleeping. She always slept as though someone had thrown her onto the bed, with one arm crooked on the pillow, fingers tangled in her own hair, her body twisted, open, ready for the taking.

Conor tightened his hand into a fist, struggling for control, remembering her words. *More time,* she'd said. How much more? A week? A day? An hour?

"Stop it!" The loud whisper startled him. It was almost an answer to his thoughts.

"Don't!" came the voice again. "You're taking up too much room!"

Conor sighed. "Becky, go to sleep."

"I'm trying. Samuel keeps pushing me."

"I do not."

"Yes, you do, you—"

"Shut up, Becky!" John grumbled.

Conor rose to one elbow wearily. "What's wrong?"

"I can't sleep," Becky said plaintively. "I want to go to Mama."

"Baby," Samuel commented acidly.

"I'm not!"

"Are too."

"Am not—"

"All right, all right." Conor sat up, rubbing his face. "What would help you go to sleep, Becky?"

"Well—"

"Mizz Travers said you'd tell us a story," Ida offered helpfully.

"A story." Conor took a deep breath. "Would that help, Becky?"

"It might." Her voice was tiny in the darkness.

A story. Conor closed his eyes, mentally flipping through his inventory of tales. As Jamie O'Brien he'd been known as a master storyteller, but those adventures were too ribald for the children. He thought back to his childhood. There had been no stories then, of that he was sure. The dragons he'd been fighting had been all too real, and there were no white knights to find him shelter at night or something to eat.

"Something with soldiers," John suggested.

Ida sounded disgusted. "Not soldiers. I want to hear about princesses and fairies."

Princesses. Fairies. The words struck a chord in Conor and brought to mind the only story he could remember.

"All right." His words silenced them. Six pairs of eyes glimmered in the darkness. "I've got a story."

She couldn't help herself.

Sari stepped outside, drawing her coat more tightly about her, closing the door quietly so as not to wake the women sleeping on the floor inside. The frigid night air cut through the thin flannel of her nightgown, freezing her legs. She curled her fingers into the thick wool of her coat in an attempt to keep them warm.

This was ridiculous. She knew it, yet she couldn't help it. For an hour she'd lain in bed, staring at the ceiling, listening to the fading gossip of her guests as they fell asleep. She'd relived the evening in her mind, remembering the way Conor had looked in the moonlight, fighting the restless desire that gnawed at her even as she warned herself that it was better to stay away.

But she couldn't forget the way he'd looked at her. She couldn't forget the painful desire she'd seen in his eyes or his tenderness when he touched her hair. She wanted to know—*had* to know—what it meant. All she had to do was see him, or hear his voice. Then she would know if he was as affected as she was, or if their kisses mattered to him at all.

The barn loomed in the darkness. Sari took a deep breath, pressing back against the closed door. Earlier she'd sent him there, thinking that she needed time to think. But once she reached her bed, she realized it was the last thing she wanted to do. Thinking would come soon enough. Now all she wanted was reassurance. All she wanted were the dreams that had seemed plausible in the cold, blue moonlight.

Just his voice, she told herself. Once she heard it, she would have the strength to go back to bed, to banish her thoughts and sleep.

Before she lost her courage, she hurried across the expanse of field that stretched between the barn and the house. Her hair blew into her face, hard little pellets of ice stung her cheeks. She stumbled against a clump of icy grass near the side of the barn, catching herself just before she fell into the wall.

She pushed away, moved along the barn to the door. She stopped there, her heart pounding. This *had* been foolish. What was she doing out here on this cold night? What did she expect? Conor was in the barn with six children, and they were probably all asleep by now. What had she been thinking—that she would sneak up into the loft and somehow wake him?

She closed her eyes. She was an idiot. If she'd waited a few moments longer, probably the longing to see him would have waned. She'd be warm and comfortable in bed instead of huddled against the barn wall in the chilling prairie night, feeling foolish and naive—

"All right. I've got a story."

Sari froze. His voice was muffled through the door, rough with weariness and quiet, but she heard him. The sound of it sent relief speeding through her.

"Does it have soldiers?"

"No soldiers, Johnny, but plenty of magic."

"But I want—"

"Shut up and let him talk!" Becky's shrill voice cut the darkness. "Okay, Mr. Roarke, you can tell us now."

Sari smiled. She could imagine Conor's face, his expression a mix of resignation and kindness. She wished she could see him.

She pressed farther along the door, resting her hands and cheek on the wood, now oblivious of the cold. What story would he tell? He was a wonderful storyteller, she remembered. Or at least he had been when he was Jamie O'Brien.

"It was the middle of a cold night. The moon was big and bright in the sky, and it lit the way for the girl who left her father's castle to walk in the woods."

"A princess?"

"Yes, she was a princess, Becky. Princess Christabel."

Christabel. Sari inhaled sharply. It felt as if

something had fallen on her heart. Her favorite poem.

"She sounds pretty."

"She was. Very pretty. She had long thick hair the color of chocolate, and her eyes were big and brown—like maple syrup. Her laugh sounded as if the finest musicians in the world had gathered to play."

"She sounds like Mizz Travers," Samuel noted matter-of-factly.

She waited for Conor's response, wondering if the description had been deliberate, wondering if he truly saw her that way or if it was a convenient fancy for the children.

"Yes," he said softly. "Christabel and Mrs. Travers look just the same."

Sari heard the soft catch in his voice when he said her name, heard the quick ache, she knew all she needed to know. That kiss *had* mattered. She was right to feel as shaken as she did. For a moment the joy engulfed her. Even if nothing came of it, even if he betrayed her again, she would remember this joy.

Conor cleared his throat. "Christabel went into the woods all alone that night to pray for her knight, who was far away. Before she could finish her prayer, she heard a moan. She thought at first it was the wind, but there was no wind that night; the forest was still."

"What was it, a monster?" Peter whispered.

"Shhh!"

"No. No monster," Conor told them. "It was a lady so beautiful, Christabel could barely speak for wonder. The lady was dressed all in white, with jewels of every color in her long blond hair. She was like a fairy queen, but she seemed very sad.

"'Who are you?' Christabel asked, and the lady said, 'My name is Geraldine, and I am so tired, I can barely speak. Please don't be afraid, please help me.' She told Christabel that she had been kidnapped by five knights, who left her there to wait for them while they rode off. She didn't remember how long she'd been there, because she was bewitched."

"By fairies?" The merest whisper of a voice.

Sari put her hand to her mouth to stop her laughter. He had them wrapped around his finger, enraptured by the tale. Almost as if he were a big brother. Or their father.

"Or so Geraldine said. Christabel was a kind princess, and she begged Geraldine to come home with her so that Christabel's father, Sir Leoline, could protect them. But when they got there, Geraldine was so quiet, Christabel was worried that the lady was sick. She grew even more worried when Geraldine began to talk—because she wasn't talking to Christabel, or even to anyone Christabel could see."

"She was talking to ghosts!" Johnny piped up.

"In a way. She was talking to spirits."

"Like fairies?"

"No, not like fairies. She was talking to the spirit of Christabel's mother, who had died a long time ago. Christabel thought she heard a warning." Conor paused. "But then Geraldine told the spirit of the lady queen to leave, and she told Christabel not to look while she changed her clothes."

"I would have looked anyway," Johnny said.

"Christabel was like you, John. She looked too. And what she saw—well, what she saw was terrible."

"Tell us!"

"She saw," Conor lowered his voice dramatically, "that Geraldine's whole side was gone."

"Gone?" Ida's voice quivered.

"Like a bear got her?" Samuel asked.

"Just like that."

"I don't like this story," Becky whined.

"Oh, it's just getting good!"

"What did Christabel do, Mr. Roarke?" Ida asked. "Did she run away?"

"No."

He would make a good father. Sari smiled at the thought. He was so good with the children, and she knew it was because he genuinely liked them, because he respected what they said. The thought filled her with wistfulness. She wondered if he even wanted children of his own, if he thought about it at all.

"Christabel took Geraldine in her arms to comfort her and fell asleep. And while she slept, she forgot Geraldine's strange ways, and in the morning she took the woman to see her father.

"Sir Leoline found that Geraldine was the daughter of his long-lost friend and he was very happy. It was then that Christabel caught the strange look Geraldine gave her—an evil look. In that moment she knew that Geraldine was not a friend, but an enemy sent from evil demons. Christabel begged her father to send the woman away, and—and . . ."

He trailed off. Sari waited, and then she realized why he'd stopped. There was no more story. *Christabel* was an unfinished poem, one that left Christabel hovering between good and evil, one that had no easy answers. It was the reason it was her favorite poem. She couldn't control the grin that hovered at her lips. What would he do? What kind of ending would he give Christabel?

"And then what?"

"Yeah, don't stop there."

He still didn't answer.

"Mr. Roarke!"

"Just a minute," he said harshly.

She heard the touch of anger in his voice, a confusion that seemed harsh and strange and far too familiar. It was as if he'd cut off emotions, it was the kind of voice that held no tenderness and no joy.

It was the voice she'd heard in those last days.

The voice that held the lies.

The memories plunged back: Evan had gone into town and Conor was there—in her house, lounging on her bed while she brushed her hair. She had been unsure whether to feel tense because he was there and Evan was due home soon or happy because she loved him and wanted him with her always—and she had decided simply to bask in the warm pleasure of his voice, of his Irish burr and whiskey-rough words.

He was running his fingers through her hair, asking her where Evan was, where Michael was, and

she had laughed and batted at his hand and told him
not to bedevil her with questions and to love her;
they had so little time.

It was then his voice had changed. The tenderness
left it, and something had come into his eyes, a darkness that was as frightening as it was momentary.

It was three days before the Pinkertons had come
in.

And it was then she'd known he was a traitor.

The memory sank inside her. Sari jerked back
from the wall, shaking, not wanting to hear more,
unable to hear another word uttered in that voice.
She hurried back to the soddy, slipping on the icy,
frozen grass, trying to feel nothing at all. This was
not what she wanted. Not those memories, not this
icy chill that deadened her heart. She wanted to
think about his tenderness, to relive the sweet ache
she'd felt when he said her name. She wanted to
remember only his quiet laughter when he spoke to
the children, and the way he'd caught them in the
magic of his story.

It was all she wanted now. The cold light of tomorrow would be soon enough to face the truth
again. But the night . . . the night was a time for
dreams.

He was still awake when the last murmur of protest faded into the darkness, and the steady rise and
fall of breathing once again filled the air. His muscles
were tight, and nervous tension made his breathing
shallow.

Telling the story to the children had been a mistake. At first he'd enjoyed it. He liked children, and tonight had reminded him of his years in the rectory, banding the younger ones together for the annual Christmas pageant. He'd been good at it then, teaching them their lines, making sure the little heathens didn't kill themselves vying for the parts of the three kings.

But the joy had ended in the split second when he realized there was no end to the poem. He'd floundered then, searching for something, anything, first wondering how Coleridge would have ended the poem, and then what the hell his father would have done.

It was that question that had stopped him. Sean Roarke had been a terrible storyteller. Conor recalled late nights when his father had bent next to the flickering flame of a candle, writing down notes to some biblical story for his sermon. The priest could remember the word of God, but he was at a loss when called upon to recite the parables that served as examples. Without those notes the exciting stories faded away to one or two lines of God's laws.

The memory had paralyzed Conor, because with it came the realization that at some point in the last few days he'd begun to put vengeance behind him. The realization shook him. The need for revenge hadn't changed, it had just taken a different turn. Suddenly he wasn't so sure that things were as black and white as he'd imagined.

In fact the only thing he was sure about any longer was that Michael Doyle had set the bomb that killed his father.

But as for the rest . . .

So many things had happened. Too many things; he needed time to sit back and sort them out. It was what William Pinkerton had taught him. Every operative must be a clear thinker, a man or woman able to force coherence from confusion. Lately Conor felt as if he'd been failing miserably at it.

He took a deep breath, struggling to put his thoughts in order. It was slowly becoming clear to him that either Sari Travers was an actress fit for Pinkerton's ranks or she had no idea where her brother was. She never talked about him, she denied having any other family to her newfound friends. It didn't change anything really. Regardless of whether Sari knew Michael's whereabouts, Conor was fairly certain Doyle would come to her. It was just that Conor was beginning to wonder if Michael would be welcome when he showed up.

The question gnawed at him, made him feel like a traitor again—and that was a feeling he'd hoped to leave behind him. Because he could not—would not—back down. Somewhere in that soddy was a letter, a picture, *something* that alluded to Michael's whereabouts.

But now the task held no appeal. After tonight the thought of betraying Sari made him sick. He had set out to charm her, to beguile her into trusting him, and his plan had worked almost too well. He had charmed her. She was falling for him the same way she had in Tamaqua. Everything was going according to plan.

Except for one thing.

Unseeingly Conor stared into the darkness. Cold fear clawed its way up his spine. He had not planned on succumbing to *her* spell. When he'd first come to Colorado, he expected to be able to seduce her as coldly as he'd seduced informers in the past—with a sharp, ruthless efficiency that left his emotions intact.

But things weren't working that way now. In all his years as a Pinkerton operative, he'd never forgotten the case. He'd always been in control of everything. Until now. Sari had done the one thing no other woman, no other job had ever done.

She had made him forget.

CHAPTER 13

THE NEIGHBORS HAD LEFT THAT MORNING, driving off over the barren prairie just after breakfast. Sari had immediately gone out to do the washing, and Charles was struggling again with the barbed wire. Without his help, Conor thought, allowing a nagging twinge of guilt. He'd muttered an excuse about an aching head and a headache powder, and now here he was, standing at the edge of the loft, looking into Sari's bedroom.

It seemed he'd spent half his life thinking about this room, wondering about it, wondering where she slept and where she kept the letters from her brother. For a moment he wished he could look at this room without ulterior motives, without thinking about anything except how much of Sari was in it.

He sighed, glancing at the rocker near the edge of the wall, where the flat roof slanted. He remembered when it had held a place of honor in her living room, one of the only graceful, beautiful things she and

Evan had owned. There had been one picture above
it—some Catholic icon, he remembered.

His eyes scanned the fine carved lines. The chair
had seemed out of place in Evan's house, only em-
phasizing the ugliness of poverty and depression.
Evan had preferred it that way.

Conor wondered what Sari had preferred.

Funny, when he was Jamie O'Brien, he'd never
thought to ask her that, never talked to her about
the privation of a coal miner's wife. What would she
have said? Probably she would have turned her head
and said nothing at all, and made him feel that he
had no business asking the question. Not that he had
of course. Being Sari's lover had given him no rights
at all.

Conor deliberately brushed away the regret that
flooded his mind at the thought, and forced himself
to focus on the job at hand. He held out the lamp,
but it barely cut the dimness of the room, and he
stared into the gloomy shadows. It was nothing like
he'd imagined it, though he could not have said what
he was expecting. Her bedroom in Tamaqua had
been as spare as the rest of the house, the one con-
cession to beauty a counterpane on the bed. It had
been white, he remembered, with bright calico birds
and leaves quilted onto it.

But the counterpane was gone now. In its place
was a quilt patched in some kind of tulip design,
riotous with scraps of color. The bed was one he
didn't recognize, with a simply carved pine head and
foot board. The well-kept wood gleamed in the lamplight. The ceiling was so low and the bed so high that

there was barely enough room to sit up in it. But he
was sure she spent hours doing exactly that. Beside
the bed was a trunk that served as a night table. A
lamp rested on it, and a stack of books rose beyond
its height.

Other than that, and the rocking chair, the room
might have been mistaken for a pantry. Bags of flour
and cornmeal leaned against the walls, canned goods
lined one end. Conor lifted the lamp higher to see,
and cats of light glittered over the glass jars, high-
lighting the jewellike colors of the fruits and vegetables within. The shadowed forms of sausages and
hams hung from the ceiling, and thin cakes of
something were wrapped in layers of cheesecloth
and piled on another set of shelves.

And the smells . . . There were so many of them,
Conor was aware only of one—a smoky, spicy scent
that invaded the little room below the rafters. It was
a damn good thing he *didn't* sleep here, he thought.
He'd be hungry all the time.

Conor stepped gingerly onto the floorboards; the
wood creaked beneath his weight. He hunched over
to avoid the muslin-draped ceiling and made his way
to the trunk. There was another one against the edge
of the loft—probably full of Sari's clothes. But it was
the one that served as her nighttable that most in-
trigued him.

Carefully Conor lifted her lamp and unbuckled the
lid. It creaked when he opened it, and the lid shuddered as it hit the wall. He felt again that stab of
guilt. These were Sari's things, things she had hidden
from the world. He licked his lips nervously, trying

to ignore his reluctance to probe through her belongings, half afraid of what he would find.

There was a scarf of some kind on the top; Conor's
hands sunk into its fleecy warmth. It was unbeliev-
ably soft, loosely woven and fuzzy, and he lifted it
out carefully, smelling the strong, pungent scent of
the cedar shavings she'd lined the trunk with. The
scarf was beautiful, and he wondered for a moment
why she kept it hidden away. But his curiosity vanished as he saw what lay beneath it.

The bolt of cloth he'd bought her. The cream silk
shone in the darkness, the dark green stripes looked
black. He'd forgotten all about it in the last few days,
but now remorse hammered at him. Conor ran his
fingers over the fabric, and his rough skin caught on
its smoothness. It was his thirty pieces of silver, his
blood money, but it was no less beautiful for that.
He'd wanted her to make something with it,
something to showcase her dark beauty, but he knew
she recognized it for what it was. He'd bought it out
of guilt, and she refused to wear it because she knew
it would make him feel better if she did.

He smiled warmly. God, it was amazing, the
things Sari knew, the things she understood. Her
sheer obstinence annoyed him, but it was also one
of the things he admired the most about her. Sari
had always been able to call a spade a spade. He'd
always called it whatever was most convenient at the
moment.

Just as it was convenient to call what he was about
to do a favor. Conor lifted the fabric out and put it
aside. He'd send it into town, have something made

for her by one of the seamstresses she claimed were so inept. Sari would be angry, and she'd know instantly that he'd gone through her things. But by then it wouldn't matter. He'd be gone.

Conor ignored the sadness that assailed him at the thought.

The other items in the trunk he fumbled through and laid aside: a boxful of Christmas decorations, tin angels and painted wooden candleholders, a satin-lined box holding a single pressed rose, a half-finished needlepoint sampler, and a few skeins of roughly dyed wool.

Conor paused as he reached a pile of framed photographs. They were wrapped in burlap, secured with twine, and he held one in his hand for a moment, wondering. His blunt fingers fumbled with the fine knot, but the string fell away easily once he broached it. Carefully he unwrapped the burlap to reveal a plain pewter frame. The back was to him, and Conor stared at it, feeling a strange reluctance to look at it. His mouth felt suddenly dry. Slowly he turned it over.

It was Sari and Evan. Their wedding picture, he imagined, since it looked as if they wore their best clothes. Sari was wearing a dark-colored dress, with braiding on the collar and cuffs, and jet buttons lining the bodice. Evan's collar was white, his suitcoat and vest black, and the hat he wore was shiny and new. They both looked as if they were suppressing huge, joyous smiles.

Conor's chest tightened, his fingers caressed the edges of the frame. She looked so young. Young and

innocent, with anticipation glowing in her dark eyes
and her cheeks plump with happiness, before years
of poverty put an edge on her softness. She was
grasping Evan's arm, and her fingers were pressed
into his coat as though she couldn't bear to let him
go for even an instant. It was as if the picture had
been taken solely to illustrate young love with all its
illusions.

There had been a time when Conor had seen echoes of that love in her eyes. Then he'd been too preoccupied to know it for what it was. Of course by
the time he'd met her, those young illusions had been
washed away and that kind of feeling had been much
harder to find. And he hadn't been looking then.

He stared at the young man who stood, shining
with pride, beside her. It could have been him standing there. It could have been him seeing that love in
her eyes, who took her home that night and every
night. It could have been him, laughing with her,
touching her, watching her struggle awake in the
morning and hearing her husky hello.

For a moment Conor imagined everything he'd
dreamed of, all the bittersweet everythings he'd
never had. Evan had been a fool to throw it all away.
He had taken a young, sensitive girl and stripped her
of her joy, her life. It was a crime Conor longed to
avenge.

But it wasn't just Evan, he knew. Evan had started
the process, but it had been Conor who had finished
it, embellished it. She had trusted him once, and he'd
not known what a treasure that trust was until it was
gone. No wonder she watched him with such trepi-

dation, as if she was waiting for him to make a mistake, to show her that he truly was the bastard he'd taught her he was.

Conor wrapped the picture again, clumsily retying the knot in his haste. Guilt filled his mouth with its sour taste. He hated this, hated it more than he ever imagined he would. There was something so obscene about pawing through her things, about wondering why she kept a dried rose in a satin-lined box and why the soft mohair scarf was stuffed away in cedar. They were her secrets, and he preferred letting her keep them. Someday someone would watch her pull them out one by one, someone would hear her whispered confessions in the dark.

It would not be him, and Conor regretted only that he would miss the chance. He would miss it because revenge came first. She would never tell him her secrets, and she would go on and find someone else. Someone to make her happy. He would go back to Chicago and think of her with regret, and sadness, but his need for vengeance would finally be appeased, and he would be satisfied.

Conor shoved the blanket back on top and slammed the trunk's lid down so hard, the floor jiggled. *Satisfied.* The word sounded so hollow; it held all the emptiness of promises kept because of obligation, not feeling. But promises were all he had now. Promises made to the living and the dead. They had taken on a life of their own, corrupting his, leading him until he felt he had no will, nothing left but obligation.

Thankfully, fulfilling obligations was something he did extraordinarily well.

Sari's muscles ached as she struggled with the heavy Dutch oven. She was sore from this morning's washing, her arms felt ready to collapse, and the thin handle burned through the towel she'd wrapped around it.

Then suddenly Conor's hands were on the handle, lifting it away from her, swinging it with strong-shouldered ease onto the kitchen table. He glanced at her, his blue eyes dark and warm. She felt his tenderness sweeping over her. Sari couldn't help her smile.

"Thank you," she whispered.

He nodded toward the table. "Sit down," he said gently, waiting until she slid into a chair before he took his own. "It smells good."

"*Ja,* it does, *Liebling.*" Charles smiled.

Sari lifted the lid from the iron pot. The savory aroma of chicken soup floated in the air, the steam clouded the small window.

"Shall we read tonight?" Conor asked.

Sari's stomach clenched when she remembered the last time they'd read.

"No poetry for me." Charles shook his head. He took the bowl she handed him. "I meant to tell you, Roarke, you will have to fence without me this afternoon." His grizzled face broke into a wide grin. "Mrs. Landers has asked me to dinner tonight."

Sari's head jerked up. "Tonight? Why?"

"Perhaps she wants Charles to try a new cherry pie recipe," Conor teased, his eyes twinkling.

Charles nodded. "*Ja,* she did say something about pie."

"But, *Onkle,* you've said nothing of this before."

He shrugged. "You were not listening, *Liebling.*"

"But—" Sari swallowed her words. Conor was watching her speculatively, and she looked away, afraid that he would see the fear in her eyes. She didn't want to be alone with him. Not now. Not when she was feeling so weak. "Look at those clouds, *Onkle.* It looks like snow tonight."

Charles sipped his coffee. His gaze was teasing. "Sari does not like to be alone, Roarke. She is afraid."

Conor's smile was soft. "I'll be here to protect you, love."

Sari ignored Conor's comment, preferring to glare at her uncle. "Can you make it to Woodrow before the snow starts?"

"You'd better leave now," Conor noted.

Charles nodded. He finished the last of his soup and rose slowly from his chair. His pale blue eyes bored into Conor's, his bushy gray eyebrows came together in a single line. "I am entrusting you with her, Roarke," he said. "You will protect her?"

Conor nodded. "You've nothing to worry about." He got to his feet. "Let me help you harness the horses."

Charles leaned forward, kissing Sari gently on the forehead. "Do not worry, *Liebling.* Trust me when I say there is nothing to fear."

Nothing to fear. Sari lowered her eyes, staring into her soup. How wonderful it would be if her uncle was right. To have nothing to fear—the idea was almost heady. Perhaps it *could* be true.

She looked up, meeting Conor's gaze. His eyes were dark with promise, his face taut with tension. Her ill-conceived hope died abruptly. She suppressed a strangled laugh. How little Charles knew about Conor Roarke, and protection, and unquenchable longing.

But she knew.

That night's supper was tense and silent, the clang of forks on tin plates obscenely loud. Sari tried to scoop up green beans, and potatoes as quietly as possible. But then all she heard were the sounds of her own swallowing, the grinding of her own teeth.

Unable to bear it another second, she set down her fork and picked up a piece of corn bread. The golden bread crumbled in her fingers and dropped onto her plate.

Conor looked up from his own meal. "Something bothering you, Sari?"

"If I told you what it was, would you help?"

"I don't know." His voice was soft. "Probably I couldn't."

Sari looked out the window wistfully, brushing off her fingers. She felt pensive and unsettled. Her fear was still with her, growing with Conor's every glance and movement, but now she knew she was more afraid of herself than she was of Conor. She was lying to herself if she thought she could control her feelings for him. In only a day those feelings had grown beyond good sense, beyond control. She'd wanted to shield herself from hurt, to take things slowly, but now even her memories weren't enough to protect her. If Conor left tomorrow, the pain would still be there—as devastating as it had been a year ago. It was long past time to resolve the anguish of the past, even if she refused to admit that she longed for a future.

She sighed. "I've been thinking about things."

He tensed. "Sari—"

"No," she said brusquely. "I want to tell you this." She took a deep breath. "Before—in Tamaqua—after Evan was arrested and I knew I'd have to leave, I thought about death. About Evan's death. About my own. About yours." She met his gaze steadily. "I was angry and hurt. I watched the papers every day, waiting for word. Waiting to find out who you really were. And then, when I did find out your name, I was sorry the sleepers hadn't gotten you." She looked away, staring into space, frowning as she remembered. "I hated you for fooling me, for taking advantage of my loneliness. Because you'd made me feel like I belonged, finally. To someone." A self-deprecating smile touched her lips. "Aunt and *Onkle* had been the only people in my life who loved me. Then suddenly there was you. But when I found out it had all been a lie . . . well, then, I hated myself. For being stupid enough to fall for your tricks, for being naive enough to believe a man like you could care for me."

She didn't look at him, but she heard his half protest, the start of sound, and she rushed on, not wanting him to interrupt before she was finished. "And at that time I wanted to die, I wanted the sleepers to find me. I couldn't bear the thought that I had caused my husband's death. Oh, not just as if I'd stood back and watched it, though I did that too. But the thought that I *made* it happen, that I'd set the wheels in motion—"

"My God." Conor's voice was harsh. "Sari, we knew of Evan's involvement before we knew anything at all about you. You weren't to blame. You couldn't have stopped it."

"You don't know that."

"Bloody hell I don't know that." Conor said. "Evan was into the Mollies so deep, nothing could have saved him. Nothing you could have done would have changed that." ·

"I betrayed him."

"He betrayed himself." Conor's jaw was tight. "If it wasn't you, Sari, there would have been something else, someone else."

She looked at him warily, wanting to believe his words, not quite believing them. "You don't understand."

Conor leaned forward. His voice was icy. "If you say those words to me one more time, love, I will wring your pretty neck. If you need so badly to assign blame, assign it to me. *I'm* the one who betrayed them. You were only a tool I used."

She winced. The truth of the words hit her like a blow. "Just a tool?"

He regarded her carefully. His face softened, his

eyes lost their icy edge. "No," he murmured. "God, no."

"Why should I believe you?"

The pain in her voice was almost more than he could bear. Conor closed his eyes briefly. When he opened them again, she was staring at him with no screens behind her eyes. And what he saw there frightened him.

His voice was raw as he spoke the lie. "You can trust me."

"I would like for that to be true," she said simply. She rose, stacking dishes and taking them to the washpan that filled the surface of the sideboard. "I want to trust you."

And in spite of the fact that those were the words he wanted, the ones he'd waited for, half of him felt sheer panic. He wanted to scream at her, to demand that she hold back, that she treat him with caution.

But the other half of him wanted her trust so badly it shocked him.

"I wanted to tell you—" Her back was to him now. "The point of my story was not that I wanted absolution. I wanted you to know how I felt when they attacked the farm. In spite of everything, I never really believed Michael would let them harm me. But I guess . . ." She took a deep, sorrowful breath. "I guess I was right about my brother all along. I don't really know him at all."

Conor waited. For a moment he wondered if he was going to ask the question. "About Michael . . ."

"Michael has nothing to do with this, Conor," she said quickly. "I washed my hands of him a year ago, and I haven't seen him since." She turned to face him, lifting her chin in challenge. "I want to go on with my life. I want the past to stay the past."

She regarded him steadily, and Conor had the uncomfortable feeling that she was holding something back, that the emotions below those coffee-brown depths were emotions he wasn't ready for.

He looked out the window. "It's starting to snow."

Worry touched her voice. "I hope *Onkle*'s made it into town by now."

"I'm sure he has. It's been hours since he left."

Their worry translated to silence. He heard the dry sifting of ice against the wooden door as the tiny flakes of snow drove against the soddy in the wind.

Conor pushed back his chair. "I'd better take care of the animals."

He slipped into his duster and stepped outside. He was immediately blanketed in the sharp shrieking of the wind. The windmill creaked and thumped at the assault. The clouds above were billowing and dark, and fine, hard-frozen crystals of ice pummeled his face, cutting his skin. Conor threw his arm over his face, grasping onto the rope tied to the corner of the house. Blizzards blew up suddenly in these parts, and it was wise to be careful even though he could still see. He looped it around his waist and tied it securely, and then went to herd the animals.

They were huddled outside the door to the barn, waiting patiently for someone to let them in. Conor's fingers were nearly frozen as he fumbled with the handle. He glanced over his shoulder at the house, wondering if Sari was watching him, wondering what she was thinking. Her revelations had startled him, and he found himself wanting to believe her. Hell, not just *wanting* to believe her. Believing her. She was being honest about Michael, he knew it, and while the thought filled him with dread and frustration, it also filled him with a strange sort of joy.

He remembered when he met her—how eagerly she'd grasped at his friendship, how shyly she'd pursued him. Suddenly Conor badly wanted to get back to the soddy, to find out more about her.

He fed and watered the animals quickly, but in those few minutes the storm had turned into a full-scale blizzard. He hoped Charles *had* made it, though he couldn't imagine Sari's uncle hadn't. Town was about two hours away, and the start of snow in these parts urged caution. No doubt Charles was waiting it out at Landers's café.

Conor drew back into the barn, pulling his collar more tightly about his throat before he curled his fingers around the rope and stepped back into the wind.

Thousands of tiny ice particles blasted his face. He closed his eyes against them and his eyelashes immediately froze together. He was blind; the piercing cold numbed his hands and feet immediately, the wind buffeted him as if he were weightless.

Conor pulled up the rope foot by painful foot, hardly able to breathe against the pressure of the wind. He reached up to peel open one eye, and the wind caught him off balance. He stumbled to his knees. He barely felt the rope in his hands as he pulled on it in an effort to right himself.

There was nothing but whiteness around him. His lungs were burning, his face was numb. Without the rope he would have been blown completely off course, lost and wandering on the prairie. He'd heard people talk about the blizzards, about how it was like walking in an eerie, blank void, but he'd never believed the tales before.

The rope grew taut. Conor tripped to the soddy wall. Carefully he pressed against it, following it around. His fingers dug into the ice-crusted grass brick; he clutched the rope in his hands until he felt the edge of the door, the smooth, cold wood.

He wrenched on the handle and the door slipped open. His feet were like blocks of ice, his breathing harsh as he nearly fell into the warmth of the room.

Sari was beside him, yanking the rope from his hands and shoving the door closed.

"Are you all right?" She asked, peeling away the ice-frosted collar of his duster. "It turned so quickly."

"It's a blizzard, all right." His lips were so stiff, he could barely form the words. Conor staggered to the stove and held his hands over the warmth. The metal was hot from hours of cooking, and yet he could barely feel the heat. "And it looks to me like we're stuck here."

"For a few days probably," Sari agreed. Her brown eyes glinted in the lamplight. "*Onkle* won't be going anywhere till it's over."

"Neither will anyone else," Conor said, turning from the stove. He was surprised at the extent of his relief. "It's just you and me, love. All alone." A slow smile spread across his warming face. "Think you can bear it?"

CHAPTER 14

COULD SHE BEAR IT? SARI STARED AT HIM AS he huddled over the stove, rubbing his hands. They were alone. Together. With no escape. The storm would keep them both in the house; she couldn't send him out to the barn in a blizzard. And without Charles there was no buffer between them.

She licked her lips unconsciously and looked at him. His hair fell forward into his reddened face, snow melted from the shoulders of his coat. He looked over his shoulder at her, his face crinkled in a smile.

"What, no answer?"

His grin sent pinpricks of warmth spinning through her heart; it almost knocked her breath away. For a moment he looked so free-spirited, so young and eager. She knew he felt the same freedom she did, and that it was a rare feeling for him and he reveled in it.

She smiled back. "I hope you won't be bored."

"Bored?" He lifted a brow. "Not a chance of that, love."

Sari moved restlessly to the window, staring out at the swirling whiteness. The snow was falling quickly, the flakes so close together that it was one big swirling mass. There was nothing but movement, constant and never slowing.

She glanced back at him. "Have you ever seen such a blizzard?"

He fumbled with the buttons on his coat, slipping them clumsily from their fastenings, shrugging out of it. Melted water shook to the floor and sizzled on the hot surface of the stove. He hung the duster carefully on the peg beside the door.

He moved beside her; she felt his heat, smelled his warm, musky scent.

"It snows in Chicago, you know. There are times when it snows so hard, you can't escape it." The wind shrieked around the house, a sharp, keening wail. "But there isn't this kind of wind in Chicago. There's nothing like this wind."

"When we first came here, I used to wake in the night, sure I heard screaming," Sari remembered. "I've heard of women who went insane because of the sound."

"But you're used to it."

She nodded. "It's strange—I know you'll laugh—but now it comforts me. It's as if there's another person out there, always telling me she's around. I have never felt alone here." She paused. "Though sometimes I've felt lonely."

"Lonely, Sari?" His voice was so low, she barely heard it. "Like you felt in Tamaqua?"

His question tightened her heart. "I've never felt much like I belonged anywhere," Sari said honestly. It was true, and the reasons for it had caused her pain once. But she was older now, no longer a confused little girl or an abandoned wife. "My mother was too drunk to pay much mind to us, and Da— Da hit us when he remembered we were there. When I met Evan . . . well, no one had ever paid attention to me like that before—as if I mattered." She inhaled deeply, steadying herself against the pain of memory. It had not dulled. She wondered if it ever would. "But he was just like Da in the end."

Conor regarded her somberly. "I'm sorry."

"For what?" She asked. "It had nothing to do with you. Evan started drinking after I lost our baby. I don't think . . . I don't think he loved me at all . . . after that."

Conor stiffened. A baby. God, he'd never known, never even suspected. A wave of anger swept him, a fierce urge to ruin the man who had blamed her. How she must have hurt at the loss. He ached at the thought of it. Conor could imagine how she'd looked pregnant, how she would have glowed with real serenity, not the false placidness she wore now. She would have been so happy.

He was surprised at how much he wanted to see her that way now. Happy, carefree. Had Sari ever been that way? Or were the burdens she'd carried as a child too fierce to allow her joy?

"Evan was a fool," he said brutally.

"Yes, he was," she said, her voice breathless. "I realize that now, looking back. He would have hated my pity," she smiled. "So I pity him."

Conor's eyes twinkled. "Too bad he doesn't know."

"He does." She brushed past him, moving to the ladder of the loft.

He watched her hips sway beneath the fabric of her skirt as she climbed the ladder, and Conor's body stirred in sudden anticipation. He swallowed, turning away abruptly to watch the snow.

The memory of that kiss against the barn surfaced with painful clarity. Too well he remembered the feel of her, the taste of her. Her scent. He closed his eyes, imagining it again. She had smelled like shoofly pie. Sweet and rich, dark and sulfury. He'd never held a woman who smelled so good.

She was back in moments, climbing down, one hand clasping a bottle filled with dark liquid. Her dark eyes were lit with a touch of mischief.

"Plum wine," she whispered. "*Onkle* wouldn't touch a drop, but Aunt Bernice put it up without him knowing it. It seemed such a waste to leave it·behind."

She went to the shelves above the stove and took down two tin mugs. She handed them to him and twisted the cork in the bottle. There was a slight pop as it pulled free. Conor smelled the heady, summery scent of plums.

He held out the cups and she poured a careless measure into each. Her step seemed almost light, her touch flirtatious as she took her cup from his hand. Her warm fingers touched his, and the shock of her skin on his surprised him with its intensity.

She seemed not to notice. Instead she went to the far side of the room and settled into a chair. She motioned to the one beside her. "Won't you sit down?"

"I don't mind if I do." Conor took a sip of the wine, following her. The drink was potent, burning and sweet as it coursed down his throat. He looked at the cup in amazement. "Bernice brewed a strong bottle of wine."

"It was her one weakness." Sari's tone was fond. "After I was married, I'd come over to visit in the afternoons sometimes. She'd have a bottle waiting. I'm sure *Onkle* suspected we'd been drinking when he came in for supper, though he never said a word."

She leaned back in the chair. "We had some wonderful times," she murmured. She looked at him suddenly. "Do you ever wish you'd had a family?"

Conor winced. "I guess I have. I don't really remember."

She leaned forward, balancing her elbows on her knees and resting her chin in her hands.

"Liar," she said.

Conor looked at her in surprise. "What?"

"I don't believe you."

He deliberately laced his voice with coolness. "A small boy in a slum orphanage thinks more about staying alive."

"An orphanage?" She frowned. "I didn't know."

"I've never told anyone." His stomach felt tight.

Conor took another sip of the wine. It churned in his gut.

"Tell me," she said softly.

Conor gripped the cup in his fingers. God, she looked so intent, so fragile and childlike. The slender bones of her face looked elfin cupped by her long fingers. Her almond-shaped eyes were innocent and beguiling. But he knew better than that. He knew there was a strength, a worldliness, in Sari that belied her appearance. A strength that could easily best his.

She was so beautiful, and she was burning inside him; he'd spent too many sleepless nights dreaming of her clasped beside him, thinking of the way she sprawled across the bed lost in dreams.

She lowered her eyes and sat back in the chair, pulling her legs up beneath her, smoothing the dark brown skirt of her dress self-consciously. "There were times when I felt like an orphan, even when my parents were alive." She leaned her head on the edge of the chair. "I can imagine what it's like to have no one."

He couldn't speak. He stared at her, unable to tear his eyes away, feeling his mouth grow dry. Conor inhaled deeply. Her eyes were tempting. He wished he could just fall into them. There was something so soothing, so comforting in her gaze. "You don't know . . ."

He saw her quick pain, the way she turned her face into her cup and took an anxious sip of wine. It knifed through him, and for the first time in his life he felt selfish for not sharing himself with her. She wanted to know about him, and God knew he'd wanted to tell her for days now. She would understand. She was the only one who would.

The thought of Michael flitted quickly through his mind, and Conor deliberately pushed it away. It didn't matter. Not now. The snow blocked out the world; there was nothing but him and Sari. And for some odd reason he wanted her to know who he was. Who he really was.

"Sari," he said gruffly, "the truth is much more complicated than you know."

"I'll understand if you don't want to tell me."

He smiled. "No, you won't. And I don't blame you." He glanced into the depths of his cup; the dark wine glinted with the lamp's reflection. "The part about the orphanage is true enough, believe me. My mother died when I was very young. I barely remember her. I don't know much about her actually. She was a whore, I do know that. An immigrant. Her name was Bridget. I never knew her last name."

He looked up, into Sari's wide eyes. There was warmth and concern in her face. "Did you ever try to find out?"

He shrugged. "Not really. I wasn't very interested in her, to be honest. I'm less interested now." The truth of his words burned through him. "It doesn't matter, Sari. She doesn't matter."

"She was your mother."

"Is there some law that says you have to care about your mother?"

Sari looked away uncomfortably. "No." She shook her head. "No."

"I spent the next eight years or so in an over-crowded orphanage in the slums of Chicago. There's not much education in those places, not much to eat unless you steal it for yourself. When I was ten or eleven, I left. There was no more room and it was mutually agreed that I could take better care of myself."

"At ten?" Sari's surprise was reflected in her eyes.

Conor grinned. "By then I was pretty proficient at stealing. It was no hardship. In fact I didn't know any other way. And then . . . then, I got sick. Some kind of fever, something. They told me afterward that I was wandering the streets in a delirium. All I know is that I was having strange dreams, hallucinations." His hands clenched the cup in painful memory. He remembered those dreams too well, remembered the fear. Even now, at thirty-three, he felt those nightmares with the intensity of a twelve-year-old.

"They told me I almost died."

She was quiet for a long time, her brown eyes hooded, thoughtful. He wondered what she was thinking and was surprised to realize that he hoped she felt for him, that he wanted, yearned for, her concern for a bedraggled little boy whose eyes were bright with fever.

When she spoke, her voice was quiet. "Who are 'they'?"

His throat tightened. "The nuns," he said finally. "I ended up on the doorstep of a rectory."

"Thank God," she breathed.

He smiled at the irony. "Yes. Thank God. When

I woke up, days later, well on my way to recovery, I thought I'd died and gone to heaven. I guess in a way I had. The priest who ran the parish decided, for whatever reason, that I had some promise, and he took me in. He treated me so much like a son, I even took his name."

"His name?"

"His name was Father Sean Roarke. He became a real father to me." Conor brought his wine to his lips, pausing before he took a sip. "He did everything he could for me. Educated me, fed me. Loved me."

She frowned. "Loved?" she asked carefully.

"The Mollies bombed my house in July," he said bleakly. "He was sick—I was taking care of him." He paused. "He died before I could get him to a doctor."

Conor caught her gaze. He fought to keep the emotion from his voice, but he heard it there, resonating from deep inside him. Anger and sadness and regret. "You said you watched the papers, that you waited to find out who I really was. That you were disappointed the sleepers didn't kill me." He swallowed. "Well, I felt dead, Sari. I felt dead."

"And now?"

He clenched his jaw. "Now I want them all."

The anguish in his eyes was so intense, Sari felt blinded. This was the anger. This was what he'd been hiding from her. He'd lost as much as she had—more, because he loved his father and she had not loved her husband for a long time and had lost her brother years before.

The thought brought a cold lump to her stomach. Even though she hadn't really believed it, she'd hoped he'd been telling the truth when he said he'd come to Colorado because he still cared about her. But now a deeper suspicion lodged in her heart. Sleepers had killed Conor's father, and there were only a few left who would have cared enough to search Conor out.

Her throat felt tight. Michael had cared enough. Michael had the means and the motive for vengeance. He had plenty of enemies, and Conor was one of them.

She remembered the last time she'd seen her brother. It had been just before the hangings, on a heavy night dark with rain.

The street was deserted, and his whispered "Sari!" had seemed to echo through the air as she'd hurried back from trying to see Evan.

He'd pulled her back into the shadows between buildings, and in the dim lamplight his movements had seemed jerky and anxious, his eyes burned with suppressed emotion. Concern, she'd thought then, but now she wondered if maybe it had been excitement instead—or anger.

"I told you not to come back," she'd whispered. *"I told you to stay away."*

"Sari, don't nag me," he'd said, pulling her close—so close she'd felt the hot humidity of his breath against her hair, smelled the liquor scenting it. *"How's Evan?"*

"I don't know," she'd said dully. *"He won't see*

me." She swallowed. "They're hanging him tomor-row."

He'd stiffened against her, and Sari had pulled away. The intensity in his eyes frightened her—she'd seen that wild light before, too often.

"They'll pay for this," he'd said slowly. "Trust me, Sari. They'll pay."

"I don't want them to pay," she'd said. "I want it to be over, Michael—do you hear me?"

He'd smiled down at her, his teeth white and glittering through the darkness of his beard. "It's too late for that, Sari, darlin'," he'd whispered. "It's too late."

Too late. Sari swallowed. A slow, uneasy dread filled her. What had Michael meant by that? Had he been planning, even then, to bomb Conor's house?

Something inside her told her he had, and though Sari tried to deny it, the thought wouldn't go away. It was like her brother to take his fanaticism to the most violent ends. It was why she wanted nothing more to do with him.

She wished she didn't know, that she could go on pretending there might be a future for her and Conor. But now she knew how much Conor had loved his father, the price he'd paid. She knew how badly he wanted vengeance. If it had been Michael, if Conor knew the role she'd played . . . that future didn't exist. It couldn't exist.

She winced. "I'm so sorry."

His gaze sharpened. "Sorry?" he asked. "Why?"

"Because." It was hard to speak through the lump in her throat, and she didn't know what to say anyway. "Because . . . of what you've . . . been through."

He shook his head; there was still that anger in his eyes. "That's not why, Sari. Tell me the truth. Tell me why you're sorry."

"You wouldn't understand."

"No? Try me."

She couldn't put words to the thought. How could she say it? *I'm sorry, Conor, because I think my brother killed your father, and I know it means you'll never love me?* What would he say to such a thing? What could he say except that she was right?

He was staring at her, his eyes demanding truths, the blue fire in them as intense as the burn in Michael's had been, in its own way as fanatical. There would be no forgiveness there, she knew, just as there had been none in her brother's eyes.

She couldn't tell him, and she couldn't lie to him. In his eyes she saw the little orphan boy he'd been, the boy who'd nearly traded his soul to survive. She wanted to touch that in him, wanted to heal it, if only for a moment, a day. At whatever cost to herself.

"Conor," she said slowly. "I'm sorry because of what the sleepers cost you. I'm sorry for my part in it. But mostly . . . mostly I'm sorry because I can kiss you, I can make love to you, but I'll never be able to make that pain go away. And that . . . that makes me sorry."

He looked up at her, and the fire of anger faded

in his eyes, replaced by a bigger, deeper fire—one that took her breath away.

"Don't be sorry, love," he said slowly, in a low, deep voice that sent shivers up her spine. "Don't be sorry. Just . . . just kiss me. Just . . . love me. Please. Make love to me tonight."

CHAPTER 15

SARI FELT FROZEN TO THE CHAIR. *MAKE love to me tonight.* She didn't misunderstand him. He wanted comfort and understanding, he wanted the mindlessness that came when they touched. But he didn't want love. He didn't want forever.

After the storm ended, they would go back to the way they had been. She would be distant and controlled, he would be the emotionless Pinkerton agent, here only to do a job. She would try to forget what he'd told her. She could not expect that tonight would change anything between them.

But what if it did? What if she took the risk of loving Conor? How much pain could she go through again if she was wrong?

The answer came quickly: as much as it took. She couldn't deny him, couldn't deny herself. Besides, she told herself, this time she'd be ready for any betrayal. The pain would be less if she was prepared for it. And in the end it didn't matter anyway. When he looked at her that way, she couldn't walk away from him, couldn't say no. She didn't *want* to say no.

She set aside her cup, uncurled her legs. He was watching her every movement with selfish fascination. *"As if he wants to drink your soul."* Miriam's words. Or Conor's words? They mixed drunkenly in her mind.

"It feels like I've wanted you forever." The velvet gravel of his voice caressed Sari's nerves. "I've dreamed of you so often. Nothing seems to stop it. Nothing."

She waited on the edge of the chair as he rose. He held out a hand, and she took it, feeling weightless when he pulled her to her feet. His hands rested at her waist, drawing her close. His lips were warm and urgent as he nuzzled the sensitive spot below her ear.

"Tell me, Sari," he whispered. "Tell me why I can't seem to get you out of my blood."

For the same reason I can't get you out of mine. Sari closed her eyes, wishing she could tell him. Wishing that it mattered that she loved him. But the only important thing was the warmth of his breath on her throat, the heady smell of him.

She wrapped her arms around his waist, pulling him closer, running her hands over the plane of his back. His flannel shirt was smooth against her skin; she felt the play of his muscles as he shifted into her.

He brushed her lips lightly with his own, and she shuddered at the warm tenderness of the kiss. She arched into him, impatient for more as he flicked the corners of her mouth with his tongue, tracing the outline of her lips, urging her mouth open so that he could explore the sweet taste of her.

She tasted sweet, and her mouth was hot and wet and urgent. Conor wanted more of her, wanted to draw her inside him. He groaned into her mouth and she answered him, twining her fingers in the hair at the back of his neck, pressing her breasts into his chest. The screaming of the snow battered the house, wrapping itself around them, removing all the walls they'd erected, leaving only two people who had nothing but each other.

It was true, he realized. He had nothing but Sari and her warm, sweet body. He wanted her more than he ever had. Wanted to bury himself inside her and take surcease in her giving. And more than that, he wanted to show her that she was his and that he wanted it no other way.

He fumbled with her dress, unfastening the inner lining. He peeled the material from her shoulders, urging it over her hips until it fell in a pile at their feet. He caressed her hips, the indentation of her waist, the full breasts straining against her muslin chemise. Conor curved his hands around her buttocks, pulling her closer, settling her over his hips.

She tore at the buttons on his shirt, spreading it open, running her fingers through the hair on his chest. Memories of lying with her in bed, tumbling together in tangled sheets damp with lovemaking, jumbled through his mind. God, how he wanted that again—skin on skin, making love far into the night, without neighbors, or the past, or responsibilities intruding.

He shrugged out of his shirt; the material fell with a soft swish to the ground. He pulled away then, searching her face, but she kept her gaze lowered, and he wanted her to look at him, wanted to see the emotion he craved—passion and longing and something else, that same unconditional love he'd always seen in the past.

But she didn't look at him, and he knew it was unfair of him to ask when he could offer her nothing in return. So instead he ran his hand up her side, cupping the fullness of her breast before he stroked her shoulder with his finger, looping the strap of her chemise and letting it fall. The muslin sagged, catching on her erect nipple, and with deliberate slowness Conor bent, kissing the top of her breast, the side, snagging the fine fabric with his teeth and pushing it out of the way so that he could curl his tongue around her nipple. Her scent was intoxicating. He'd never known a woman like her, never been so ensnared by the perfume of woodsmoke and soap or the sheer, beautiful softness of skin.

Conor pulled back, tangling his hand in her coiled hair. He strung it through his fingers, pulling her head back so that he could take her mouth. He'd meant it to be a gentle kiss, but the longing that racked his body consumed him. She was like fire, hot and soothing at the same time. She tasted of plum wine and forgiveness, and the combination was almost more than he could bear.

"Touch me," he whispered into her mouth. She complied with an eagerness that left him weak, tear-

ing at the buttons of his pants, trailing her finger
slowly over him. Damn, this wanting was like an ob-
session. All he could think about was how good it
felt to be inside her, how much he wanted the balm
her soul gave him. Her hair was soft against his
hands, her breasts brushed his chest as she leaned
closer.

He backed against the chair, suddenly too feeble
to stand. He sank down, pulling her with him until
she was sitting in his lap.

With a quick curse of impatience he lifted her
slightly. Her eyes were so dark, they looked almost
black in the lamplight. He grabbed at her skirt,
bunching it in one hand over her thighs, fumbling at
his pants with the other.

Sari couldn't look away. His eyes held her locked
in place. His fingers dug into the smooth softness of
her thighs, the muscles of his chest and throat were
taut with control as he urged her upward. She felt
his hand drag at the ties of her drawers and then a
sharp tug brought the material down around her
hips.

Her knees dug into the coarse fabric of the chair,
but before she could move, his hands were on her
again, his fingers curling in the soft hair at the junc-
ture of her thighs, his thumb caressing her. Stroking,
dipping, driving her insane with need.

Sari moaned, unable to do anything but press herself against him, arch her back in response to his
ceaseless movement. Oh, he knew just what to do.
She threw back her head, felt her own hair, warm

and soft and heavy across the naked skin of her back.
And then his mouth was on her breast, his tongue
laving the sensitive peak, curling and teasing.

"Sari, love." His whisper was hot and moist
against her flesh. "Ah, Sari, how I need you."

She heard the whimpering and didn't realize it was
her own. She heard the sound of the snow beating
against the house, screaming in the wind, and it echoed the sound of her own mind, of the need that
swirled around her, overwhelming her, controlling
her.

She took a deep breath, then leaned her head
back, offering her throat to him. Offering her soul,
if only he knew it. He was holding his breath, it
sounded harsh and drawn out as he released it. The
sound sent shivers through her body, and Sari
gripped his shoulders. His heat was burning her, her
breasts, her hands, her mouth were aching for his
touch. "Please," she moaned breathlessly. "Please."

His hands left her, tightened on her hips and
pulled her down. She gasped as he sank into her and
Sari's eyes flashed open. She met his gaze, blue with
desire, burning with promise. She tried to move, but
his hands kept her still, held her prisoner.

"Slowly, love," he whispered. "Take it slowly.
Make it last for both of us."

She slid her hands downward, through the thick
hair on his chest, over muscles tight with tension,
and began the slow, twisting movement. His eyes
closed, his fingers tightened on her buttocks.

She writhed against him, twisting beneath his
hands, pressing down, wanting him deeper, deeper,

where she could feel him against her very core. She clutched his head, tangling her fingers in his hair, closing her eyes against the feelings sweeping through her. There was nothing like this, there never had been. How could she fight it? Why did she want to?

Her questions fell away in darkness. There was only the excruciating, peaking pleasure. Her words were incoherent, her pleadings vague murmurs as the release tore through her. Sari felt her body throb and tremble, felt her own hot rush in the same moment she heard Conor's hoarse cry, in the same moment she felt him shudder against her. His fingers dug into her back, pulling her into his chest, and Sari collapsed against him, cradled in his arms as the aftermath throbbed around them, caressed them.

And in that moment, safe and secure in his arms, with the sound of the snow whirling around them, Sari knew that nothing had changed.

She was still in love with him.

The feeling had never really disappeared, never been beaten into submission by lies and hate and betrayal.

She'd denied it, and if she were wise, she would go on denying it. Her feelings for Conor didn't blind her to what he was; they didn't take the past away.

She heard his deep breathing, felt the steady rise and fall of his chest beneath her cheek. The soft hair curled against her skin scratched at the corner of her mouth.

"Ah, Sari, how I need you." His words came circling back to her through the daze of repletion. She

remembered how his face had looked then, how she'd searched his eyes and seen into his very soul.

What she would have given to have found love there.

Conor rolled onto his side, gathering Sari into his arms, smiling at her soft murmur when she curled sleepily against him, nestling her round buttocks into his groin. He had missed this. Missed waking up in the middle of the afternoon to find her tangled in the blankets, missed the curious ways she twisted her body on the mattress. His chest tightened at the thought that he should savor it now. Once the storm stopped, this interlude would be over. It would be time then to finish this job one way or another and get out.

He buried his face in her hair, breathing in its clean scent, closing his eyes against its softness. How nice it would be to stay like this for the rest of time, without Pinkerton's constant demands, without the never-ending threat of danger and death. Perhaps it would be better to be a farmer.

For a moment Conor let himself imagine it. Milking cows, feeding livestock, stringing fence, and breaking his back to break the tangled sod. Hard, honest work that ended when the sun went down, when a man walked into a kitchen filled with the scent of ham and beans and sugar pie. He imagined Sari standing at the stove, her face flushed, her hair falling into her face. But when she turned, there was a smile on her lips and welcome in her eyes.

God, it actually sounded good.

He was getting too involved. The thought of leaving her, of hurting her again, made him weak. She had become more important than just a means to an end.

He wasn't sure when it had happened. Until tonight he would have sworn he had it in control. It was frightening to realize just how much he'd been lying to himself. Her serenity soothed him, her presence was a balm to his battered spirit. Since he'd been on the farm, even revenge for his father's death had faded in importance.

That was what frightened him the most. He was afraid the anger would die, that he would step back and allow Michael Doyle and the others simply to walk away, unharmed, to live with only their consciences to punish them. The fear was only exacerbated by the words that nagged at him when he was tired and aching, the harsh memory of Sean Roarke's last breath: *"Don't go after them."*

Don't go after them. Conor closed his eyes, tightening his hold on Sari. The memory was there, and instead of fighting it, he let it come, let himself remember the horror and the fear of holding his broken father in his arms, feeling the man's frail body shudder in his grasp. Once again he heard the gurgling whisper: *"Don't go after them. Leave it to—"*

—God. Conor finished the sentence in his mind. He knew his father's sermons well. Retribution was not the duty of man; punishment was for God only. Doyle and the others would find their hell on Judgment Day.

His father had believed that. His father would tell

him to stay in bed, to enjoy Sari and forget about vengeance. His father would tell him that the risk of losing her—of losing his own soul—was too great. If he went after her brother, Sari would never forgive him, even as she insisted that Michael was dead to her. If he killed Michael to avenge Sean Roarke's death, Conor knew he would have made the decision to leave Sari forever, to bear her hatred.

For the first time he wondered if he wanted to make that decision.

Sari moved in her sleep, snuggling closer to him, moving her head so that her hair caught on his shoulder, the silky strands trailing over his skin. Conor stared up at the ceiling, letting the pure pleasure course through him. She felt so soft and warm, so forgiving and loving. Her giving aroused feelings of tenderness and need inside of him that he hadn't felt in a long time, not since Tamaqua.

He didn't want to admit that he was starting to rethink his reasons for pursuing revenge, and he especially didn't want to admit that it was due to Sari. He wondered if his father was right. Was there a God who would sentence Michael Doyle and the others far more effectively than Conor could?

Maybe he'd been wrong all this time. Maybe he *could* just walk away. Or was it even possible anymore to live without scheming and lying, without violence and constant betrayal. Could he live a normal life, raising a family on the plains, loving a woman?

It had never sounded good before, but now suddenly the idea took hold. There was the promise of a future in a farmer's life. Family, children, love, and warmth where before there'd only been emptiness. This was what he needed, this warm, unconditional understanding, this hope.

Conor buried his face in Sari's hair, smelling the warm, sweet scent of her, and suddenly he wanted that kind of life more than he'd ever wanted anything. It went against everything he'd ever known about himself, but for the first time he began to believe it was possible to find those things. He would court her and learn to love her. He would learn this land as well as Charles had learned it. He would do it all. He *could* do it all.

He buried the nagging thought that maybe he couldn't.

CHAPTER 16

"DAMN!" CONOR JUMPED BACK FROM THE
stove, dodging the spattering grease. He jerked
around as a scorching droplet landed on his skin.
"Christ, that's hot!"

Sari looked up wryly from the book she was reading. "I find it difficult to believe you grew up in a
rectory."

He shot her a dry glance. "So did my father." He
wiped at his arm with a towel, then once again
picked up the heavy metal fork. "Unfortunately I
never outgrew swearing. Though I did learn to tem-
per it somewhat."

"Which meant you didn't do it in front of your
father."

He smiled. "Precisely." He stepped back, wincing
as he turned the slabs of scrapple in the skillet and
they spat back at him. "I do remember sending a
certain Sister Ursula running from the room, how-

ever. Something to do with 'rejecting proper discipline,' I believe she called it."

"My goodness, it sounds fatal."

"I wasn't too fond of being smacked on the knuckles with a ruler." He grinned at the memory. "By then I was no longer afraid they'd kick me out if I disagreed with them."

Sari's lips twitched with laughter. "What did you do, smack her back?"

"Nothing so drastic." He shook his head. "I grabbed the ruler and broke it over my knee. And then I called her every foul name I could think of. Which, at that time, was a formidable list."

"I imagine," Sari murmured. "And then what happened?"

She had never seen Conor Roarke look sheepish before, and Sari stared in surprise as his eyes lowered and his mouth twisted strangely. Something tugged at her heart.

"Within half an hour I was in my father's office," he remembered. "He had this way about him—this funny hesitation. Sometimes he'd stop in the middle of a sentence while he tried to figure out exactly how to say something. I thought he was too angry with me to speak. It wasn't until months later that I realized it was just the way he was." He poked at the scrapple with the fork, idly moving it around the skillet. "I remember how harried he looked. His hair was standing on end, and he kept running his hands through it as though it helped him think."

"Had he much experience with little boys before then?"

"I don't know." He shrugged. "I guess he'd dealt with the parish children on occasion. But it wasn't until I'd been there nearly a year that he set up a small orphanage in the rectory."

His mouth twitched with a smile. "Before that I don't think he'd ever dealt with anyone quite like me. I'd been on my own for a long time. It was difficult for me to follow rules."

"Impossible, maybe?"

Conor chuckled. "Yeah. The first week I was there, after I was stronger, I tried to sneak out in the middle of the night with the rosaries." His blue eyes twinkled as he caught her look of disbelief. "I thought I could sell them."

"But they caught you?"

"Sister Ursula again." He nodded. "God, she was a horror. She was about the biggest woman I'd ever seen. I wasn't worried so much that she could chase me down, it's just that I couldn't get *around* her—"

"Conor!"

He laughed, and Sari was amazed at how much it changed his face. His cheeks were cut with deep dimples; wrinkles nearly hid his eyes. And it was so infectious. His laughter made her want to join in, made it impossible *not* to join in.

"Well, it's true," he protested. "But the sister and I worked out a sort of grudging respect for each other in the end." He paused. "She was transferred to New York the year before I left Pennsylvania. I got a letter from her a few months ago saying how sorry she was. She said she'd pray for my soul, since my father didn't need praying for."

"Thank God someone's seeing to your soul." Sari struggled to interject a lighter tone.

He flashed her a grin. "And if I know Sister Ursula, she's praying damn hard." He lifted a plate from the shelf above the stove and piled the thick, fragrant slices of the spicy pork-and-cornmeal loaf onto it. Taking a basket of freshly baked biscuits from the sideboard, he set them both on the table before he stepped behind her. His arms went around her, pulling her close as he bent and buried his face in her hair.

Sari closed her eyes, reveling in the feel of his lips through the hair she'd worn loose especially for him. She caught her breath as he nuzzled her throat.

"Put the book away, love," he whispered. "Breakfast is ready."

He left her then, too suddenly, and took the seat across the table. Sari folded her book and pushed it aside, reaching for a plate.

"I didn't realize you were such a cook," she teased, forking a piece of scrapple and dishing canned pears onto her plate.

"How do you imagine I survived for so long on my own?"

"On your own?" She lifted a dark, well-shaped brow. "I didn't realize you had to do your own cooking—at least not in Pennsylvania. Seems to me the rent at Lawler's covered room *and* board."

He spread molasses on a biscuit. "Apparently you never ate at Lawler's."

"No," she admitted. "I never did. Evan used to

say there was no need to pay for food when I could cook it at home."

"If I had been Evan," he said softly, "I would have taken you everywhere. I would have made damn sure that everyone knew you belonged to me. And I would have killed anyone who touched you."

Her heart skipped a beat, but Sari forced herself to reply teasingly. "If Evan had been that possessive, you'd be dead."

"I should be," he replied soberly. He paused, his jaw tightened as he looked down at his plate. "Did you ever get a chance to talk to Evan after they arrested him?"

She frowned. The memory of Michael came sneaking back, along with that guilty regret. With effort she pushed it away. "No. They wouldn't let me in."

"You were his wife."

She shrugged. "Perhaps if Evan had wanted to see me, it would have been different." She tried to keep her tone light, but she knew by the way Conor paused that she hadn't fooled him.

"Evan refused to see you?"

"He . . . I . . . ." Sari took a deep breath. "He never did forgive me."

"Forgive you? For what?"

"What wasn't there to forgive?" she asked. "For betraying him. For . . . for you. He didn't find out that you and I had been . . . that we had a relationship . . . until the trial. I don't think he'd come to terms with it yet."

He was quiet for a moment. Then Conor cleared

his throat. "He'd come to terms with it," he said brusquely.

Sari frowned. "How do you—"

"I went to see him just after they took him into custody. By then most of the gang suspected I was the spy, but they didn't know for sure. Pinkerton thought it best if I paid one last visit to Evan, just to see if I could get a few more answers." He looked up at her, his eyes expressionless. "The reason the case went on so long, Sari, was because we wanted to get them for something big. We'd had them on the little things for months, but we just couldn't pull together enough evidence to accuse them of conspiring to murder. We hoped that Evan would be the key."

"I—I don't understand what you're trying to say."

"I spent about an hour with him." Conor looked at his plate. "Evan was nothing if not clever. He wouldn't tell me a damn thing about the Mollies, but I could tell he was excited about something. He was nearly on the edge of his seat waiting to spring it on me."

"Evan had a lot of secrets," Sari said tightly. Her stomach clenched.

"Yes." His eyes met hers. "Evan knew about us. That was what he wanted to tell me. He knew we were lovers. He'd known for months."

"But—but that's not possible!" Sari stared at him in disbelief. "He would have killed you! He wouldn't have tolerated it—he would have killed us both."

"It amused him," Conor said. "He was trying to figure out how to use it against you. It was a game to him. I just . . . I want you to know. . . . Don't torment yourself thinking about how you—how *we*—betrayed him, Sari. He'd broken his vows to you already."

She turned away abruptly, catching her breath. It was just one more thing to add to Evan's list of transgressions. He'd been expert at taunts, at the special kind of verbal torment only a husband could supply. Her only consolation was that he undoubtedly regretted it later, when he realized Conor was the traitor. It must have tortured him, wondering if his "game" had cost him his life, wondering if she'd given Conor the information that led to Evan's hanging.

Sari took a deep breath and looked up at Conor. "Evan's dead," she said slowly, toying with her fork. "And what was between my husband and me was over long before I met you. I don't want to talk about Evan anymore."

His icy eyes were penetrating in the moments before his lips curved upward in a gentle smile. "I'm sorry I mentioned him."

"Let's pretend you didn't."

"All right. Let's pretend."

The storm was increasing outside, the sound of the wind and the snow so constant, Sari had ceased to hear it. The tiny, icy particles whistled through the cracks and crevices of the house, blowing across the floor like sand and melting near the stove. The snow had piled up high enough to cover the window. When she looked outside, all she saw was a wall of snow. That morning she had taken a warm flatiron to the glass in an attempt to melt the ice, to see the daylight.

But in spite of that she never wanted it to end.

She looked toward Conor. He was sitting in the rocker, flipping through the pages of a book. His dark hair fell over his forehead, his finely shaped lips were pursed in concentration. Once again Sari smiled in contentment. How easy it was, being here with him, locked into habits that felt familiar and comfortable even though they were less than two days old. She felt as though she'd stolen something infinitely precious and now was just savoring the moments until it was taken away again. As long as the storm raged on, they were safe. Protected and secure in a world containing just the two of them.

The turning pages rustled in the relative silence, and Sari hugged herself tightly. *I love him.* The words made her giddy. She formed her tongue around the phrase, trying it out silently, mouthing the words. *I love him. I love him. I love you.*

She sighed, knowing she would never tell him. At least not now. She wanted nothing to spoil these days, wanted no lingering pain to taint her memory. Only in her imagination did Conor respond with "I love you too." The reality was just as it had always been. The job and vengeance came first. There was no room for love. There was no room for her.

She told herself it didn't matter. She was tired of battling things she couldn't change, tired of living with betrayal. She didn't want to think or analyze. She wanted to love, even if it meant she would ultimately be hurt again. It was better than fighting all the time.

The relief that went through her at the thought was astounding; she nearly laughed out loud at the force of it.

Conor looked up, as if sensing her mood, and smiled. "What is it?"

"Nothing," she answered. "A joke I remembered."

"Tell me."

"I don't remember it that well." She went to him, resting her hands on the armrests and leaning over him. Her hair fell forward, washing down his shirtfront, curtaining part of her face. He pushed it away gently, tucking it behind her ear. "Something about a city boy trying to be a farmer." She lifted the corner of the book he was reading and closed it over his thumb. "*Alfalfa: Techniques and Procedures for Growing from Mexican Seed.* Are you serious?"

"What's wrong?" he asked lightly. "Can't you see me bent over a plow, cursing in the sunshine?"

"Of course I can." A teasing smile touched her lips. "With your gun tucked into your belt and William Pinkerton sending you telegrams every other day." She lowered her voice in a parody of the Pinkerton boss. " 'Another emergency, Conor. We need an experienced man.' "

Conor laughed. "Poor William would be humiliated to hear himself sound like that. He'd say something more like: 'Top secret, Roarke. Only you can do it.' "

"If that's the future, I can see you won't get much alfalfa harvested."

"Or planted, for that matter." Conor laid the book aside and pulled her into his lap.

Sari locked her arms around his neck, leaning into him. Her knee jabbed into the side of the chair. "Have you ever thought about having a family? About settling down?"

She caught a glimpse of surprise, of sudden vulnerability, but then the shutters went up over his eyes. He was wondering what to tell her, she realized, and the knowledge sent a shaft of pain through her. "I've never had the time for that, Sari."

"But you've thought about it."

He shrugged. "Once or twice."

"When you were young and idealistic probably." Sari kept her voice light, though the tension that tugged at her heart grew tighter and tighter. "How lovable you must have been then, before Pinkerton got his hooks into you."

"And I'm not lovable now?"

Sari shook her head. "Not at all. No woman in her right mind would fall in love with you."

"Only insane women."

She chuckled. "Or a woman with no mind at all."

His hands tightened on her hips; Conor stared at her face. "Which one of those women were you?"

She couldn't tell if he was teasing or not. Sari worked to keep her smile. "When I was in love with you?"

He nodded.

"I believe I was dangerously close to being a woman with no mind at all."

He studied her for a moment. He smiled, a sad, wistful smile, and the expression sank into her stomach.

"You lie so prettily, love."

She said nothing, waiting for the next question. The inevitable question. *"How do you feel now?"* How would she answer when he asked it? With the truth, or with the lie that would protect her again?

But he didn't ask. Instead he pulled her closer, burying his face between her breasts. Sari held him there, bending her head over his until her hair rained onto her hands and his shoulders.

"I didn't know you'd lost a baby," he said softly, whispering against her heart, the words so soft, she barely heard them. But she did hear them, and she heard his concern, the pain she didn't understand.

"I—I thought I'd told you about that."

"No." He pulled away, his blue eyes surveyed her calmly. "I never knew."

"Well, it's not really the kind of failure you tell everyone about." It had been so long ago. Nearly seven years. But she could still remember her fierce joy at the life inside of her, the fulfillment that touched every part of her life. . . . And then the overwhelming, devastating pain.

She couldn't look into his face. Conor had not been a part of that time, and it was still so private to her. "I loved being pregnant," she said slowly. "It was the best thing that ever happened to me."

He was quiet for a moment, and she wondered if he was going to ask her the other question. After she'd lost the baby, everyone had been too courteous to ask how it had happened. But then, they hadn't needed to ask. Evan had volunteered the information freely, telling anyone who even seemed interested about his aunt's terrible premonition, and how Sari had ignored it.

Evan had always believed the miscarriage was Sari's fault. When he'd told Sari about his aunt's vision, she had laughed it away, feeling so secure in her pregnancy that an old woman's superstitions seemed silly. Evan had never forgiven her. It had irrevocably ruined a marriage that was disintegrating anyway. Evan seldom touched her after that.

She looked at Conor, waiting for the question. Instead he caressed her jaw with his finger.

"What happens now, Sari?" He asked quietly. "When you ran away from Tamaqua, from the past, did you have a plan? Did you want to settle down, remarry, have a family?"

Her throat tightened. He was asking the questions she wanted him to ask, but not because the answers had any relevance to his own plans. There was only mild curiosity in his voice—no strained emotion, no hopeful edge.

She told herself it didn't matter. She'd known from the beginning he didn't plan to stay. And if there was nothing for her in the future, she would grab today and make it as precious as she could. She had decided to love him, to trust him, and she would do it and hope that one day he might decide to love her back. Even just a little bit.

She opened her mouth to speak, to make some light, teasing comment that didn't show how much his question hurt. But the soddy was suddenly, eerily quiet. The cold silence rang in her ears, loudly and painfully.

Conor looked toward the door. "What the hell is that sound?"

"There is no sound," she said. "That's what you hear. Silence. The blizzard's stopped."

His eyes met hers, and Sari saw the quick desperation, the profound regret in his gaze. She knew those same expressions were mirrored on her own face.

The world was back.

CHAPTER 17

IT HAD BEEN THREE DAYS SINCE THE BLIZ-
zard had ended. Since Charles had ridden home that
first day, there'd been no chance to be alone. It had
been three days of seeing Conor across the room and
longing to touch him, three days of catching his intimate glances, three nights of lying awake, aching
with need.

Sari looked up at him as he stared down at the
chessboard they'd placed on the floor—an innocent
game, and one that had been taking the place of
other games, other intimacies. Now just watching
him made Sari burn. The endearing way his hair was
tousled, the laughing mouth—she could not keep
her eyes off him. Which was why she was ready
when he took his bishop and knocked over her king
and reached for her.

"Don't!" Sari shrieked, half laughing as she
scooted backward on the floor, out of Conor's reach.
"It's not fair! You're cheating!"

He lunged forward, toppling the chess pieces off the board, sending them scattering across the cowhide. He was practically on top of her. He locked his hands around her waist. "You've taken unfair advantage of me from the beginning. I'm not cheating, I'm just evening the odds."

"Oh, you'll say whatever—"

"—works," he finished. His face cracked in a teasing leer. "And this is working quite well." He fell onto his side, pulling her with him as he rolled onto his back. Sari found herself on top of him, her skirts tangled around her knees.

She rested her palms squarely on his chest, pushing away. "Why is it so impossible to play a normal game of chess with you?"

"I believe I told you. You have an unfair advantage."

"Which is?"

"Every second I look at you, I'd rather be in this position."

Sari felt the heat of a blush work its way over her face. The man said the most outrageous things. She never quite knew how to react to them, though she liked his frank compliments and the way he studied her through lowered lids when he thought she wasn't looking. It had been such a long time since anyone had looked at her that way.

"I think," she said archly, "you'd better learn to control it. *Onkle* could come in any minute."

"What would he do?" His eyes twinkled.

"Put a gun to your head, most likely."

"I think I can withstand such a threat." His hands

lowered to her hips, he pulled her closer until Sari
felt his heat through her skirt. "What do you think,
love? Should I sneak up to your room tonight?"

Her stomach felt hollow; warmth spread all
through her body. She smiled, leaning closer so that
her hair tickled his face. "I don't know if I should
let you," she said. "You don't deserve it."

"I don't?" He rose to brush her throat with his
lips. "What are you punishing me for?"

"For cheating at chess." Her voice was breathless.

"Ah, love." He brought a hand to her chin, tilting
her face down so that she was forced to look into his
eyes. Blue, blue eyes. "It's only cheating if I win."

His voice was like a spell, wrapping around her,
mesmerizing her. Sari wanted nothing more than to
feel him touching her, to feel him inside her.

His thumb caressed her jaw, bringing her closer.
His lips were inches away, she felt the warm moist-
ness of his breath and saw the dark desire in his
eyes—

The front latch turned, and Sari sprung away, pulling down her skirts and brushing back her hair as
the door swung open. Charles walked in, stamping
snow from his boots.

"How do you stay warm in the barn, Roarke?" he
wheezed, taking off his hat and throwing it onto the
table. "It is freezing out there."

Sari picked up the chess pieces, ignoring the blush
staining her cheeks. She tried not to look at Conor.
He hadn't moved, and she knew if she turned to meet
his eyes, he would smile that lazy, mocking smile
that turned her blood to fire.

The thought of it made her fingers tremble; she knocked over a pawn and tried unsuccessfully to right it three times before it stood again on its rightful square.

"Playing chess?" Her uncle's voice floated past her.

Sari nodded vigorously without looking at him. "Yes. There was nothing else to do, and I'm tired of reading—"

"Who was winning?" he asked, his pale eyes twinkling.

Conor rose on one elbow, his mouth cocked in a half grin. "Sari was giving me the beating I deserved, I'm afraid. You taught her well."

"It is best to remember that chess is a strategic game. Every move counts." Charles shrugged out of his coat before moving to the stove to pour a cup of coffee. He took a sip and looked back out the window. He shook his head, smiling tenderly. "Bernice loved chess. We would play it at least twice a week. She was not a woman to waste moves."

"Sari learned that as well." Conor looked at her as he spoke, and Sari heard his promise, saw the sly sparkle of innuendo in his eyes.

She got to her feet, stepping away from the chessboard. "Perhaps you two should finish the game," she suggested. "Since you're both so fond of it."

Charles's face lit at the idea. "If you would like to, Roarke."

"As long as you're not too much better than I am," Conor said. "I do have some pride, and being beaten by Sari was almost too much for me."

His voice sounded light, but Sari felt his gaze on
her back as she moved to the loft ladder. She took a
few steps up, and then stopped, knowing he was
watching the movement of her hips, and afraid her
uncle would notice. She waited until Charles took
the few steps from the kitchen.

"Very well, Roarke," he challenged. "I will give
you the first move."

"Oh, God," Conor said. "I don't like the sound of
that."

Sari climbed into the loft, closing her eyes and letting the soft darkness swallow her. Conor and Charles's words blended together, and she stopped
listening as she stumbled the short distance to her
bed and sat on the edge.

The shadows were soothing; Sari closed her eyes
and tried to relax. But it was impossible. She kept
imagining the smooth movement of the muscles of
his back, remembering the whispers of passion that
shivered over her skin like Tamaqua mist.

She wished it were easy to walk away from him,
to love him with her body and not her mind and soul.
But she had never been able to do that before, and
she knew it was useless to try now. Conor was in her
blood, had been since the day she'd first seen him,
cocky and too bold at the Christmas dance in Tamaqua. She thought he'd grabbed a little piece of her
heart then, and now his hold on it was impossible to
break. She wondered if she would be able to stand
it when he left.

But she had promised herself not to think about
it. She loved him with everything in her that knew

how to love. She did not want to think of a time when she might hate him again just as intensely.

The men's talk dwindled to silent concentration as the game wound on. Charles was a good player, and Conor was easily outmatched. Besides, he was distracted as hell. He kept remembering the sway of Sari's hips beneath her skirt, the subtle bouncing of her breasts as she climbed the ladder. She was up there now, no doubt in bed, with her face buried in a book. He could imagine how she must look, with her hair unbound, trailing over the soft rise of her shoulder, her breath slow and even—

"Checkmate." Charles sat back, a wide grin creasing his face.

Conor started. "Where? I didn't see."

"That is right, you did not see." Charles wagged a finger. "You would be a good player, Roarke, if you had concentration. But no, you wander off, caught in a dream like a small boy."

Conor smiled. "A very pleasant dream."

He was surprised to see Charles's face darken. The man rose abruptly, stretching his legs and walking distractedly to the window. "It is getting late."

Conor thought of Sari upstairs. "Yes."

"Would you like to come to the back house? To share a pipe?"

Conor was startled by the question. Charles had never asked him to his soddy before. He had the impression the place was the man's retreat, that even Sari didn't go there often. It was an honor, no doubt, but one he didn't want to take the old man up on. The picture of Sari in bed came to him again. His breath quickened.

"It *is* late," he began.

Charles nodded shortly. "*Ja*. But there is still enough time for a smoke. Come along."

It was an order, then. Conor got to his feet, sending a remorseful glance into the loft. A soft light glowed up there. She was reading, as he'd thought. Perhaps she'd even fallen asleep, her arm crooked over the book.

He cleared his throat. "Good night, Sari."

Her answering good night was so quiet, he barely heard it. Damn, he wished Charles would just say he was too tired for a smoke.

But the older man was pulling on his coat, and reluctantly Conor did the same. Charles blew out the lamp on the table and called a quick "*Gute Nacht, Liebling*" before he opened the door and motioned for Conor to follow him into the cold night.

There was still snow left from the blizzard, and it crunched beneath their feet, slick from the day's melting and the night's frigid winds. But the sky was cloudless, dark blue and heavy with stars. Conor thought he saw the shadows of the mountains in the distance, but it could just as easily be a trick of the high mountain air and the deep darkness of night.

It was silent except for the wind and the sound of their footsteps. The wind whipped his hair into his face, and Conor buried his chin farther into the collar of his duster. He glanced toward the barn. It looked dark and lonely suddenly, especially in light of the dim yellow glow coming from the house window. He was chilled to the bone, and wondering what Charles wanted to talk about left him tense and edgy. It was not a good night for a long, companionable smoke.

They reached the smaller soddy, and Charles shoved open the creaking door and went quickly inside. Conor followed him, standing back in the shadows of the door until the sputtering of a lamp echoed in the darkness and the room burst into pale light.

The room was still warm. The coals in the sheet-metal stove held their heat from hours ago. Charles threw open the grating and tossed in straw that had been braided into logs, coaxing the makeshift fuel into fire. Then he took off his coat and motioned toward one of the stiff wooden chairs that bordered a small table in the corner.

The room was hardly as elaborate as the main house. There was no loft, the ceiling was low, and the muslin that covered it billowed inches above their heads. A narrow bed had been built into one corner, propped up at either end with heavy wooden crates and covered with nondescript wool blankets. But farming journals lined a shelf that ran the length of the wall above the bed, and a framed tintype showed a beaming Charles and glowing Bernice. There was not much else decorating the room. Charles's soddy was utilitarian, a bedroom only, and not a home.

Conor took off his coat and sat in one of the chairs at the table, watching while Charles dug in a small

wooden cupboard for a tin box. He pulled it out tri-
umphantly, setting it on the table with a hollow
clank. He pried off the lid, taking out a healthy fin-
gerful of fragrant tobacco and packing it into a pipe.

He lit it with expertise, puffing life into it and taking several deep drags before he handed it to Conor
with a sigh of relief.

"It is good to have another man around the
place," he said, leaning back in his chair. "Sari will
not admit it, but she feels so too."

The smoke coursed down Conor's throat, rough
and soothing at the same time, and he let it curl
around his lungs before he blew it out in a long
stream. "Does she?"

Charles nodded and took the pipe. "She is afraid
of the sleepers, though she is too proud to say so."

"There's nothing wrong with being afraid. Especially not of them." Conor paused, remembering.

"*Ja*. They are ruthless."

"I'd be ruthless too if there was no money and
nothing to eat." Conor took the pipe again and inhaled. "Nothing worse than a man whose children
are hungry." He made the apology before he thought
about it, and started at the realization of what he'd
said.

"That is not an excuse," Charles said harshly.
"When I was mining in Lancaster—years ago—we
were poor and starving, too. Even then you did not
find good Deutschmen killing one another."

"There were different reasons," Conor insisted.
He remembered when he was playing at being a

Molly, how easily that desperation crawled inside him—even when he knew he didn't have to endure it, even when he knew he wasn't going to stay.

"You are defending them?" Charles's eyes narrowed.

Conor took an uneasy breath. "No," he shook his head. "No." But he knew it wasn't as simple as that. They weren't all like Michael Doyle, like Evan Travers. Many of the Mollies had been decent, hardworking men who'd tried the only way they knew to change things; that it had been a bloody and violent way may have been inevitable. Once, Conor had viewed that way as evil—as something that needed to be stopped. But after two years in the coalfields he only knew that he didn't know anything. Morality was as accommodating as an innkeeper, it all depended on who was paying for the room.

"Evan," Charles began slowly, puffing on the pipe, "Evan was not a man who cared for compromise. Violence would always have been his way, and that of his friends."

Conor remembered the man he'd once called a friend. "Evan knew what he wanted."

"And he took it." The bitterness in Charles's voice was startling. Conor glanced at him in surprise. The old man's thin lips were pulled into a frown.

"Some would call that decisive."

"Some did not have their daughter as the prize." Charles shook his head, handing over the pipe. "Oh, I know Sari is not my daughter, though she came to us when she was just a child and I have always loved her as if she were my own. She was a good child, with a quiet strength." He smiled. "Bernice used to say that Sari was as strong as a bull, with the gentleness of a lamb."

Conor liked the whimsy. It fit her.

"But even as a child she was sad," Charles continued. "Bernice and I worked to make her happy, to be her parents. When she began to smile again—that was a fine, fine thing." He sighed. "Evan was all bluster and no substance, but he caught our Sari. She was a child, she could not know what Evan was. She married him, and every day I saw her become again the child her mother failed. Her joy was gone, she was not my Sari."

The pain in Charles's voice tore at Conor. He recalled the way Evan had treated his wife, the way he barely spoke to her, always ignored her. The one time Conor had seen Evan touch Sari, she appeared so surprised, Conor had been sure it was his imagination. He almost wished Evan were still alive so that he could kill him with his bare hands. He wanted to watch the blood drain from Evan's face, slowly and torturously, to kill him the way Evan had killed Sari.

Or tried to. She was so much stronger than any of them realized.

Charles was still talking. ". . . and I do not wish it to happen again."

Conor blinked, wondering if he missed something important. The tobacco made his head fuzzy. He said the first words that came into his head. "I understand how you feel."

"Good." Charles nodded satisfactorily. "Then you

will understand when I ask what your intentions are."

Conor stared at him blankly. "My intentions?"

"Toward *meine Nichte.*"

Conor swallowed, unable to answer. He was still wondering himself. He wanted to be so careful this time, not to lead her to believe he could give her what he still wasn't sure he could. "I—I don't know."

"I see." Charles took a slow drag off the pipe. "I am not blind. You were alone during the blizzard, when I was in Woodrow. I can only guess what happened, but I cannot be far from wrong."

"No." Conor said roughly. "You're not wrong."

"It is for Sari to decide what she wants, but I would have her get the choice. You will ask her to marry you? I thought you might have done it in Pennsylvania, if Evan was gone."

"I was doing a job in Pennsylvania."

"So you say."

Conor's voice was harsh. "I'm a Pinkerton operative, Charles. I'm not sure I can stop being that."

"You are telling me you care nothing for her?"

"No," Conor shook his head. "I'm telling you nothing of the kind."

"Then?"

"I can't tell the future, Charles. I don't know what's going to happen." He took a deep breath. "I'm trying to take things a step at a time. I don't want to hurt her."

"You will stay with Pinkerton, then?" Charles asked.

"I don't know." Conor spoke slowly, trying to think, grabbing answers from thin air. "I'm not sure I can be anything else. Sari doesn't deserve that. No one deserves it."

"What about love?"

"What about it?" Conor looked away. "Does a man have to learn how to love, Charles? Or does it just come naturally? I don't know the answers. I don't know if I *can* love Sari." He shook his head, and the sadness of his own words made his chest ache. "I don't know if I can leave behind years of lying."

"Have you tried?"

"What do you think I'm doing? I don't have any experience with this."

"I think you have more experience than you know," Charles said quietly. "I have faith in you, Conor Roarke. Now you must have faith in yourself."

CHAPTER 18

CHARLES'S WORDS HAUNTED CONOR—HE thought of them during the short, freezing walk to the barn, and later, when he lay curled in his bedroll, listening to the frigid winds whip around the building and the soft snorting of the animals below. *"Now you must have faith in yourself."* Such easy words. Sentiments he'd heard before, echoed in his father's gentle voice. *"You must believe in yourself, Conor."* At twelve Conor had scoffed at them, believing the old priest had no concept of the life Conor lived, that those words had no bearing on any reality he had ever known.

And now he was still scoffing.

Conor folded his arms beneath his head, staring up at the darkness. He had always thought he wasn't the kind of man who would ever have a family. The job took everything he had. The best Pinkerton operatives were single men, men who had no connections, hardly any family. Men willing to take risks because they had so little to lose.

He thought he'd been a man like that. He'd taken the risks and thought he was invulnerable. And then his world had crashed in on him in a hail of plaster and wood and ash, and he'd realized just how vulnerable he'd been.

Conor squeezed his eyes shut, feeling the tears start behind them—still tears, even after so many months. He didn't want to lose that again. He didn't want to love someone enough to hurt.

But he wondered if he even had a choice anymore. He wondered if maybe Charles was right, if Conor could be the man Sari wanted, if he could love her enough to change. It meant being something he wasn't sure he could be, becoming the kind of man who could take satisfaction in working the land, in the warm security of a family, of children.

It meant giving up vengeance.

He thought of Sean Roarke's face, of those kindly eyes, the wizened features, and waited for the anger to come. And though it was there, though he felt it growing in his heart, the regret was stronger now, a sadness that tightened his throat and burned his eyes. Sadness now, more than anger, and Conor realized that his anger had been lessening bit by bit—since he'd arrived at this farm, since he'd looked into Sari's eyes and seen a forgiveness he hadn't wanted, a trust he didn't deserve. She had reason enough for distrusting him, and yet she didn't. She had opened herself to him again, had trusted that he was telling her the truth.

And he paid her back by deceiving her.

He thought about those days during the blizzard, the things he'd learned about her, about Evan, and realized nothing was black and white. Conor no longer believed Sari had deliberately betrayed him. She had told Evan nothing, and if she had warned Michael away, well, he was her brother. He was her only family. Conor would have done the same.

He believed her when she said she'd washed her hands of Michael, that she hadn't seen or heard from him in a year. She had never believed in their cause; she had despised the violence of their ways. He had heard her speak harshly of her brother in Tamaqua, and Conor had no reason to think she was lying now. No reason except for his own foul—and foolish—suspicions.

He'd been a Pinkerton agent too long. Had grown used to distrusting people, to attributing motives to those who had none. He'd grown used to lying and pretending, had given so much to the job that honor and love were emotions he'd forgotten how to have.

Or had he?

The wind was screaming. He heard the whisper of icy snow blowing against the door. It was a cold, cold night. But his heart . . . his heart felt warm again. For the first time in a very long while.

At first the knock blended with the howl of the wind and the hiss of snow—a soft tap, a muffled scrape. But then it grew in intensity, and Sari sat up in bed, fumbling with the lamp. *Conor,* she thought, and her heart leaped at the hope that he'd come to her.

Hastily she grabbed the lamp and hurried from bed, nearly stumbling down the ladder in her excitement. It had been so long—three days now—and the thought of touching him again, of feeling his warmth against her, made her almost giddy.

She fumbled with the door, a greeting ready on her lips, and pulled it open. It was barely cracked when he pushed through it, bringing snow and wind with him, shoving her back before he collapsed against the rocking chair.

It wasn't Conor.

It was Michael.

Sari shoved the door closed. "Michael—"

He collapsed on the floor, a lump of ice-covered wool. His breathing was loud and raspy; his whole body shuddered with it.

"Michael." Sari set aside the lamp and went to him. "Oh, Michael."

He looked up at her. His eyes were watery and red, the heat from his skin nearly burned her. "Sari," he whispered, and the rawness of his voice shocked her, the harsh, choking sound of it. "Sari, darlin', I'm afraid . . . I need just a bit . . . of help."

Sari pushed away his hat so hard, it rolled across the floor. Her brother's forehead was hot; sweat matted the dark curls of his hair. She shoved at his coat. "You're burning up. Where's the wound?"

"No . . . wound."

"Then, what? What happened?"

"Fever," he said. "Caught it a few days—" He

broke off, coughing so hard, he couldn't catch his breath, shaking in her arms. When he recovered, he smiled weakly at her. "I know . . . I said I would leave you be."

Sari's heart constricted. That smile of his, weak as it was, caught her, just as he had to know it would. It reminded her of other times, childhood times, of the older brother who had been irresponsible and carefree, who had charmed her with his fanciful stories.

"It's all right," she said softly. "I was just . . . surprised. I didn't expect to see you."

"Came to visit," he said. "Me and Timmy and . . . Sean O'Mallory."

Sleepers, every one. Sari frowned. "They just left you here?"

"Didn't think . . . you'd care to have 'em stay." He struggled to sit up, the movement had him coughing again, hard enough to bring up phlegm. She grabbed the handkerchief from his pocket and wiped his mouth.

"Just stay still," she said.

"I . . . won't be a bother. Put me in . . . the barn, darlin'. I'll be fine."

The barn. Sari froze. Conor was in the barn. Conor, who was looking for the men who had killed his father. And though he hadn't said it, she suspected—knew—that Michael was one of those men.

"You can't stay here," she said desperately. "Michael, you can't."

Her brother frowned. "Sari, darlin', I've said . . . I'm sorry."

"It's not about being sorry." Sari hesitated. She glanced at the door, wondering how much to tell her brother. Whatever Conor felt for her, vengeance meant more to him. She would not be able to keep him from taking it if he knew Michael was here. And as for her brother . . .

Sari bit her lip, wishing she knew him better. She had no idea how much vengeance was enough for Michael. Was bombing Conor's house, killing his father, enough? Or did he need Conor's blood as well?

Michael was staring at her, a puzzled look darkening his already dark face, his brown eyes dilated with fever. She looked down at him, studying his features, taking in the dark hair and the handsome face, the mouth she knew could quirk in an endearing smile. He was her brother. Except for Charles, he was the only family she had left, and even though she'd claimed he was dead to her, even though she'd ordered him from her house and her life a year ago, she could not just toss him into the cold.

Her chest felt tight, her heart leaden. *He was her brother.* It was why she'd warned him away from Tamaqua all those months ago. It was why she'd told him her suspicions about Jamie O'Brien. She had not even told her husband those things. And because of it, Evan died.

In spite of everything she still didn't want that fate for Michael.

She touched his hair, wound her fingers through curls damp with sweat, and took a deep breath. "Michael," she said, "promise me that if I tell you

something, you won't . . . tell me you'll understand."

His thick brows came together. "What?"

"Promise me."

"Darlin', I can't . . ." He started coughing again,
shaking in her arms.

Sari held him tight against her. "Please, Michael.
Promise me." When he nodded, she hesitated, trying
to think of the right words. There were no right
words. Nothing but the truth.

"You'll have to stay in *Onkle*'s soddy." When he
started to protest, she cut him off with a shake of
her head. "You don't understand, Michael. There's
someone else staying in the barn."

Michael's eyes narrowed. "Someone else? Who?"

"Conor Roarke."

The name was as explosive as she'd known it
would be. Michael jerked up so quickly, it set off
another round of coughing. When she tried to hold
him closer, he fought her arms.

"Damn it, Sari," he managed finally. His eyes
were blazing now, as much from fever as anger, and
though his voice was hoarse and rasping, it had re-
gained strength. "That traitor's here? Why is that
. . . little sister? Are you . . . sleepin' with him
again?"

Sari jerked away so quickly, he fell back against
the floor. "That's none of your business," she said
tightly.

"Like hell it's . . . not."

"My life is my own," Sari said. "I've told you that

before. I'll help you, Michael, but my . . . relationship . . . with Conor is not your concern."

"He . . . betrayed us."

"That's all in the past."

"Maybe for you."

She glared at him. "For you too, Michael, or you can go back into the cold."

His face tightened. She saw the exhaustion blanketing his features, the pale draw of it in his face. He leaned back on one elbow; he was so weak, his body shook with the effort. He hesitated, and then he nodded slowly. "All right, lass. For . . . now."

Sari rose and held out her hand. He grasped it tightly, and she staggered as he leaned into her, pulling himself to his feet. His legs were unsteady, and she wrapped her arms around his waist, letting him take strength from her, feeling the heat of his body against her cheek.

Together they went to the door. With his weight against her, she could barely manage it, but she pulled the door open. It slammed against the soddy wall with the force of the wind; ice particles swirled in, stinging her face and her hands, burning through the flannel nightgown she wore. She shoved her feet into the boots she kept just inside the door; without her heavy socks they were enormous on her feet, flapping around her ankles, but there was no time to do anything about it.

She glanced outside. The barn was dark and silent; the only sound was the shriek of the wind and Michael's strained breathing in her ear. The thin snow crunched beneath their feet as they struggled around the corner of the soddy, toward the back. With her brother's weight and the wind, it seemed miles instead of only yards, but finally they were there. There was little moonlight, but she saw the shadow of Charles's door—darker against the sod bricks. She knocked once and fell against it. Their bodies thudded against the heavy wood.

"*Onkle,*" she whispered. "*Onkle,* it's me."

She didn't know if he could hear her above the wind, but he must have heard something. The door was yanked open. Charles stood behind it; the long nose of the rifle he held gleamed in the scant moonlight.

"It's me, old man." Michael wheezed. "Put the gun . . . away."

Charles frowned. "Sari?"

"And Michael," she answered. "*Onkle,* it's Michael. He's sick."

"Michael?" Charles frowned and sighed. There was a split second when Sari thought he might deny them, might order her brother away, but then he leaned the gun against the doorjamb. "Come in, then," he said wearily. He put his arm around Michael's waist, taking some of his weight, and together they got her brother into the room and over to the bed. Michael sagged into it, clutching his chest.

Charles closed the door and lit the lamp. The faint brightness barely filled the shadows of the tiny soddy, but it was enough for Sari to see the disapproval on her uncle's face.

"Michael," he said slowly. "Why did you come to us?"

"I'm . . . ill," Michael said. "Maybe dying."

"Not dying," Charles disagreed. "Though it is what you deserve."

"Please, *Onkle*," Sari said.

Charles turned to her with a frown. "He brings trouble to you whenever he comes," he said. "Does he know Roarke sleeps only a few yards away?"

"As long as he's in the barn," Michael said. "And not . . . in my sister's bed."

"Michael!"

He gave her that smile again, though it was more strained this time, his breathing harsher. But her uncle ignored him.

"Why are you here, Michael?" he demanded. "And do not tell me you are passing through. Colorado is far from Tamaqua."

"I wanted . . . to visit my . . . sister."

"I thought she has told you to stay away."

Michael sagged onto the bed, wiping at his forehead. "I missed her."

"*Ja.*" Charles snorted. "Like the mouse misses the cat."

"You have . . . never . . . liked me, *Onkle*."

"*Ja.*" Charles agreed coldly. "Because you are trouble, Michael Doyle. You are like the bad coin."

"Enough," Sari scolded. "Leave him be, *Onkle*. I've told him he can stay a few days—until he's better."

"You're an angel, darlin'."

She threw her brother a warning glance. "If he

doesn't keep irritating me." She turned to her uncle. "I'll get him some broth if you'll see he's kept warm. I . . . I don't want Conor to know he's here." She ignored Charles's questioning glance and glared at her brother. "I want you to stay out of Conor's way, Michael, do you understand me?"

Michael shivered with sudden chills; his smile was weak. "Why is that, Sari . . . darlin'? Afraid he'll . . . hurt me?"

"No," she lied.

"Ah, then. Afraid I'll . . . hurt him?"

"You've already tried it once, haven't you?"

He frowned. "What . . . do you mean?"

Sari took the few steps toward him. She leaned over him, catching his gaze, holding it. "Tell me something, Michael. Tell me the truth. Did you kill Conor's father?"

She heard Charles's quick indrawn breath behind her, and she motioned for him to be quiet.

Michael looked genuinely confused. "His father? Why the hell would I do that?"

Relief rushed through her, but she'd heard enough of her brother's lies to wonder if this was another one. "You weren't part of it, then?"

"Part of . . . what?"

"Conor's home was bombed last July. His father was killed—" Sari stopped when she saw the dawning light in her brother's eyes. Her relief died, her chest felt too tight to breathe. "You *were* part of it."

"We didn't . . . know his father . . . was there," Michael breathed.

His words brought a strange, tight despair, a faint

nausea. Sari drew back, bracing herself against the table, closing her eyes. He *had* been a part of it. He'd killed Conor's father, and she wished now she didn't know. The uncertainty was better. Suspicion was better. She turned away, catching her uncle's gaze, seeing the sympathy there, and she wondered how she would get through the next days knowing the truth, how she could put on her prettiest dress and dance with Conor at the Christmas dance knowing that her brother had killed the only person Conor had ever loved—and that he wanted to avenge that death with everything inside him. He would never forgive Michael, and she couldn't blame him. She wasn't sure *she* could ever forgive Michael that.

The heaviness of tears started behind her eyes. Sari turned away from Michael abruptly. "I'll get some broth," she said. She pulled open the door and stumbled outside into the dark and icy night.

Charles was right behind her. He said nothing as he followed her to the main soddy, but she heard him there, heard his footsteps and the purpose in them. He waited until they were inside and her coat was hung before he spoke.

"He is trouble, that one," he said quietly.

Sari didn't look at him. "He's family."

"And for that I curse the devil."

"*Onkle* . . ."

"I cannot pretend I am happy to see him, *Liebling*," he said. "He has caused you pain his whole life, even when he was small. That boy has a thirst for violence; it runs in his veins like blood. You cannot deny that."

"He's my brother."

"That is an accident of birth, no more."

Sari took a deep breath. "I can't turn him away. Not like this."

Charles shook his head sorrowfully. He crossed to the stove and poured himself a cup of coffee, but he didn't drink it, and his expression was very sad and very grave. "You cannot keep taking risks for him, Sarilyn," he said. "It is time that boy learned to pay the piper. You cannot forever be saving him."

Her uncle's words fell into her stomach like a stone. "He's sick—"

"There is always a reason."

"You want me to turn him out in this cold?"

"You told him a year ago to stay out of your life. Show him you are serious."

Sari stared at him in disbelief. "I can't believe you mean that."

Charles nodded tersely, his jaw set. "I do. It is long past time."

"But this is only for a few days."

Charles sighed. "It is too long," he insisted. "But if you will not change your mind, at least be wise. Tell Roarke the truth. Tell him Michael is here."

"I can't," Sari said bitterly. "You don't know Conor the way I do. Michael bombed his house. He killed Conor's father. And Conor wants revenge. He wants it more than anything. He would kill Michael if he had the chance."

"Perhaps before Michael kills us."

Sari stared at her uncle in horror. "*Onkle,* you

can't mean that. Michael's family. He wouldn't hurt us."

"No?" Charles lifted a brow. "What about the other night? What about the raid?"

Sari's heart fell. She shook her head stubbornly. "We don't know that was him."

"Who was it, then? Roarke said the Mollies have put the blackmark on you, Sarilyn. Do you not believe that is why Michael is here?"

"He's my *brother.*"

"He's a killer." Charles said vehemently. "He stopped being family long ago, *Liebling.* Would you put us all at risk by allowing him to stay?"

Sari looked down at the floor, unable to face her uncle's accusing eyes. "I think you're wrong."

"Are you so sure that you would bet your life on it?"

"I can't throw him out," she said. "*Onkle,* he's sick. He's my brother."

"That is an old loyalty." Charles's voice was so quiet, she had to strain to hear it. "Things have changed."

"Perhaps. But I . . . when our parents weren't there . . . he took care of me. I owe him, *Onkle.*"

"You risked your life once before to save his," Charles said. "Is the debt so big, you feel you must do it again?"

"It's not like that."

"What is it like, then?" Charles asked. "Sari, I am begging you. Do not be foolish." When Sari said nothing, he sighed. "If you would do this, Sarilyn," he said, his words slow and deliberate, "then you must tell Roarke that Michael is here. At least we will have some protection then."

"That protection comes at too big a cost," she said angrily. "I told you—he's after Michael."

"If you tell him about Michael, if you tell him not to harm your brother, he would do as you ask."

She started. "You believe that?"

"He loves you, *Liebling.*"

"He's never said such a thing to me."

"Perhaps not, but he does. He does not want to hurt you."

Sari met her uncle's eyes. "I wish I could be so sure."

"Sarilyn—"

She held up her hand, stopping his words. "No more, *Onkle,*" she said wearily. "Please. No more. I'm tired and I . . . I want to think."

Her uncle's lips tightened, but he nodded—a terse, hard nod—and put down his cup of coffee. "Good night then, *Liebling,*" he said, going to the door. "Remember what I have said."

"I will."

She watched as he went outside. The screech of the wind seemed to swallow him up, and then the door closed and he was gone and she was alone.

Sari looked up at the loft, at the lonely darkness, and shuddered. Her uncle's words rang in her mind. *"He's a killer,"* and the words seemed to take form, to fill the shadows. She harbored no delusions about Michael's role with the sleepers. Evan and the others had tried to keep it from her, but she'd known anyway. Michael's charming words, his easy smile—

they hid the heart of a fanatic, and one who believed violence and murder were his God-given rights.

Michael *was* a killer; she had always known that. But in her heart he was still her brother, still family, and a man didn't kill his own family.

Or did he?

She hated the question; she hated the way it made her feel. She wanted to be able to trust Michael, but there was a niggling doubt inside her, a heaviness that burdened her heart. If she was right about trusting him, then everything would be fine. He would get well and then he would leave. But if she was wrong . . .

If she was wrong, she was putting them all in danger.

Sari shivered and pulled her shawl more tightly about her. She was not wrong, she told herself. Michael was ill, and he'd come to her for help. He wouldn't betray her. She would make him promise not to harm Conor. Then, once he was better, he would go away again, and this lie would be safe between them, something Conor never had to know. She wouldn't have to worry about Conor killing her brother.

The lie helped everyone: It saved Michael's life, it kept Conor from dirtying his hands with murder, and it left her with her brother and her lover—two men she loved—still alive.

It helped everyone.

She told herself that, and she forced herself to believe it. Still she heard her uncle's voice in the back of her mind, his condemnation of her brother. *"You cannot forever be saving him."* No, maybe not. But she had a weakness when it came to Michael, and her brother knew it. They had spent their childhood taking care of each other, and she guessed old habits were hard to break. But it was more than that, more than even Charles knew. Michael was her brother, and the truth was that she still loved him, even if she didn't like him very much. Even if she despised the life he lived. She had saved his life once before—she would not be part of his death now.

But she knew she was lying to herself when she insisted that her love for her brother was the only reason she didn't tell Conor he was here. There was another reason too—one she hated admitting even to herself. Because she knew, in spite of what her uncle said, what Conor would do if she told him Michael was in the back soddy. Conor couldn't turn his back on his father, or his honor, or his pride. He would kill Michael, even if she begged him not to.

Vengeance meant more to him than she did. It was a truth she knew deep down in her bones, as certain as the beating of her heart.

And as long as she didn't put it to the test, she could believe maybe it was different.

CHAPTER 19

SHE STOLE OUT INTO THE COLD, TUCKING the covered bowl of stew beneath her arm. The steam heated the wool of her coat, the smell floated on the dry air. The snow had died away; it was nothing more than thin puffs of ice dragged up by a cold and unforgiving wind. Her breath came in clouds of steam as she hurried the few yards between the house and Charles's soddy, and she couldn't keep herself from searching for any sight of Conor, even though she knew Charles had taken him out to the fields. He would keep Conor out of the way long enough for her to see to Michael, as much as Charles disapproved of the deception.

The pressure in her chest lessened, but it didn't go away completely, and it wasn't until she opened the door to the smaller soddy and went inside that she relaxed at all.

Michael was sleeping, his breath still coming hoarse and raspy from his chest, gurgling with the liquid in his lungs. Her uncle had made up an onion poultice, and the small room stank with the sweetness of cooked onions.

Sari closed the door and set down the bowl of stew. She unwrapped the scarf from her head and laid it across a chair, and then she moved to her brother's side, touching him gently.

He woke immediately, his brown eyes clearing at the sight of her, his face cracking in a weak smile. "I thought you'd abandoned me, darlin'."

She motioned to the plate on the table. "I brought you something to eat."

"Bless you." He struggled to his elbows, coughing slightly at the movement, sweat breaking out on his forehead. The mess of onions and brown paper slid from his chest, and he pushed it aside so that it fell to the dirt floor. "Old folk remedies," he muttered. "I told the old man it wouldn't help."

"It is helping," Sari corrected him. "You already sound better."

"I don't feel better."

"You were nearly passing out last night. Surely you feel stronger today."

He smiled at her, and though it wasn't as brilliant as usual, it was still warm and charming. Sari felt herself responding, just as she always did, with a smile of her own.

"That's the way," he urged hoarsely. "That's the Sari I know."

Her smile died. Sari brought the bowl of stew over to him. He grabbed it eagerly, spooning into it with a primitive hunger. She let him eat a few bites before she spoke again.

"You can't stay much longer," she said. "It's only a matter of time before Conor discovers you."

"So let him discover me, then." Michael spoke through a mouthful of stew. "I'd like a chance to even the score with the bastard."

"Didn't you already do that when you killed his father?"

Michael turned to her, his eyes blazing, his spoon poised above the plate. "He caused the death of nineteen men, Sari," he said brutally. "Your friends. My friends. Your husband. *Nineteen* men. In the Bible it says, 'An eye for an eye.' That's thirty-eight eyes. I've only taken two."

The horror of his statement numbed her. "That's the Old Testament," she said hoarsely. "The New Testament says to turn the other cheek. And they broke the law, Michael. Evan too. *You* broke the law. If they'd found you, you would be dead."

"So I would. Would you mourn me, Sari? The same way you're mourning your poor dear husband?"

Sari felt herself pale. "That's not fair."

"Isn't it?" Michael asked roughly. "You weren't exactly a faithful wife to him."

"No," she said evenly. "But I didn't betray him either."

"I didn't say you did."

"No, but you thought it. You all thought it. Admit it, Michael. You thought I gave information to Conor. You believed it along with the rest of them."

"What else were we to believe?"

"How about that I didn't know anything? Evan and I didn't have a good marriage—not even a bearable one. He didn't talk to me about the Mollies' plans, and neither did you. How would I have known anything to tell Conor?"

"You knew he was the Pinkerton agent," Michael said stubbornly.

"Not until much later," Sari argued. "Not until I told you. I saved your life by telling you."

"But you didn't tell Evan."

His statement felt like a blow. It was the truth. She couldn't deny it. She hadn't told Evan that she suspected Conor was the traitor. It had been too late by then for Evan to avoid being implicated, but not too late for him to escape.

She had let him go to his death.

She had even wanted it.

Sari looked down at the floor, at the pile of greasy onions, of oily paper, and felt that sadness, that emptiness, well up inside her. She'd had to live with Evan's death every day since she'd stood there in town and watched him march to the gallows, his white shirt gleaming in the sun, the blood-red rose pinned to his chest looking like a wound.

She would never forget that day. She would never forget how he refused to look at her, or how his sister and mother had stoned her with their eyes. The small community had drawn away from her; she felt their collective blame in every sigh and every breath, in every unsaid word. She could not have remained in Tamaqua another day after the hangings. Eventually they would have come to her house in the middle of the night. Eventually she would have had to pay the price for her perceived betrayal. Sleeping with the enemy—how brutal the words sounded, how terrible they were.

"You don't know how it was," she said slowly, quietly. "You don't know."

"Evan never laid a hand on you, Sari," her brother said. "I know that for sure. If he had, I would've killed him."

"Not a hand, no," she said. She raised her eyes to his. "But there are other ways to hurt someone, Michael. It doesn't have to be a blow."

Her brother's face closed, eyes hardened, lips tensed. She wasn't sure whether he was working to control his anger at Evan or at her. His eyes shut briefly and he leaned his head back against the wall.

"Sari," he said. "You used to be such an obedient girl."

"Those days were long ago," she said bitterly.

"Before Da died."

"Yes." That was all that needed to be said. Just that *yes*, and she knew he was thinking back, as she was, to those days before their parents had died, back when they were a family and she and Michael had been close. Before Da died in the mines and Mama had followed him shortly after, dead of a fever that made her delirious and strange. Before Sari had been taken in by Aunt Bernice and *Onkle* Charles, and Michael had chosen a different path altogether.

In his own way he was like Conor, she thought. He'd been ten when their parents had died, and already angry. Their father's death in a mining accident had only exacerbated that anger. Michael had joined one of the boy's gangs in town, and though Bernice and Charles had taken him in as well, Michael rarely slept there, never ate there. He was in trouble almost from the moment their parents had died, raging against fortune, against life, and then, later, against the railroad and the company that ruled the miners' lives. The days when she and Michael had been children who depended on each other were long ago and faraway, vague memories, half-remembered dreams.

She looked at him now and remembered how well he'd been her brother once. How he'd taken care of her in the wake of their parents' neglect, kissing her scraped knees and feeding her bread and cheese when their mother was too busy sneaking shots of whiskey to make dinner.

She thought he'd forgotten those things, had forgotten what they'd been to each other, and so it surprised her when he turned to look at her, and his dark eyes were warm. "I haven't made things easy for you, have I, lass? Not these last years."

"No," she said. "You haven't."

"Do you hate me?"

Sari sighed. "I don't hate you, Michael," she said wearily.

"But you wish I would go away. You said as much once before."

"We don't lead the same lives. We don't care about the same things. I . . . I don't like your methods. The violence, the . . . killing . . ." She looked at him frankly. "Yes, I wish you would leave me out of them. I wish you would go away."

"There are no other ways now," he said bitterly, and that light of fanaticism, of hatred, glittered in his eyes. "The company's made sure of that."

She got to her feet. "Michael—"

"All right, all right." He grabbed her hand, forcing her back to her seat. "I'm sorry. Just tell me something, darlin'. Why's Roarke here?"

She jerked her hand from his. "I don't want you to hurt him. Promise me you won't."

"Sari—"

"Promise me."

He sighed heavily. "I won't hurt him—at least not while I'm here," he assured her. His lips broke in a grin, his teeth shone, eerily white, through the darkness of his close-cropped beard. "I promise you. But I don't trust him, and I want to know why he's sniffin' around my sister. Unless it's the same reason he was always sniffin'."

"Michael!"

"Sari, darlin'. Just tell me. I want you to be safe."

She laughed shortly. "That's interesting, given why Conor said he was here."

Michael's brows rose in question.

"He says there's a blackmark against me. That he's here to protect me from assassination."

Her brother sobered. He glanced at the wall, his jaw tightening, and it was those gestures more than anything that told Sari the truth of what Conor had told her.

"There is a blackmark," she said quietly.

"You have to understand," Michael said. "They think you gave him information. That you betrayed us."

"And you didn't tell them differently?"

Michael gave her a desperate look. "I couldn't tell them different, Sari. I didn't know." He scowled. "But I did tell them not to touch you. That I wouldn't allow it."

"But they didn't take the blackmark away."

"No, they didn't," Michael agreed.

"So is that why you're here?" she asked, and her heart squeezed with the words. "You were their assassin. Does that mean you've come to kill me? The raid on the soddy . . . was that you?"

To his credit he blanched. "I don't know what you're talking about," he said. "There's been no raid."

"But there was," she insisted. "*Onkle* was beaten."

"Not by us," Michael said. "Jesus, Sari. You're my sister. It may not mean much to you, but I do love you. You saved my life; I'll do what I can to make sure they don't take yours."

Sari felt numb. Her brother's admission shocked her; she hadn't truly believed Conor when he told her she was marked; she had believed Michael had the power to prevent it. That he didn't surprise her. That he'd had nothing to do with the raid . . . She didn't know what to think about that, wouldn't let herself think.

She stood again, backing away from him. "The

sleepers are dead, brother," she said firmly. "That way of life is over. Pinkerton crushed it. It's time you and the others understood that."

His face tightened. "You're wrong—"

"Nineteen men died—not because of Conor but because they broke the law. How many others have to die? How many, Michael?"

"It's not over," he insisted. "We have plans. There are ways. . . ."

"I'll see you hanging from the gallows yet," Sari said. She rose and grabbed her scarf from the table, wrapping it around her hair before she turned to look at him. She saw the anger on his face, that brilliance in his eyes, and wished he were different. Wished everything were different. "I want you to understand one thing, Michael. I'm not helping you get well just so that I can watch you die. This is the last time I help you. The last time.. The Christmas dance is in two days. I want you gone by then."

He eyed her steadily. The silence fell between them, stark and heavy, and then he nodded—a short, hard motion. "I understand, sister dear," he said, and there was a touch of mockery in his words and no affection at all.

Sari knotted her scarf around her chin and stepped out into the cold.

Conor struggled with the fence. The barbed wire ripped at his heavy gloves as viciously as the wind whipped at his face. Particles of ice blew off the evaporating snow on the ground, biting at what little skin wasn't covered by hat or coat or scarf, but he was sweating so with exertion that the frigid blasts almost felt good.

He paused, letting the fence sag, wiping his face with the back of his hand and staring out at the bleak gray and white horizon. This was a hard land. Harder, he expected, than most, but he was beginning to see promise in the far-reaching plains. There was something strangely peaceful about the prairie, something lonely too. He liked the way the land went right to the edge of the horizon, stopped only by the shadowy range of the Rockies that loomed up as if to say, "Stop right there. No farther for you."

He thought of how it would look when these plains were planted, when wheat and corn nodded their heavy heads in the wind. He wondered if he would like the change, and then smiled at the thought. A month ago just the idea of this land put a chill inside him, made him feel lonely and strange. Now, suddenly, he was imagining how it would look months from now. Imagining himself standing here, watching the changes.

Conor Roarke, a farmer. God, how his friends would laugh if they knew.

Conor frowned at the thought. *Friends.* He tried to put faces to the word and couldn't, and it dawned on him then, standing there in the freezing wind with barbed wire glinting mean and ugly in the cold sun, that he didn't have any friends. He'd had the Mollies, the men he'd laughed and played with—lied to—for two years. The men he'd turned in to the law with a sense of duty that didn't allow regret.

He'd had his father.

And he had Sari.

He wondered if she would laugh at the notion of him tilling the soil. Wondered if she ever imagined it, if she ever thought of what it would be like if he stayed.

He'd been wanting to ask her that question for days now, but he hadn't had a chance to talk to her alone. Charles was always around, and when he wasn't, Sari was mysteriously gone—out to milk the cows or tend the animals, he supposed, and wondered if he would ever know all the things that had to be done on a farm. If she even wanted him to learn.

The question burned inside of him. Lately she'd been evading his gaze; there had been an edge of tension in her body that hadn't been there before. He knew Sari well enough to know what it meant. She was having second thoughts; probably she was regretting those days during the blizzard. She had a tendency to think about things too much; no doubt she'd already decided what the future should be—and whether or not it included him.

Conor glanced down the line. Charles was farther down, working his own line of fence. Conor waited until the old man looked up, and then he waved at him and motioned toward the house. Charles waved back at him, telling him to go on, and Conor stepped away from the fence and walked toward the soddy, determined to find Sari this time, to talk with her.

He was nearly to the house when he saw her. She was hurrying from the back of the yard, her chin lowered, her face buried in her scarf. Her step was quicker than he'd seen it before, almost furtive, and she was carrying something in her arms, holding it tightly against her chest.

He smiled at the sight of her. Quickly he took the last steps and pressed against the soddy wall, waiting until she rounded the corner. When she did, he reached out and grabbed her arm, pulling her against his chest.

She squeaked a scream, dropping what she held in surprise. It clattered to the ground and rolled—a bowl, he saw, splashing what was left of what had been inside across the thin snow.

"Conor," she said breathlessly. "You startled me."

"Sorry, love." He smiled at her, and then he swooped down and retrieved the bowl, handing it to her with a flourish. "Feeding someone?"

"The . . . the birds," she said. She motioned limply to the back of the soddy.

"Oh?" He raised an eyebrow, teasing her. "They like stew?"

"Yes." The word came out on a rush of sound. She backed away from him, clutching the bowl again to her chest. Her brown eyes shifted—to his feet, to his chest, to the wall behind him. "You aren't working on the fence?"

"I'm taking a break," he said. "It occurred to me it's been some time since you and I were alone together."

"Oh." She laughed slightly; there was a nervous edge to it that he found endearing. "Yes, I guess so."

"So how about making me a cup of coffee? It's a cold day, and I've been working hard."

"Of course." She took a deep breath—so deep, he wondered if the air burned her lungs—and stepped to the door. He followed her inside. The warmth of the soddy felt good, the smells of corn bread baking and beans and ham fragranced the air. He closed the door behind them and leaned against the wall, watching as she laid the bowl aside, and then unwound her scarf from her hair, leaving tendrils loose and dangling against her neck, curling to her shoulders. She took off her coat and hung it on the peg beside the door, and then she went to the stove and picked up the enormous tin pot that always stood at the ready, full of hot coffee.

Conor unbuttoned his duster and took off his hat, feeling warmed by the very sight of her. Such grace she had, the way she poured coffee, with her neck bowed to reveal that soft skin of her nape, the way the muscles in her arm flexed as she set the heavy pot aside. The way she turned. . . .

She met his gaze; her cheeks colored. "You're staring at me," she said.

"Yes."

"Why?"

"Because you're so beautiful." He took the cup from her and set it on the table, and then he curled his arms around her, settling his hands on her waist, pulling her close. He nuzzled her neck; she smelled of icy air and coffee. "I've missed you these last days, love."

Her hands pressed against his chest, a subtle pressure. "I've missed you too," she said, though he heard something else in her voice and felt the tension in her body.

He'd been an operative too long, he thought. He read people too well. There were times, like now, when he wished he didn't, when he would have preferred to live in ignorance about how someone else was feeling, what she was thinking. But now, all he felt was that tension in Sari, that pushing away.

He stepped back and looked into her face. She looked at his chest. Conor cupped his hand beneath her chin, bringing it up, forcing her to look at him.

"What is it, Sari?" he asked softly. "What's bothering you?"

Her eyes widened in feigned innocence. "Nothing."

"Don't lie to me. You haven't looked me straight in the eye for days. What's wrong? Have I done something? Said something?"

She shook her head. "No. You've done nothing."

"Then what is it?"

She pulled away from him. Her hands fluttered in a half-finished gesture as she turned to the stove. "It's just . . . it's nothing."

He frowned.

"I've been thinking about the Christmas dance," she said. "That's all. I don't . . . have anything to wear."

He thought of the cloth he'd stolen from her trunk. The cloth that he'd had Charles take into Woodrow with him that night of the blizzard. Mrs. Landers could sew, Sari's uncle had promised him. Mrs. Landers could make the dress Conor envisioned. But it wasn't done yet; it wouldn't be done before the dance tomorrow night.

"You could wear sackcloth and still look fine," he said. "And I don't believe that's what's bothering you."

She looked at him over her shoulder. That faint blush still stained her cheeks; she looked breathless and distracted. "Well, it is," she said defensively, and then she turned all the way around and stepped purposefully toward him. She grabbed his hands in hers and leaned into him, kissing him hard on the lips, molding her mouth to his.

"I've missed you," she whispered again, and there was a power in the words that convinced him.

Conor smiled. He pulled her closer, spoke against her mouth. "You'll be beautiful at the Christmas dance whatever you wear," he said. "You can't tell me there'll be anyone else dressed as fine."

She laughed. "Calico and gingham most likely."

"Well, at least I have fancy teacakes to look forward to," he teased. "And lemon punch."

"Stack cakes and cider," she teased back, kissing him again. "And a fiddler playing 'Turkey in the Straw.'"

"No waltzes?"

"I believe the preacher is still calling it the devil's invention," she said. "He's only about fifty years behind the times."

"Well, for innocent girls I can see how it could lead to a life of sin. All that . . . touching." Conor shuddered in mock horror.

Sari laughed out loud. The sound of it jangled like bells through his soul. "I believe all those years in a Catholic parish have surely left their scar upon your spirit. No doubt you'll go to heaven after all."

"And after all the time I've spent trying to prevent it."

She tapped his mouth lightly with her finger. "Well, you've failed miserably, I'm afraid."

"I'm too much of a worldly soul," he said. "Because all I can think is that heaven is right here—where you are."

He was half teasing, half serious, but the words changed her. He saw it immediately; the way she tightened up again, the stone-solid set of her shoulders. She pulled away, looked away, and there was such seriousness in her face, along with a desolation that flitted through her eyes so quickly, he was left wondering if he'd seen it at all.

He reached for her, feeling that desperation inside of him, the fear that she would retreat too far, that he wouldn't be able to find her. His hand closed around her wrist, tightened around those fine, slender bones. Her gaze snapped to his.

"Sari," he said, and he heard that desperation on his words, that strange breathlessness. "Sari, love, we have to talk."

He thought for a moment that she would deny the truth of it, that she would pull away and go back to the stove and tell him no, but she didn't. She looked at him for a long moment, and then she said, "I know." She disentangled herself from him, wrapped her arms around her chest, and he saw something that looked like fear—or, not fear, but a loss of hope, a loneliness, that made his heart feel swollen and sad.

"But not today," she said. "There are . . . things . . . I need to think about."

"Things?"

She gave him a small, sad smile. "Just things, Conor," she said gently. "Please."

He nodded, though her answer took away the lightness he'd been feeling for the past days, added a weight to the hope that had started inside of him. He looked beyond her, to the mildewed newspapers on the walls, the darkness barely held at bay by the lamp, the steam rising from the heavy iron pot full of beans. It felt damp and dark suddenly, and the day seemed to have soured around him.

"Something's wrong," he said again.

She shook her head—a little sadly, he thought. "Go back to the fence," she said. Then that odd smile again. "Go be a farmer."

"A farmer," he repeated. "You think I could be?"

"I don't know," she said. "Can you?" And then she turned away from him, grabbing her apron from the hook beside the stove and tying it on, leaving him completely even though she didn't quit the room. Leaving him with the question dangling in his ears, and the strange, unfamiliar thought that she didn't care about the answer. That she already knew what it was.

CHAPTER 20

CONOR TOOK THE BITS BETWEEN HIS hands, warming them with his breath and his body temperature before he finished harnessing the horses. Tonight was the Christmas dance in town, and they couldn't have picked a more hellish evening for it. The cold lanced through his coat, seeped into his bones. He checked the hot rocks wrapped in straw on the floor beneath the wagon seat, warming his hands before he shoved them back into his pockets. Then he glanced toward the house.

Almost in answer to his thought, the door opened. Lamplight slanted across the snow, and onto that bright carpet Sari stepped, looking refined and graceful as a princess even though that old wool coat was bundled around her like a blanket, the ubiquitous butternut scarf covered her hair. All he could see of the dress she wore was the hem peeking beneath the coat.

She caught his gaze and smiled, but it was a subdued smile; Conor caught the edge of tension beneath it. She was nervous, he realized. He remembered the day they'd gone into town, how she'd acted the same way then, how the curiosity of the townspeople seemed to bother her, and he guessed that was where her tension came from now.

He smiled back at her, as gently and reassuringly as he could. "Don't worry," he said. "I won't leave your side."

She looked puzzled for a moment, and then she turned away. "Did you remember to put the pies in?"

"They're in the back," he answered, coming forward to take her hand and help her into the wagon. She settled herself in the middle of the seat just as Charles came out of the soddy, closing the door behind him.

"You didn't forget the blankets?" Charles asked.

"It's too damn cold to forget." Conor waited until Sari's uncle climbed into the seat beside her, and then he came aboard himself, taking the reins into his hands. "I hope this dance is worth freezing to death," he teased. "Because it feels like we're going to."

Sari nodded distractedly. "I've been told it's a fine time."

The wagon started off, jerking across the snow, the steel-shod wheels crunching on the ice. They fell into silence; it was too cold to talk on this frigid night. The horses puffed in icy little clouds of steam, their hooves slipping even with the wool socks Conor had pulled over their forefeet.

He felt Sari beside him, sitting stiffly, the warmth of her body radiating through her coat. It was humiliating to admit how much her presence affected him, but the truth was, it did. The last few days he'd thought of nothing but this dance, of holding her again, of leading her across the floor while she leaned into him and laughed. It made him remember other dances, that first dance in Tamaqua, when he'd watched her coming down the stairs clad in blue-striped silk and thought she was the prettiest thing he'd seen in a long while.

That was the first time he'd met her, and he remembered now how she'd enraptured him from that second, how he'd watched her the rest of the night, had been unable to take his eyes off her even when someone told him she was Evan Travers's wife. He should have seen the trouble starting then, he knew. She affected him too easily; he should have stayed as far from her as he could. It was what a smart operative would do.

But then, when it came to Sari, Conor was rarely a smart operative.

He glanced at her, and she stared straight ahead, her expression tight. He thought about their conversation yesterday. He should have told her the truth about why he was here. He should tell her everything: his suspicions about her relationship with Michael, the fact that he was here looking for her brother, the ambivalence he was feeling about vengeance. He should tell her the truth, and discover if she could still love him after. If she loved him now.

He was almost afraid to know the answer. If she

truly loved him, if she trusted him . . . That kind of confidence terrified him. He'd gone into the most dangerous situations a man could face. He'd confronted outlaws and criminals, bombs and guns and fires. He'd gone into the blackest depths of the earth and come back alive. But this thing with Sari, this was the biggest risk he'd ever taken. And he felt horribly ill equipped to face it. Hell, he wasn't even sure he could.

But he was willing to try. If Sari loved him, he would try.

The well-lit windows of the Grange hall beckoned them as they finally pulled into Woodrow. The building glowed like a beacon from the end of what passed for the main street of town. The yard was covered with wagons and livestock. Hoarse shouts and laughter echoed in the darkening night. Excitement crackled in the air, sparkled on the lamp-lit snow.

"Oh, it's beautiful," Sari breathed, her voice muffled by the brim of her bonnet. "I didn't realize it would be so grand."

Grand? Conor looked skeptically at the small building. The gaily decorated hall was not festooned with the tiny glittering lights of chandeliers, nor did its steps sparkle with reflections cast upon hundreds of glittering jewels nor shimmer with the movement of velvet and silk skirts. It wasn't one tenth as opulent as most of the parties he'd seen in Chicago.

But laughter pealed through the air, followed closely by the squeaking chords of a fiddle. Women picked up their calico skirts and tripped gaily up the

steps, their eyes bright with anticipation, their remade gowns as beguiling as rich taffetas. The steps
of the men were just as light—perhaps more so—as
they gazed into the laughing faces of their women.
The air shimmered with intimacy and romance, and
despite himself Conor was caught up in it.

He smiled. He *could* grow comfortable with this
life. Chicago could have its luxurious parties with
women who flirted but never laughed, with conversations billowing above the hum of an orchestra and
ladies careful not to spill punch on jewel-toned satins. He'd take Woodrow any day, with its fiddler and
laughter and women dancing boisterously in blue
gingham.

He looked at Sari sitting beside him, her cheeks
red from the wind, her eyes sparkling in the light
spilling across the snow, and Conor was caught up
in the excitement. He reined in the horses, jumping
down to lend Sari a helping hand. Together he and
Charles led the animals to the temporary shelter
erected behind the building.

"Charles! Conor!" Will Schmacher came forward,
extending his hand. "Good to see you all could make
it."

Charles shook the man's hand firmly. "We would
not miss it," he said. "I hope you have not started
the party without us."

"Hardly a chance of that. We all been waitin' for
Sari's mince pie."

"I wouldn't want to disappoint you, Will." Sari
said, smiling softly. "Do you think two will be
enough to go around?"

"Not when I can eat one by myself."

"I think Berthe will probably make you share." She laughed. "It is Christmas, you know."

She reached into the wagon bed and pulled out the basket that held the pies, swinging it clumsily over the side. Will reached for it, lifting it easily.

"Let me help you with that, Sari." He offered his arm. "I trust your menfolk won't mind if I take you on inside. It's darn cold out here."

Conor's heart squeezed at the thought of her entering the hall alone, without him, and he realized he'd been harboring images of himself as one of those happy men escorting their wives up the icy stairs. Except Sari wasn't his wife, and he didn't have the right to monopolize her.

He cleared his throat. "See you inside, Sari."

She nodded, weaving her arm through Will's and swaying into him as they stepped precariously over the ice. Conor watched her dark head lift to Will's as they walked away, and he turned back to the horses, suddenly wanting to be done with the unloading and unharnessing. A shiver of anticipation coursed up his spine when he thought of walking into the decorated hall and taking Sari into his arms for the first dance—

"Conor Roarke?"

He looked over his shoulder. The man standing behind him looked vaguely familiar, though Conor couldn't place his pockmarked face or serious expression. "Yes?"

"I'm John Clancy. I've got a telegram for you."

Conor hesitated. He dropped his hold on the harness and brushed off his hands. From the corner of his eye he saw Charles stiffen. Trepidation filled him. "A telegram?"

"It came in yesterday, actually." John Clancy looked sheepish. "But I couldn't get out there, and Pa said you'd no doubt be coming to the dance." He held out the thin, yellow paper. "It's from Denver."

Denver. Peter Devlin was based in Denver. He was one of Pinkerton's oldest operatives—and the first to recommend Conor be placed on sabbatical. There was no love lost between them. Conor's trepidation turned into foreboding. He took the missive from John's hands. "Thanks."

"I'm sorry it wasn't sooner—"

"It's all right. Thank you." Conor dismissed him curtly, turning to see Charles's intent gaze. "Don't wait for me," he said. "Go on in, I'll follow in a minute."

For an uncomfortable moment Charles looked as if he would protest, but then he nodded and quickly finished loading hay into the feed box. "I will see you inside," he said.

Conor waited until Charles disappeared around the corner before he leaned against the wall and stared at the envelope in his hand. Other men bustled around him, hurrying to get inside. Their talk floated about his ears, fading into incomprehensible sounds. For a moment Conor stared at the envelope, feeling a surge of dread he couldn't push away. For a moment he wondered if he had to open it. Perhaps he could throw it away, pretend he never got it, pretend Pinkerton didn't exist. But he couldn't and he knew it.

Clumsily Conor ripped open the envelope and pulled out the thin sheet. The words danced in front of his eyes before he could assign them meaning, and then he drew in his breath harshly. DOYLE SEEN STOP MEET ME FIVE SHARP TOMORROW AT ELEPHANT CORRAL IN DENVER STOP USE CAUTION STOP. Conor stared at the words in shock.

Michael was here. Here in Colorado. The knowledge put a sick heaviness in Conor's gut; he thought of Sari the last few days, how she'd avoided him, slipped away from his hands. Was it because she wasn't sure how much to trust him, as he'd thought?

Or was it because she was in contact with her brother?

The suspicion was nagging and uncomfortable, and Conor forced it from his mind. He made himself think of the blizzard, and Sari's heartfelt words. *"I washed my hands of him."* She'd meant it, he was sure. He had looked into her eyes and believed her. *That* was what he had to remember. That was the only important thing.

He looked at the Grange hall, at the lights sparkling on the snow. He had to decide to trust Sari now—or never trust her. The time had come to make the most important decision of his life. He shoved the telegram into his pocket, sprinting past the horses, the men who stared after him in surprise. He had to find Sari, and when he did, he would ask her how she felt. He would find out now, tonight, if Sari loved him enough to trust him, if she loved him enough to help him find the man he hoped was somewhere inside him. And if she did—oh, God, if she did, he would send a telegram to Denver, tell Devlin to go to hell, that his warning was unnecessary. Because if Conor knew Sari loved him, he would do as his father had asked—as William Pinkerton had asked—and put aside revenge and hatred and anger. For Sari he would forget about finding Michael. He would make vengeance part of his past.

Sari stood at the edge of the room, her toe tapping to the raunchy chords of the two fiddlers despite the tension that tightened her shoulders and the muscles in her neck. She wanted to relax, to enjoy this night. She'd been looking forward to it for weeks, more so in those days before Michael had come, when she had fantasized about dancing over these floors in Conor's arms, when the vision had brought pleasure instead of a steady sense of dread.

But things were different now. Now she couldn't stop thinking about Michael. He was better. In the last days the fever had faded. He had promised to be gone tonight, as she'd demanded, and she hoped he was true to his word, but even that thought didn't ease her anxiety. There was too much hatred in Michael's voice when he talked about Conor Roarke. Too much anger. She could not rid herself of the notion that Michael would try something, that he would make another attempt at revenge, in spite of his promise.

Onkle's words haunted her. *"He's a killer,"* and

once again—as she had several times over the last
few days—she thought about warning Conor, and
dismissed the idea just as quickly. Only now she felt
a deep, heavy foreboding, a guilt she couldn't quite
ease. *It was better this way,* she told herself. If Conor
found out . . . if Conor found out, she would not be
able to keep either of them from taking their revenge.

All she could do was hold Michael to his promise
and hope he would be gone. She was tired of this;
the strain of lying was exhausting her. She was
afraid, every moment she spent with Conor, that he
would sense her discomfort, that he would somehow
sense Michael was here, within his reach. She
thought of the conversation they'd had in the kitchen
just a day ago. Conor had known something had
changed. He was a Pinkerton agent, skilled at finding
out things. When he'd seen the bowl she dropped on
the snow, she'd been sure he would figure it out.
When he hadn't, when he'd accepted her story about
the birds, her relief had been overwhelming. But she
wouldn't always be able to come up with a story.
And she couldn't keep avoiding him.

She took a deep breath, forcing a smile at a couple
that eased past her, and wished she were like them
tonight. Wished she could smile and dance and
laugh. She wanted to sway beneath the shimmering
tin stars hanging from twisted swaths of red and
green bunting, to kiss under the tiny, wilted sprigs
of mistletoe hanging in the doorway. She wanted to
dance until her cheeks were flushed and perspiration

gathered beneath her breasts, to walk out into the freezing air and whisper secrets in a lover's ear. In Conor's ear.

But her secrets would only tear them apart, and she would not be whispering them to anyone. Sari squeezed her eyes shut. She hoped Michael was gone already. She hoped he stayed gone.

The door opened behind her; the wind that came in with another couple blew tendrils of hair loose from the coiffure she'd taken such care with. She had styled it special tonight, wrapping the heavy strands in a French twist and tying scraps of lace from her remade gown into it. The dress she wore was her Sunday best—a fine, blue-striped corded silk that had been altered so many times, she wasn't sure when she'd first purchased it or what the style had been. Now it was fairly simple, as befitted life on the plains. It had a small stand-up collar and a slim-fitted bodice, with tiny pleats on either side of the button-down front. The sleeves fitted tightly to her arms all the way to her wrists, and the full skirts that had once seen a bustle were gathered on either side and fastened at the back with a large bow.

It was pretty enough, and a few days ago she would have been satisfied wearing it to the Christmas dance. But now it only made her think of the green-striped cream silk tucked away in her chest upstairs and the man who had bought it for her. Now all she could think about was the trouble she'd taken with her appearance and what a waste of time it was. Because deep in her heart she'd wanted to be beautiful for Conor, and she knew there was no purpose

in it. She and Conor had no future—Michael's visit
had only confirmed what she knew in her heart already. And if she'd had a passing fancy that maybe
that could change . . . well, she knew now that it
wouldn't. Michael was her brother, and he would
always come between them.

The image of her brother was so strong in her
mind that when the door opened and Conor came
rushing inside, she felt a momentary twinge of
panic—as if Michael were standing before her. The
blood tingled in her fingertips. Her brother was
gone, she reminded herself, and then added a prayer:
"Please, God, make him be gone."

"There you are." Conor was at her side, standing
close enough to whisper the words in her ear. "Waiting for me?"

She turned to him, forced a smile, and hoped it
was a good one. "You were outside so long, I
thought you might have frozen to death."

"It sure as hell felt like I had," he answered. He
smiled, but there was an odd tension in his face; his
good humor sounded as forced as hers felt. He took
her hand, squeezing it between his fingers, and led
her into the hall. The dancing had started. The fiddlers were playing a boisterous tune, and petticoats
flew as partners stomped across the floor, raising
dust for the boy near the wall to wet down with his
sprinkler can.

"Anyone you'd rather dance with?" Conor asked
her. "Or can I claim all your dances now?"

Sari forced herself to answer in kind, even though
her stomach was roiling and her throat was tight

with tension. "What would people think if I danced them all with you? You'd ruin my chances of meeting some nice, widowed farmer. I'll let you be my partner for one."

His face darkened a moment, his fingers tightened around her hand. "There's no farmer here worth your time," he said roughly. "Dance with me."

He still wore his coat, but he pulled her onto the dance floor anyway, swinging her into his arms and starting the steps. He was good at it, she thought, seeing how easily he moved, how the motions came to him without thought or care. It reminded her of when she'd first met him—that dance in Tamaqua, the one where he'd swept her off her feet with only a few words spoken in a charming brogue, a pair of warm and ready arms. Evan had not danced with her that entire night, but as Jamie O'Brien, Conor had ignored the scandalized looks and partnered her for two.

The memory was one of the good ones, one not tarnished by what happened later, and it eased her tension now, brought her swinging back into his arms with a smile. She was wrong to worry so about Michael, she decided, lifting her skirts and moving into the reel. He'd promised to be gone; surely he would leave. There was no sense in letting him ruin her pleasure in tonight.

So when the fiddlers began a slower dance, Sari responded to the light pull of Conor's hands, moved into his arms with little resistance. There was no future in their relationship, but there was tonight. There was now.

His hand nestled in the small of her back, keeping her close. She felt the movement of his hip against the fabric of her dress, the press of his leg against hers. She looked up and found he was staring down at her, his blue eyes dark and intense, his expression serious.

"What's wrong?" she asked, laughing. "Did I step on your foot?"

He frowned. "No. Why?"

"You're frowning quite fiercely."

His expression relaxed. "Sorry. I seem to have lost my charming touch this evening."

His hand tightened against her, pulling her closer. She smelled bay rum and the lingering freshness of cold air and the warm, wet wool of his coat. "I suppose I'll forgive you," she said, "if you tell me what's bothering you."

That look in his eyes sharpened. "Do you really want to know, Sari?"

It was the way he said it, that too-serious, too-intent way, that made her think he knew about Michael. Sari's stomach dropped, her heartrate sped. He knew. They hadn't been careful enough. All those treks across the frozen yard with plates of food—she should have known Conor would catch on. He was a Pinkerton agent. Of course he would discover it. . . .

She was so lost in her thoughts, it took her a moment to realize he was dancing her across the floor to the back door. There were people standing there, eating plates of dried-corn casserole and chicken and coconut cake, talking and laughing, and she saw the surprise on their faces as he danced her right through them, stopping only because the door loomed in front.

Sari was breathless when he pushed it open; she gave a fleeting smile to Will Schmacher as Conor dragged her out into the cold air, feeling a moment of panic when she thought of how quickly the word would make the rounds. Before the night was over, the entire town would know that Conor had whisked her away outside, where her neighbors and their prying eyes could only guess at what was going on. Unfortunately their imaginations were far too vigorous for her comfort.

But before she had time to think any more about it, Conor pressed her against the wall of the Grange, shielding her from the cold wind with his body. There was little moon tonight, it was mostly covered by clouds, and a light, whirling snow hovered around his shoulders, danced in his hair. His hands were at her waist; his breath was warm and moist against her face.

"Sari," he breathed, and then he choked a little— a half laugh—and turned away for a moment. When he looked back again, there was a determination in him she hadn't sensed before.

"Sari. I've been thinking about us."

It was foolish, how easily the words made her heart jump, how she felt that silly little rush of joy even though she knew there was no point. She worked to keep her voice steady. "And what have you decided?"

"I've decided I—Christ." The words came out on

hard rushes of air, as if he had to say them quickly before they were gone. Sari waited. He leaned his forehead against hers, tightened his hands on her waist. "I've decided I need to tell you the truth," he said.

The words were so raw, so edged in pain, that Sari stiffened. The dread she'd fought all night settled in her chest, harsh and heavy.

"The truth," she repeated dully.

He nodded and took a deep breath. "You were right when you accused me of not coming back because of you," he said slowly. "Protecting you was a convenient lie."

"But the raid . . ." She spoke the words carefully, remembering Michael's disclaimer, her own suspicions. "There was the raid."

"It was set up."

She could barely breathe, could hardly talk. "You mean you—"

He nodded. "I hired men to come out. I wanted to frighten you so that you'd let me stay." His hands tightened on her as if he was afraid she'd run if he loosened his hold at all. "They went a little too far. I never meant for them to hurt anyone."

"Well, they did hurt someone. They hurt *Onkle*."

"I'm sorry for that. You don't know how sorry."

She felt as if she were falling into darkness, into a fear that was fed from deep inside her. Sari tried to find his eyes in the night. His face was shadowed, but she heard the desperation in his voice as he rushed on.

"I came back for Michael, Sari. I thought he would

search you out, and I wanted to be on the farm in case he contacted you in any way. We—the agency— heard he was on his way here. I figured maybe I could find a letter or something to tell me when he might show up."

She clenched her fists. "Did you find anything?"

His breath came out in a long, slow whoosh of air. "No."

"So you thought I was hiding something. You thought I was lying to you—"

"Yes." He cut her off with the wicked brutality of that one word. "Listen to me, Sari. How well did I know you a month ago? I don't know, I really don't. Sometimes these things just run together in my mind. I wasn't sure if what I felt for you in Tamaqua, what I *knew* of you, was something I had imagined, something that made it easier to act the part—or if the feelings were real. God, sometimes . . ." he paused; she sensed him struggling for the right words. "Sometimes you get so that you don't trust what you think is real. There are so many damn lies."

"I didn't lie to you," she said slowly.

"I didn't know that for sure. You'd warned Michael in Tamaqua, and I couldn't forget that."

"Because he killed your father?"

"Yes."

"And that's why Pinkerton sent you? Because of your father?"

He took a deep breath. "Pinkerton didn't send me."

She stared at him in stunned amazement. "The agency didn't—"

He shook his head. "I'm on sabbatical, Sari. The agency has a policy against vendettas, and William knew how I felt about Michael. They didn't want any part of it. He warned me not to come, and I ignored him." He rushed on, as if expecting her to interrupt. "I couldn't let it alone. Michael *killed* my father, Sari, you have to understand. I figured he would make his way to you. I thought you might be helping him. So I thought, if I could get you to trust me again . . ."

"You came here intending to use me," she said, each word an effort. It was what she'd suspected when he first came, and now the thought that she'd been right, that he *had* used her again, was like a stone in her heart. It was exactly as it had been a year ago, when he'd left, and she'd waited, knowing he couldn't have meant to go, waiting for him to come back. It had been months before she could believe he had used her, months before she could start to hate him.

"I'm sorry." His harsh whisper broke into her thoughts. "I can't tell you how sorry I am. I was wrong. I love you. I'll become a farmer on these blasted plains if that's what you want. I'll leave Pinkerton for good. Just tell me you love me. Just tell me if—after all this—you still can."

"I was wrong. I love you." Sari stared at him, hearing the words she'd always wanted to hear, but they were false somehow. He had just told her the truth, and she heard in his voice the hope that she might forgive him, that she would choose to love him beyond his lies. In his words she heard a future.

She looked into his face, into the shadows. She

felt his breathing as if it were her own. "Conor," she said slowly. Her heartbeat drummed in her ears, so hard it seemed to blot out all other sounds. "What about Michael?"

He stiffened, and she knew the truth in that moment, even if he didn't say the words. He paused for a long moment. "What about him?"

She pulled away from him, pried his fingers from her waist, and stepped from the circle of his arms, and she wasn't sure whether it was just her skin that was cold or whether it was her blood that ran chill and freezing through her veins, wrapping her heart in desolation and a loneliness she knew too well.

"What if he showed up again. Would you go after him?"

He paused. The uncertainty in his eyes was blinding. "Not . . . not if you don't want me to. Not if you tell me you can . . . love me."

She looked back at him, heard his desperation and his pain, and she felt sorry. "That's the condition, then?" she asked. "If I love you, you'll leave my brother alone?"

He frowned; she saw the confusion in his expression. "Yes," he said.

"And then what, Conor? What if I decide to love you and Michael happens by? Do I have to worry that you'll kill him?"

He leaned into her, cupped her cheek in his rough palm. "Sari, love, it doesn't matter. Michael doesn't matter to me anymore—"

"He killed your father, Conor. How can he not matter?"

She saw the truth of her question in the way he closed his eyes, the slight catch in his breath. And she thought of the price of loving him. Thought of Michael huddled in the bed in her uncle's soddy, his face flushed with fever, and knew that if he came to her again like that, she would not turn him away.

"Tell me something," she said slowly. "If I say no, if I tell you I can't love you, will my brother's life be in danger?"

"Sari—"

"Just tell me." Her chest felt so tight and swollen, she couldn't breathe. "Tell me."

She felt the nearly imperceptible tightening of his hand against her face, heard him swallow.

"It's as you say," he said carefully—too carefully. "He killed my father."

"And you can't forgive him that."

He dropped his hand. "No," he said. "God, no, I can't forgive it. But I'll try to forget it, Sari. I'll . . . I'll put it behind me—"

"It will never be behind you, Conor," she said sadly. "You'll think of it all the time. Until you've reconciled it in your own soul, you'll never be at peace with it." She looked away, into the swirling, dark snow. "And that will always be between us."

His hold tightened—so hard, she felt his fingers press into the soft skin of her arm. "Sari, please. Try to understand. I'm trying the best I can. But Michael's a murderer, for Christ's sake—"

"He's my brother," she said. She pulled back from him, gently, sadly. And then she walked away.

CHAPTER 21

THE RIDE BACK TO THE FARM WAS QUIET,
the squeak of the wheels and the clip-clop of the
horses punctuated the silence. Several families had
asked them to stay on in town, but Sari had refused.
She didn't want the soft companionship of friends,
the too-intimate comfort. She was nervous and
tense. All she could think about was Michael and his
promise. All she could think about was Conor.

She stole a look at him, sitting stern and silent
beside her. She felt his tension hovering in the air
between them. Where his sleeve brushed her, his
arm was solid and strained; there was a chill in the
set of his jaw and a distance in his expression that
brought regret and sadness settling into her heart.

He hadn't searched her out again. When she left
him, she'd gone back inside, found Miriam, and tried
to lose herself in her friend's excited chatter. But she
watched for him. It was a long time before he came
back inside, and—except for one quick glance to lo-

cate her in the crowd—he didn't look her way again.
When the dance ended, he was waiting by the
wagon, his eyes burning in the dim light from the
lamp resting on the snow. He had not said a word
to her, merely helped her into the wagon and
climbed aboard himself, and in the long ride since
he had not uttered a single syllable, not even when
Charles asked him if he'd enjoyed the dance. He'd
nodded, a short, terse nod, and his unspoken words
fell into an uncomfortable silence.

When they reached the farm, it was past midnight.
The shadows of the house rose out of the darkness
of the prairie—a darker black against the black.
There were no lights anywhere that she could see,
no sign of life, and Sari breathed a sigh of relief.
Michael must be gone. She waited until Conor left
them off at the door and took the horses and wagon
to the barn, and then she turned to her uncle.

"I hope to God he's gone," she said.

Charles's face grew thoughtful. *"Ja."* he said
slowly. His eyes followed Conor to the barn. Together they watched as he climbed down and opened
the barn doors. "Did you and Conor fight, *Liebling*?
He seems sad tonight."

Sari turned away. "It's nothing," she said, though
the words formed a lump of regret in her throat. "I'll
go see if Michael's left."

She left her uncle standing by the soddy door,
heard his murmur of protest die in the dry ice of the
air. She hurried around the corner to the smaller
soddy, clutching the loosened tails of her scarf to her

mouth as an endless prayer ran in her head. *Please
let him be gone. Please let him be gone.*

The soddy door was slightly ajar. Beyond it she
saw nothing but darkness. Sari closed her eyes
briefly, feeling a rush of relief so strong, it nearly
made her faint. She pushed the door open wider.
"Michael?" she asked. "Michael?"

There was no answer. She stepped inside. It was
so dark, she could see nothing; not even shadows.
But she heard nothing either. No harsh breathing, no
talk, no movement.

"Michael?" she said again. The name thudded
into the darkness.

He was gone.

"Thank God," she whispered.

"Ah, now. You'll hurt my feelin's, talking like
that."

Sari froze. She whipped around, nearly falling into
her brother's chest. "Michael! You're supposed to
be gone. Damn you, you *promised* to be gone."

"And I'm going, lass," he assured her. "You just
came back a little sooner than I expected. Timmy
and Sean just got here."

She looked past him. She saw them in the dim
moonlight, in the shadows they left on the snow.
Two men leading three horses, standing warily near
the soddy.

"Get out of here," she said. "Conor's in the
barn—"

"We saw him." Michael said tersely. His jaw tightened. "That bastard—"

"You promised to leave." Sari pushed at him. "Now, go. Please."

He nodded. Then, surprisingly, he leaned close. Close enough that she felt the coarse wiriness of his beard against her temple. "I'm . . ." He cleared his throat as if it embarrassed him to speak. "I'm going," he said. "But not without telling you something, lass. Timmy and Sean—they're saying the word's come down. They got a telegram in Denver. Roarke's after me, and the other sleepers— Timmy and Sean and the others—they want you. I've warned 'em off, but it'd be best if you picked up a gun and learned to use it."

She worked to keep her expression even. The shadows of the other two men shifted in the darkness. "I know how to use a gun," she said quietly.

"Good." He took a deep breath and backed away. "I'll do what I can, Sari. I love you, darlin'. I won't see you dead."

She nodded. It felt as if the blood had left her fingers, drained from her face. "I know you'll try."

"Yeah. I'll try."

She felt his kiss on the top of her head, the warmth of his lips pressed against her hair. Then he turned and motioned to the men waiting for him. They started toward him, their footsteps and their horses' hooves sounding too loud in the night. She glanced toward the barn. There was no movement there.

Michael walked across the snow to the others. She heard his quiet laugh, heard his whispered "Let's go then, laddies," as loudly as if he stood right beside her. Sound carried so well on the plains, and the wind . . . the wind seemed to bring the meanness of Timmy's stare right to her; the evilness of it raised gooseflesh on her arms.

"Get out of here," she whispered. "Ride away."

And then she heard it. The quiet cocking of a gun that echoed in the keening of the wind. And she felt him behind her, felt his fingers as he grabbed hold of her arm, holding her in place. He stepped up beside her.

"Well met, Michael Doyle." His voice took on the false Irish brogue he'd had in Tamaqua, the voice he'd worn as Jamie O'Brien. The barrel of his gun aimed steadily at her brother. "It's been a long time. Too long. Care to chat awhile?"

Conor felt Sari stiffen beside him. He tightened his fingers on her arm, not caring if he hurt her, not caring about anything except for the fact that she'd lied to him. She'd lied to him about her brother, and he'd been foolish enough to believe her. The thought made him crazy.

He tightened his finger on the trigger of the Colt and waited for Doyle to turn around, and when the man did, Conor felt a jolt of hatred so intense, his hand shook on the hilt of his gun.

"Well, well," Michael said slowly. His voice was rough and lazy and completely unsurprised. "So glad you could join us, Roarke. Have you come to join my little sister in saying good-bye?"

"You and I have some unfinished business."

"Aye, that we do," Michael said. "And we will talk." He motioned the others forward.

Conor recognized Timmy Boyd and Sean O'Mallory. He released his hold on Sari's arm, gave her a little push. "Go inside," he said roughly.

She turned to him. He was gratified to see fear in her eyes, and something else—regret, maybe. "Conor," she said in a low, urgent voice. "Conor, there's something you don't understand—"

"Undoubtedly that's true," he said. "Now, get inside."

She looked desperately at her brother. "Michael—"

"Do as the man says, lass," Michael said. "It's not safe for you out here."

"I'm not going anywhere." She crossed her arms over her chest and raised her chin—Sari's signs of battle. Then she stepped away from him, from her brother, until her back was against the wall of her uncle's soddy. "The two of you can say what you have to, but I'm not leaving."

Michael sighed. "You were such an obedient girl once, darlin'." The words held affection, the familiarity of an old jest.

Conor felt sick. "Don't be stupid, Sari."

"I'm not being stupid," she said quietly. "Say what you have to."

He recognized that stubbornness in her voice, and he wondered why he was fighting her. She wanted to stay; well, then, let her stay. If she was strong and smart enough to lie to him, she was strong and smart enough to protect herself.

He turned back to Michael. The other two had not dismounted; their horses pawed nervously at the ground. But there wasn't a nervous twitch in Michael's big body. He seemed completely relaxed—as well he should, Conor thought. There were three of them, and only one of him. *And one big gun,* he amended silently.

"It's been a long time since we've had the pleasure," Michael said, smiling. "I've been looking forward to seeing you again."

"I've been looking forward to killing you," Conor said.

"Such anger in your voice, Roarke. Surely we can be friends? We were once." Michael spread his big hands, laughed shortly. "I've missed your stories, laddie. Tell me one now."

"A story?" Conor lifted a brow. "I can tell you a story, *friend.* I can tell you a story about a priest who never hurt anyone. A good man who met his end when a bomb exploded in my house."

"A priest." Doyle nodded with exaggerated sadness. "It's a sorry tale. But no sorrier than a man who betrayed his friends, and left them all to hang. One priest for nineteen men. Too bad he was a man of God, but that's the way it goes sometimes, eh? A nasty bargain."

Conor's eyes narrowed.

Michael smiled. His teeth flashed in the blackness of his beard. "We wanted you, Roarke. But you're a stubborn man. Too stubborn to die."

Conor caught his breath, remembering the way the Mollies had gathered at the train depot in Shenandoah to kill him. He'd eluded them then and gone to his boardinghouse, where he'd waited up all night, revolver ready, staring through tattered curtains at the moonlight bathing the mountains.

"Protected by that whore, he was," Timmy interjected, scowling.

From the wall Sari gasped.

Michael spun on his heel. "Shut up about her," he said. "She's my sister, don't forget."

Conor waited. Tension coiled inside him, along with a sweet, hot anger, the emotion he relished.

Michael looked back at him. "I want you to leave her alone, Roarke," he said. He nodded toward his sister. "She knows nothing about what I do. Nothing. She'd be just as happy if I disappeared forever."

It was a strange thing to say. Conor wondered if it was true, but he didn't glance at her to see her expression. Told himself he didn't care.

Michael watched him steadily. "Whatever it is that keeps you hanging round my sister, Roarke, you'd better decide if it's worth her life. Because every minute you're around her, you put her in danger." He glanced at Sari; his expression softened for a moment. He murmured something to her, something Conor couldn't read—an apology maybe. Then Michael motioned toward Timmy. "He thinks she betrayed us all. He doesn't believe me when I tell him she knew nothing. And he wants her, Roarke." Michael's voice lowered; it crackled like breaking ice in a spring thaw. "He wants her dead. And he hates you almost as much as I do. Now, I might be able to keep him from hurting my sister, because he loves me like the brother he never had. But I can't keep him from you. And if you're with her . . ." He shrugged, and smiled again. "He can kill two birds with one stone. Understand me, laddie?"

Conor did. He understood too well. Sari's life was in danger as long as he stayed near her. The thought of it ached like a fist in his gut. But it didn't hurt him the way her lies had. It didn't make him feel empty and foolish and cruel. *"I washed my hands of him."* She'd said the words; he heard them now in his mind, the echoing of her voice, her inflection. He knew she'd said them. But her brother was standing there before him, that thin smile on his lips, and moments before, she had been standing with him, wrapped in his arms, her head bent close to his.

Now Conor understood her evasions. He understood the glances away and her avoidance of him the last few days, and he cursed himself for believing her—loving her—so completely he hadn't seen the lies. She'd been protecting her brother, and she was a terrible liar, and still he hadn't seen it.

Conor thought of her in the moonlight tonight, against the outside wall of the Grange hall, looking at him with sad eyes and saying, *"Until you've reconciled it in your own soul, you'll never be at peace with it."* He'd thought then he'd seen regret in her eyes, and pain, but now he knew it was only deception.

His heart felt hard as stone, but still her words bedeviled him. *"You'll never be at peace. You'll never be at peace."* He looked at Michael Doyle and knew it was true. He would never be at peace, but now he thought he could live with that. He could live with it because his father was dead, and the man who had

killed him was standing in front of him now, a mocking smile on his lips and cold anger in his eyes, and
Conor felt fiercely that only Michael's death could
assuage that hollowness inside him. If the price was
his own peace—well, he would pay it. Because the
only reason he'd ever had not to was standing against
the wall and watching them, and she had lied to him.

She had lied to him.

He raised his gun, aimed for the spot between Michael's eyes, and cocked the hammer. "I want you
dead, Michael," he said as coldly as he could. "Nothing else matters to me. Nothing else."

But he didn't pull the trigger when Michael
laughed and turned his back to him, and he didn't
pull it even when Michael mounted his horse and
looked over his shoulder.

"Good-night, my friend," he said, smiling. "We'll
meet again, you and I. Then we'll finish it."

And Conor just stood there. He stood there and
watched the man who had killed his father ride
away, disappearing with his cronies into the dark
vastness of the prairie night, and then he uncocked
the gun and let his arm fall uselessly to his side.

"You'll never be at peace."

The words mocked him, and he cursed himself.
Because Sari had lied to him, yet he still could not
kill her brother in front of her. And though he told
himself he hated her, that was the biggest lie of all.

She waited for him to say something. The night
grew large and silent around them, but he didn't
move. He stared off after her departing brother,

watching until long after their shadows disappeared into the darkness, standing so still she would have thought him a statue if she hadn't heard the heaviness of his breathing.

Sari didn't move from the soddy wall. She pressed her hands into it, so hard she felt the imprint of the tough, frozen grass through her gloves. She felt frozen to the wall, pinned by the sheer force of Conor's presence, by the anger that floated between them, heavy and palpable in the dry air, and she wanted to go to him, to take his hand and tell him the truth and beg him to change his mind about her brother. She wanted to scream at him, "I love you," and have it be enough for him.

But she knew it never would. So she stood there and waited, and after a while he turned his gaze from the prairie. Turned that cold, cold gaze on her. She shivered. The iciness of his eyes made the winter air feel warm.

"How long has he been here?" He asked the question slowly, so quietly she had to strain to hear him.

"A few days," she said.

"In the soddy?"

Sari licked her lips. "He was ill, Conor. He had a fever. I couldn't turn him out into the cold." She lifted her chin, facing him evenly. "He's family, Conor. He's my *brother*."

"He's a murderer."

"So are you."

That jolted him, she saw without satisfaction. His jaw clenched, his fingers tightened around the gun. "You lied to me."

Sari laughed bitterly. "We've lied to each other. You came after him. I protected him. I may not agree with his means, but do you honestly believe I would put him into your hands?"

"He broke the law."

"And you were going to arrest him and take him to the sheriff?" she challenged. "You were going to let the courts decide?" When he didn't answer, she went on, and all the pain and emptiness she'd felt since the dance came hurtling to the surface. "I didn't think so. You mean to kill him, Conor. You mean to kill my brother. You told me not two hours ago that if I loved you, you would give up this stupid vengeance of yours, that you would let him be."

"That was two hours ago," he said, his voice hollow. "And you didn't make the bargain, did you?"

She hated the sound of his voice. It was so empty, so flat. And she hated the look on his face. She saw the glittering of his eyes even in the darkness, saw the solid tightness of his expression. Sari turned away.

"How long have you been lying to me, Sari?" he asked. "Since Tamaqua?"

"I haven't spoken to my brother in a year," she said steadily. "I didn't lie to you about that. I hadn't seen or heard from him until four days ago. But I can't change the past, Conor. I can't change the fact that I warned Michael to run or that he killed your father. I can't change the fact that I'm afraid—of you, and of Michael, and of this . . . this *thing* between you. I don't understand that kind of hatred. I don't want to be a part of it."

"But you are a part of it, aren't you, *love*," he said, and there was such sarcasm in his tone, it made her shudder. "You deceived me—"

"You're a fine one to talk about deception, Jamie O'Brien," she reminded him.

"Tamaqua was a job," he said tightly.

"Maybe to you. But those men who died were friends of mine. They had families. They had children. And I . . ." she took a deep breath. "I fell in love with a man I thought was fine and honorable. Imagine how I felt when I found out everything was a lie."

He laughed bitterly. "The same way I feel now, I imagine."

"Is it?" Sari asked, and her whole body felt clenched and tight as she moved toward him. "Do you even know how to love someone, Conor? Do you even know what it means?"

He stiffened as if she'd shot him. "Go to hell."

Sari stopped. Only a few feet away, but it could have been miles. He was that much a stranger to her. "You go to hell," she said sadly. She walked toward the soddy, beyond him, and in those few steps it felt as if the past had loomed before her, swallowing her up, smothering her, blacking out the future she'd never believed in, the future she hadn't dared to want. "Just don't come back. Don't come back to me, Conor Roarke."

He left for Denver in the morning. He got on the train and sat on the hard seats and gazed out the window, watching the flat, treeless country roll by, brown and lifeless under a gray sky, hearing the wheeze and clang of the engine as it dipped uncomfortably into unsettled portions of the track and heaved out again. Now and again a lone soddy came into view. At one he'd seen a woman shade her eyes and turn toward the wind just to see the passing train. She'd waved and then turned back again, as if suddenly realizing she wouldn't see any return hellos, and the unbearable loneliness of the motion made his sadness swell inside him, choking him.

Conor turned away from the window, shifted on the unpadded wooden seat. It was freezing in the little car. The tiny stove in the corner provided little heat, and what it did give was greedily swallowed up by those passengers huddled around it. Not that it mattered. Nothing mattered. Not the cheap coach car filled with dust and the smell of sweat nor the overflowing spittoons that puddled brown and sticky on the floor. Not the noisy chomping of the couple eating hunks of sausage next to him.

The only thing that mattered was the self-hatred inside him. He had known it would come. It had been there when his father had died, along with a nauseating sense of loss and fear and that horrible, inescapable loneliness. It had been there when he turned away from Sari that last time in Tamaqua, had kissed her good-bye and promised to see her tomorrow and known he was never coming back. And now it was here again, tearing a hole inside of him, leaving him with that emptiness . . . that horrible emptiness.

Except it was worse now than it had ever been.

Worse because, for a while, for a few moments, he'd harbored a hope that things might be different. That he might have a different future. But it was an illusion, just as it always was.

There had been a moment, when he'd turned from the barn to see Sari's shadow against the dark plains, along with three others, that the hope was still there. A moment when he didn't think immediately of betrayal, but instead thought she was in danger, that the shadows he saw with her must be outlaws. By the time he'd crept up behind them and eased around the back of the soddy, that hope was dead, replaced by another, stronger feeling. Replaced by anger. He should have known, he thought. He should have suspected the lie. She'd been showing the signs of it for days, with eyes that wouldn't look at him and words that were nothing but evasions. But he'd forgotten by then how she'd lied to him about Michael in Tamaqua. She had sworn she hadn't seen him, and yet her brother was gone. Had disappeared into the Pennsylvania mountains as if he'd been warned that hell was about to come crashing down around him.

Conor thought of the ashes of his home, the skeletal frame of a brick chimney silhouetted against the red-pink sky of sunrise. He thought of holding his father's frail, broken body in his arms, and the whispered plea, *"Leave it to God."*

He couldn't leave it to God. Those few days when he'd told himself he could, when he'd been willing to trade it all to hold Sari in his arms—those days were gone. Deep inside he'd known it wasn't possible to walk away from it, that the fire of vengeance burned so deep in his soul that only blood could put it out. He'd thought love would be enough for him, but now he knew that Sari was right when she'd thrown those last words at him. *"Do you even know how to love someone, Conor? Do you even know what it means?"*

He'd wondered for a long time if he was capable of love. He was too used to lies and betrayal, to not trusting what he saw or what he felt. Love was a fickle emotion; easily changeable, easily damaged by even a single lie. Or at least it was proving to be that way for him. He knew some couples, some people, whose love for each other seemed solid as the earth itself, still holding together through even the worst of tragedies, through white lies and blacker ones. He had always envied them, had always hoped to find that for himself. Unconditional love.

He laughed softly to himself. Was there even such a thing?

Not for him, he decided. Sari's face floated before him, her dark hair, her shining eyes, and pain gripped his heart so hard, he could scarcely breathe. But then he thought of Michael, standing there, laughing, and the pain faded away.

No, it wasn't love. Just infatuation. Just an illusion brought on by the cold Colorado prairies and the warmth he'd glimpsed in that little town's heart.

He told himself he felt relief at the thought.

But all he really felt was empty.

CHAPTER 22

CONOR WALKED SLOWLY, HANDS SHOVED
into the pockets of his coat, head buried against the
stinking, icy wind. The loud voices of men coming
from the clubs and restaurants he passed blended
with the din of barking dogs and the rattling suck of
carriages speeding down the muddy streets, splashing muck and sewage.

He ignored it all, barely looking up, uninterested
in the rubble of razed buildings or the shadows lurk-
ing in corners untouched by the soft yellow glow of
gaslights. Once, the noise and commotion of Denver
would have soothed him. It was familiar to him, the
way towns were always familiar. They all held the
same restaurants and saloons and whorehouses.
They all held the same comforting press of strangers—people who cared nothing for you. People easy
to get lost among.

But tonight . . . tonight Conor found himself wishing for the quiet of the prairie, the whistling wind

that wasn't littered with the sound of dogs barking
and horsecarts clattering. The cold darkness that allowed a man to really see the stars.

The thought surprised him, and Conor frowned
and forced himself to concentrate on the bright lights
of the gambling hells on Blake Street. The building
he was looking for was just ahead. The sprawling,
ungainly club took up most of a block, the sign that
hung from its arched stone doorways had a crude
elephant drawn on it, with the word *Corral* below.
The Elephant Corral was one of Denver's most fa-
mous gambling dens. No doubt Devlin had placed
the meeting there, knowing that the two of them
would be unobtrusive in its crowds.

Quickly Conor went inside. Noise and smoke assailed him immediately, making his head ache. He
pushed past tables of men playing faro until he saw
Devlin seated at a small table in a corner. Purposefully Conor strode toward him.

"Roarke." Peter Devlin nodded his graying head
in greeting as Conor took a seat. "Care for a drink?"

"Not really," Conor said. He glanced away from
the agent's shrewd green gaze, eyeing the exits.

"I appreciate the fact that you decided to come."
Devlin snorted. He took a sip of his drink, his blood-
shot eyes focusing on Conor. "No one had heard
from you."

"I'm on sabbatical," Conor said.

Devlin smiled tightly. "You've been part of the
agency too long. William asked us to . . . keep an eye
on you. He was worried."

"Everything's fine."

"Is it?" Devlin's bushy brows rose. He leaned forward. "We knew you were in Colorado. We've had our men tracking Doyle since he showed up in Saint Louis. William thought there might be trouble."

"Don't worry about it," Conor said brusquely. "The agency needn't get its hands dirty."

"Look, Roarke. You and I have our differences, but I've always admired the way you work. This is a filthy business all around. Don't let yourself get mired in it, for Christ's sake. Doyle belongs in prison. Let us find a way to put him there. This vengeance . . ." Devlin laughed harshly. "Well, we're not a bunch of ignorant immigrants, if you know what I mean."

"Careful, Devlin. Your narrow-mindedness is showing."

Devlin flushed. "You know what I mean. We're sworn to uphold justice. Leave things to us. Go on and court your pretty little Irish lass, and—"

"Leave Sari out of this."

"All right. All right." Devlin raised his palms in surrender. He sat back in exasperation. "Well, I tried anyway."

"You can tell William you did a fine job," Conor said. He started to rise. "Now, if you'll—"

"Sit down, Roarke," Devlin said quietly. "I told you. Doyle's been seen in Denver. . . ."

"I saw him. He's with Timmy Boyd and Sean O'Mallory," Conor said shortly.

"You've seen them?"

"In Woodrow."

"Christ." Devlin's hand curled around his drink.

He took two quick gulps, draining it. "Damn it. We're too late."

"Too late?" Conor frowned. "What the hell are you talking about?"

"You should have telegraphed me, Roarke," Devlin said. "You should have told me you saw them before you came here."

"What difference does it make?"

"A lot of difference." Devlin licked his lips. "A hell of a lot of difference. Jesus, Roarke . . . I got a telegram from William yesterday. There was a message that went out from Timmy Boyd two days ago, back to Tamaqua."

Conor's chest tightened. Dread settled in his mouth like lead. "To Tamaqua?"

Devlin nodded shortly. "It was short. All it said was: *We'll take care of it.*"

"Take care of what?"

"We think it was a response to the telegram sent out to them about a week ago." Devlin took a deep breath, and in his eyes was a sympathy Conor had never expected to see. "They followed you from Chicago, Conor. They followed you to Sari Travers. She's been blackmarked."

Conor felt the blood drain from his face. Blackmarked. It was what he'd told Sari all those days ago, when he'd first needed a reason to stay on the farm. But it had been a lie, a fiction he'd created to frighten her. In the light of it, Michael's words from the other night took on a frightening meaning. *"And he wants her, Roarke. He wants her dead. . . ."*

It was no longer the simple anger of one man, or the hatred of another. It was orders for assassination.

"Christ." Conor got to his feet. "I'm going back," he said shortly. He leaned over the table, so close to Devlin that the man sat back in his chair. "Wire William. Tell him to send someone else out here. Tonight. I want help, goddammit, and it'd better come quick."

"Conor—"

"Just do it." Conor waited for Devlin's nod, and then he turned on his heel, pushing out through the crowd and back into the littered, stinking streets of Denver. Sari was in danger. He should have known it, should have realized there was a reason for Michael and the others to be in Colorado. He should have put it together; why the hell hadn't he put it together?

He knew the answer almost the moment he asked the question. He hadn't put it together because he'd been so torn apart by Sari's lack of trust in him that he hadn't looked beyond it. That lack of trust had wounded him simply because it was so well deserved. She had lied to him about Michael, but he had lied to her first. In Tamaqua he'd lied for two years. Two years of going to her bed and making love to her and pretending to be someone he was not. Two years of loving her without intending to stay. No wonder she hadn't trusted him.

The realization flooded him, chilling him. He had never been anything more than a liar and a cheat. And Pinkerton had put those skills to good use. *The end justifies the means.* He'd believed the words once. But now . . . now he thought of a woman with melting brown eyes, and he was no longer so certain. No longer certain of anything.

Except that he could not let her die.

Beyond him he heard the train whistle. Conor set off at a dead run.

Sari lifted the pail of milk, feeling the strain in her arms and her back as she walked from the barn into the cold morning air. She glanced up at the heavy clouds forming overhead. There would be more snow tonight. More snow to gather in an icy layer on the ground, more snow to trudge through tomorrow and the next day. The thought made her tired. But then everything today made her tired. She hadn't slept well last night; she'd been awake when dawn started over the horizon, awake to hear the rattle of harness and the lone hoofbeats crunching over the prairie. Conor, riding away from here. Away from her.

She squeezed her eyes shut, forcing away tears. She didn't know whom to blame for that, herself or Conor. She should have told him the truth last night, as he'd done. She should have trusted him. But then again she wondered if it would have made any difference, if his leaving was simply inevitable.

Conor had asked her during the blizzard what she planned, whether she wanted a family, whether she wanted children. She would have been lying if she'd said no. It *was* what she wanted. A husband who loved her, children playing in the yard—the sound of their voices blending with the chirp of crickets and the stomping of corralled cattle. She could see it so clearly in her mind; she could almost smell the coffee on the stove and hear the giggles of children trying to sleep, the soft rasp of her husband's voice warning them to be quiet.

Conor's voice.

But the things she wanted were not things Conor could give her, and he wasn't worth her tears. Love meant nothing to him. She didn't think he even knew what the word really meant. For him it was an emotion easily roused, as equally dismissed when it no longer served his purposes. He'd said he loved her, but she'd seen his eyes last night, and she knew the truth. He would never trust anyone enough to love them.

She felt sorry for him, but mostly she was sorry for herself. Because she loved him, and it hurt that he hadn't trusted her—and that she hadn't had the strength to trust him in return.

Across the field she saw her uncle. He walked slowly, his hand pressed to his back, and Sari felt a flash of anger that Conor wasn't here to help him anymore. Charles was long past the age where he should be working so hard. He'd already spent his youth and his strength toiling in Pennsylvania, and without the help of a younger, stronger man she feared her uncle would never be able to break this hard, unforgiving sod.

Quickly, she hurried to him, splashing the warm milk against her skirt, where it turned cold instantly. He met her halfway across the yard.

"Are you all right?" she breathed, reaching him.

Charles smiled slightly and nodded. "*Ja, Nichte,* do not worry so."

"I can't help but worry." She took his arm. "Come inside. Let me fix you a poultice. There's no need to work any more today."

He pulled away gently. "There is always need to work, *Liebling.* Look at those clouds. I cannot finish the fencing in the snow."

"Maybe we should hire someone to help you, then."

"We cannot afford hired help."

"Perhaps John Graham—"

"Ah, Sarilyn, the man has his own work to do." Charles patted her arm reassuringly. "I am fine, I promise you. But I could use some dinner. It is growing late."

Sari colored. "I'm sorry. I—I haven't been myself today."

"So I see." Charles smiled.

"It's just that—"

"Roarke is gone," he said. Her uncle sighed. "I had hoped things would end differently. I have not been to a wedding in some time."

The words made her sad. "There won't be a wedding, *Onkle,*" she said gently.

He nodded. "I know." He took her arm, and together they started back to the soddy. "But he will regret this, *liebling* I promise you that. It takes more effort to fight what a man really wants. Roarke does not yet understand how much he loves you, but he will. He will."

"That's small comfort."

Charles chuckled. "*Ja.* it is that. But for now we have each other."

Sari smiled, though her heart was heavy. "Yes, we have that."

They were nearly to the soddy when she heard the sound of hoofbeats. For a moment her heart jumped. For a moment she thought maybe it was Conor. But when she turned around, she saw three horses making their way over the prairie, and the disappointment that crashed over her nearly made her sag against the house.

"Who could that be?" Charles asked, turning around. "You were expecting someone?"

"No." Sari shook her head. She set down the pail of milk and started toward the horses. She had only taken a few steps when she recognized them. Timmy Doyle and Sean O'Mallory. And behind them was her brother.

Sari froze. "You'd best go inside, *Onkle,*" she said.

He came up beside her, peering into the distance. "Who is it?"

"Michael."

Her uncle's expression hardened. "I thought you told him to go."

"I did."

The horses were in the yard now. The riders reined them to a stop and dismounted, and Sari caught the look on her brother's face. Too serious, too strained. The promise he'd made to Conor last night came rushing back to her. *"We'll meet again, you and I. And then we'll finish it."*

She knew by Michael's expression that the time was now.

"Hello, lassie," he said, and though his tone was friendly enough, he didn't look at her. His eyes roamed the yard, stared at the barn as if he could see through the walls. "Hello, *Onkle*."

Charles spat. "Not your *Onkle*," he said. "You ceased being *mein Neffe* many years ago."

Michael laughed. "Still don't like me, do you, old man?"

She hated that laugh of his. That cold, nasty laugh. Sari touched her uncle's arm, murmuring a warning. "Don't cross him. Not today."

Her uncle pulled away, ignoring her. "You are no longer part of this family," he said, straightening proudly. "Sari has told you that. I have told you. We have come a long way to be free of your kind. You are not welcome here. You will please leave."

Sean O'Mallory came forward, a smile on his ruddy face. " 'You will please leave,' " he mocked. "Aye, we'll leave, old man. Once you tell us where Roarke is."

"He's gone," Sari said. "He left this morning."

Michael sighed. "Sari, darlin', please don't lie to me. I've got Timmy on a thin enough leash as it is."

Sari glanced at Timmy Boyd. He was staring at her as if he could melt her flesh from her bones with his eyes. She shuddered and turned away, but it was too late to keep the fear from starting deep inside her. She struggled to stay calm. "It's not a lie," she said. "He went to Denver."

Timmy stepped forward; his thin face sharpened with a nasty grin. "If you don't mind, we'll just be havin' us a look around."

Charles stepped in front of her. "I want you off my land."

"Just a look around, old man," Michael wheedled. "If we don't find him, we'll be off. It's simple as that."

"Get off my land," Charles demanded again. "You do not belong here."

"*Onkle*," Sari warned. "Let them look. We have nothing to hide."

"They do not belong here," he insisted stubbornly.

Timmy's grin widened. "I think we belong anywhere we want, you old fool," he said. "And I'm not leavin' till we have a look around. Of course, you have another choice." He reached inside his coat, drawing out a revolver and pointing it at Charles's chest. "We could always leave a dead man."

Sari grabbed her uncle's arm and squeezed hard, pulling him back. "Go on," she said to Timmy. "Have your look around. Then leave us be." She flashed an angry look at Michael. "As you promised."

He inclined his head slightly in acknowledgment, but his expression never changed. He reached for his own gun and leveled it at them, though she knew it was just for show, so that these friends of his would know they could count on him. "Come on, laddies," he said to the others. "Let's get to work. And you two"—he looked at Sari—"go on inside."

"Keep an eye on 'em, Mick," Sean said.

"I will. Don't you be worrying about that." Michael motioned with his gun.

"You think you are such a big man," Charles said. "But you are nothing, Michael Doyle. I am ashamed to call you kin."

Michael's face hardened. He gestured again with the gun, and Sari tightened her fingers on her uncle's arm, pulling him with her as they went to the house. Sean kicked the door open, even though it was unlocked, nearly breaking it from its weak leather hinges.

"Light the lamp," Timmy demanded when they were inside, and Sari did it quickly. He grabbed it, holding it aloft and peering into the corners where sunlight from the window and the open door didn't reach.

Michael jerked his head to the table. "Sit down," he said. "This may take a while."

Charles balked, and Sari felt the tug of fear. "Come on, *Onkle*," she said in a low voice. "Let's not cause trouble. They'll be gone soon enough."

"Not soon enough," Charles said.

Michael glared at him. "Sit down, old man."

Charles sat, and Sari set the pail of milk on the table and took the seat beside him. Sean tromped through the house, kicking at trunks and pulling aside chairs as if he expected to see Conor cowering behind them. Timmy was in the loft. Sari heard him yank open the lid of her trunk, heard it thud against the wall. She winced, thinking of him up there. Picturing him looking under the bed, pushing aside the hanging hams to see into the corners, pawing through her personal things, defiling every one.

The thought made her feel sick. She closed her eyes, tightening her fingers on the edge of the table. She wanted them gone, wanted Michael to take his friends and go far, far away.

"What's this?" Timmy said, coming to the edge of the loft. He was holding one of her nightgowns—a fine batiste, lavishly embroidered. It was one of the gowns she'd brought on her honeymoon, one she rarely wore now. "Ain't this a pretty thing," he minced, holding it up before him.

Michael glanced up. "Put it away, Timmy," he said. "We're looking for Roarke, remember?"

"Aye, I remember." Timmy grinned, and then his face changed; he leered at her. "You wear this for Roarke, Sari?"

Sari felt herself flush, and she felt Charles tense beside her.

"It's all right," she whispered. "Let him—"

"Leave her be, Tim," Michael warned.

"Come on, Sari," Timmy continued, ignoring Michael. "Did you wear this when you fucked—"

She felt Charles's move before she saw it, a sudden lurch to the side, a quick reach to the rifle angled in the corner by the window. He had it up against his shoulder before she could say a word, was cocking the lever and aiming at Timmy.

She could never say afterward exactly what happened. From the corner of her eye she saw Michael whip around, saw the sunlight glint off the cold metal of his gun. She heard Sean's scream and then her own, and then she heard the crack of gunfire, saw the flash of powder.

Charles spun, and there was another shot. Then the rifle was falling and so was he, collapsing on the table, upsetting the pail of milk so that it splashed across the surface—

"He shot me! Christ in hell, he shot me!" Michael was shouting, clutching his arm. Blood seeped through his fingers. "The bastard shot me!"

Sari jumped from her seat. *"Onkle!"* she shouted. She grabbed at him, but he was limp and heavy. The milk was spreading, pooling and spilling onto the floor, stained with pink that was rapidly growing redder and redder.

"My God, my God." She grabbed at him, pressing her ear to his back, listening for breathing, feeling for movement. *"Onkle. Onkle,* please . . ."

He was breathing, but it was shallow and strained.

Sean was leaning over Michael. Timmy stumbled down the loft ladder.

"He shot me," Michael moaned. "He shot me!"

"You shot *him!"* Sari lifted her head and screamed the words. When Michael looked at her, his eyes dark in the paleness of his face, she turned back to her uncle. With effort she pulled him from the table, nearly fell with him to the floor. The men on the other side of the room made no move to help her, and she wasn't sure she would have let them touch him. She knelt beside him, seeing the hole in his chest, blackened around the edges, the seeping blood. His eyes were closed, his face drained of color

except for the thin line of blood trickling from the corner of his mouth.

"Oh, my God," she whispered, leaning close. She lifted his head, cradling it in her arms. She looked at the three men standing there, stunned. "Somebody get a doctor!" she screamed at them. "Get him a doctor, damn you!"

"Sarilyn—" Her uncle's whisper was strained. "*Lieb . . . ling*, it is . . . too late."

"No." Tears blurred her vision, fell onto her lips. The fear grew so big in her soul, she could taste it mixing with the weak salt of her tears. "*Onkle*, no, it's not. It's not too late. Just hold on. Hold on." She looked at her brother, who just sat there in silent shock. "Get a doctor!"

Michael's lips moved, though Sari heard no sound.

"Calm down, lass," Sean said.

"He's dying, damn you!"

Her uncle shuddered in her arms. "I . . . love . . ."

Desperation surged through her. She offered a prayer to every deity she could think of. *Don't let him die. Please, don't let him die.*

But it was too late. She knew it by the hoarse clattering of his breath, and then by the way he went limp in her arms. She thought she heard the breathing of a word. "Bernice . . ."

And then he was gone.

Sari stared down at the lifeless body in her arms. "No," she whispered. Then, louder, "No."

Too late. She laid him on the ground, buried her face in her hands, unable to look at the face she'd loved so well, not wanting to believe. He was gone.

He was gone and she had nothing left, nothing of him but this still-warm, empty body that suddenly wasn't him at all.

"I'm sorry, darlin'," Michael said softly. "I didn't mean to shoot him."

She didn't look at him. "Then you shouldn't have pulled your gun."

"It was an accident."

She turned to face him. "You are no longer my brother," she said, marshalling her anger, her grief, into quiet, too-calm words. "I want you out of my house. I don't want to see your face again."

"Sari—"

"Get out."

It was all she could say. She looked back at her uncle, at his silent body, and she felt the tears running down her face, over her cheeks and her jaw, and she didn't move. She heard them behind her, their quiet shuffling out of the soddy. Heard Michael pause at the door. But he didn't say anything, and finally he, too, was gone, and she was left alone with the cold, keening wind and the dull sunlight, and hands that were sticky with her uncle's blood.

CHAPTER 23

CONOR RODE UP TO THE SODDY DRENCHED in sweat, panic still racing through his veins. He'd made the trip as quickly as he could, and when he saw the stillness of the little farm, he was sure he hadn't come quickly enough. He dismounted and left his horse standing there in the yard, and took the few steps to the front door of the house at a dead run, nearly falling through the door that hung loosely—too loosely—on its hinges.

"Sari!" Her name burst from his lungs; he skidded to a stop when he saw her. She was standing just inside, staring into space, her hands curled around a cup of coffee. His first emotion was relief; he'd come in time. Then he saw her expression. That dead-eyed, empty expression.

And he knew he was too late.

"What happened?" he asked.

It seemed she looked right through him. She didn't seem surprised to see him, and she didn't ask him to explain his question. Instead she nodded toward the table, and he turned and saw the body.

"Christ," he said, striding toward it. "Oh, Christ." It was Charles, and he was dead—there was no denying the stiffness of his limbs or the sagging of his face. He looked like all dead bodies looked—like a shell and nothing more, an almost obscene imitation of sleep.

Conor stood there staring, felt the disbelief sink through him and then the denial. He was too familiar with it, with this unbelieving shock, this denying sadness. Too familiar with the grief.

"How—how did it happen?"

"Michael was here," she said, and her voice was as lifeless as Charles's body. "He and Timmy and Sean. They were looking for you, and *Onkle* tried to warn them away with the rifle. He shot Michael in the arm, and Michael . . . Michael shot him."

Her words were so matter-of-fact, and the pain he felt at them, the blame, welled up inside of him, filling him so that he couldn't ignore it, couldn't push it away. There was no place for it to go. He looked at Sari, too silent, too still. He wanted to take her in his arms, but he knew she wouldn't allow it—and also knew he would crumble if she pushed him away. So he didn't touch her. He just stared at the man on the table—that good, kind man. Charles was gone, and Conor's grief tightened his chest until he couldn't breathe. Charles was dead and this land he loved would never be touched again by those old, caring hands, and it suddenly seemed too much, too meaningless to be borne.

Conor squeezed his eyes shut, trying to ease that terrible, lonely pain, and thought, *No more.* He was so damn tired of death, of sacrifices. Tired of lies and betrayals that never seemed to end.

He opened his eyes and looked at Sari. "Where's Michael now?" he asked.

She looked at him as if he'd slapped her. "Michael?" she asked. "Good God, is that all you care about? A man's been killed—a man who was good and honorable—and all you want is your damned revenge!" She slammed the coffee cup on the sideboard; coffee splashed over her fingers, dripped to the floor. "You and your damned job, your damned agency. Look what it's brought!"

Conor shook his head helplessly. "Sari, I never intended for this to happen."

"Of course not," she said, sarcasm dripping from her words. "You knew about the blackmark. You knew they would come back here. Yet you left anyway. So much for your 'protection.' You decided I lied to you, and that was all that mattered. *I* didn't matter. *Onkle* didn't matter."

"Sari—"

"It's just like it was in Tamaqua."

Each word felt like a blow, and Conor just listened helplessly, unable to stop her, letting her punish him because he deserved it. Christ, he deserved it too well.

"What kind of man are you, Conor Roarke? I thought I knew you. I didn't want to trust you and you kept making me do it. You lied until I was exactly where you wanted me, and you had the gall to run away because I lied to you." She pointed to her uncle; her hand was shaking. "Look at this! He's dead, and it's all your fault. Are you satisfied now?"

Silent sobs shook her. Conor went to her. He pressed his hand against her cheek. Her skin was cold. Icy cold and wet with tears.

She shrank away from him. "Don't touch me," she spat. "It's too late. I don't want you. I can't forgive you any more. Not you—nor Michael. I want you to leave." Then, when he didn't move, she turned to him with reddened, angry eyes. "Leave!"

He watched her for a moment, and then he shook his head. "I'm not going. Not this time."

"Don't you understand?" she asked desperately. "Don't you see? It's too late." Her voice faltered. "It's too late."

The words cut into his heart. So sad. So lonely. They made Conor think of that long and silent train ride, of the woman waving from her soddy in the middle of the barren plains. He thought of the emptiness inside him—that emptiness that had only disappeared when Sari loved him; those few days before the Christmas dance, when they had been together and the world had seemed different somehow— brighter and cleaner and better—when the plains had not seemed so lonely after all. He had made so many damn mistakes. So many . . .

Conor's chest tightened. She was pale and shaking. He wanted to take all her anger and sadness into himself. Christ, he would if he could.

But forcing her to accept him now would kill

whatever feeling she had for him, he knew it. She would only resent him later, for once again making her feel things she didn't want to feel. It would stay between them forever, and that wasn't what he wanted. Not now. Not when he finally knew what he had to do.

It was time to find Michael.

Time for it all to end, one way or another.

"I'll bury him," he said shortly. "And then I'll leave. But not for good, Sari. Not for good. I promise you that."

"Don't promise," she said. "Don't promise me anything."

She walked away.

It took him a day to dig the hole deep enough. The shovel rang against the frozen ground, he chipped at it little by little until it gave way. Rivulets of sweat rolled from Conor's temple down his cheeks, but he didn't pause. The grave had to be deep enough to keep Charles's body from the scavengers, and Conor would at least protect Charles more in death than he had in life.

He was constantly aware of the way she stood behind him. Standing, never sitting, never varying her posture or saying a word as she watched him dig. Now and then he would turn to look at her, and meet her blank eyes, see the way the wind whipped her hair. But she never batted it away, never moved.

By the time he finished, the sun was setting. Sari had washed her uncle's body and changed his clothes. The old man looked peaceful in death, and

Conor remembered that he'd seen that peaceful, contented look on Charles's face before, many times. Charles Donaldson had been a man happy with his life. He'd known love as well as pain, happiness perhaps more than sorrow. Conor envied him that. It was probably a fallacy to believe that Charles's life hadn't held the torment his own had, but Conor wanted to believe it. It was suddenly terribly important that there be something redeemable about being alive, something that meant more than guilt and uncertainty.

He watched Sari as she knelt by the grave, one hand pressed against the soil. Her dark hair blew about her head, obscuring her face, but he saw the way her fingers clenched in grief and anger. He wished he could comfort her, but he could think of no gesture she would accept from him.

His heart felt heavy. Somehow, somehow he had to earn her forgiveness. God knew he couldn't walk away from her—not this time. He hadn't known much real happiness in his life, but what he had known had been with Sari, and now he prayed he hadn't destroyed it forever.

He cleared his throat and looked over at Sari. Her face was devoid of tears. Conor felt a swift stab of unbearable sadness. This was the Sari he knew, the one he remembered. She was so strong, and yet he knew she was strong from necessity, not from desire. No, there were no tears, but he knew she held a pool of them deep inside.

She turned back to the grave. Conor closed his eyes at her whispered "I love you. Rest in peace."

The words carried on the wind. Then Sari rose to face him. Her face was shuttered, her eyes empty.

"Thank you for burying him," she said quietly. "I couldn't have done it."

Conor followed her as she turned and went back to the house. He watched her careful step, the skirts that blew against her legs. "I'm going to go now," he said heavily. "You won't have to worry about protection. Michael won't be bothering you again."

"Why? Because you'll kill him?" she sneered. "You're such a hero. Get off my land."

Conor leaned the shovel against the wall. "I'm going to find him," he agreed. "Because it's time to resolve things, Sari. It's long past time. Not just for me, but for you too."

"I don't want you to do it for me," she said. "I don't want your kind of vengeance. Do it for yourself, if you want, but don't lie about it. At least don't lie. It's not for me, and it's not for the best, and you're as bad as he is. You and your 'eye for an eye.'" She laughed shortly, mirthlessly. "Get off my land."

"That's not what this is, not anymore."

She was silent, and he didn't wait, knowing she was too deep in her anger to care about what he said, knowing that she was looking for a chance to hurt him as badly as she hurt. But still there was something inside him that waited for her to stop him, to call him back as he made his way to his horse.

He stepped up to his horse, mounted slowly, and then couldn't keep himself from looking back at her. She stood quietly, waiting.

"I love you, Sari," he whispered. "I'll be back, whether you want me back or not."

His answer was the quiet sigh of the wind.

Sari buried her face against the cow's side, pressing her eyes and her lips against the warmth to keep the tears from coming, taking some small comfort in the familiar routine. The farm didn't stop just because *Onkle* had died; time didn't stand still. The animals still needed to be fed and the cows milked. And as long as she did those things, she didn't have to think too hard. She didn't have to remember the sharp crack of Michael's gun or the sadness in his eyes afterward. She didn't have to remember her uncle's lifeless face or Conor's *"I love you."* They were things she didn't want to have to come to terms with, things she didn't want to understand.

She kept expecting to wake up and find this was all a dream. Any moment she expected to hear her uncle's footsteps, to hear the thick, guttural edge of his German-accented words.

Her heart ached. Sari longed to cover her ears, to muffle the ceaseless screaming of the wind. She imagined she heard her own sorrow in its keening cry. Her peace was gone. She was alone, with only the wind and the cows for company.

And it was all because of Conor. All because of Michael. All because of their blind, stupid hatred for each other, the vengeance neither of them could relinquish.

Elsa snorted and shifted, and Sari looked down into a full bucket of milk. The scent nauseated her,

forcibly bringing back the memory of the milk pooling around her uncle, the thin red trail of blood. . . .

Sari pushed back the stool and straightened, setting the milk aside. She stared up at the loft, at the
makeshift room that had been Conor's home for the
last few weeks, and rage swept through her. This
time she embraced it. Sari snatched up her wool
skirts and climbed the ladder.

She smelled his scent first. The musky, fresh-air-
and-leather smell drifted to her subtly, twisting her
heart and bringing tears again to her eyes. Sari
dashed away the tears with the back of her hand.
Damned if she would hurt over him now. Damned
if she would remember the way he touched her, the
gentleness of his words. Her foot snagged in the
blankets of his makeshift bed, and she fell hard,
landing facedown in the harsh, scratchy wool. Once
again his scent filled her nostrils.

"Goddamn him!" She pushed herself up, shoving
the blankets aside, kicking them over the edge of the
loft to land with soft thumps on the floor below. He
said he was coming back. If he did, she'd show him
just how much he was welcome. She'd burn every
damn thing he owned. She'd set a bonfire people
would see in Julesburg. And when all his belongings
had turned to ash, there would be nothing left in her
heart either.

Sari sent the last of the blankets over the edge,
then crawled to his saddlebags, huddled in the corner. The leather was supple with use, and heavy. She
yanked them loose and shoved them across the floor.

She watched them fall with almost insane pleasure, heard the muffled shattering of glass when they hit the ground. Something had been inside them. She hoped it was something precious, something he treasured. Something that would help make up for the way he'd hurt her, for the way he'd left her life in ruins.

But the thought didn't have the power she wanted it to have, and there was nothing left to throw but straw. Sari stood on the edge of the loft, staring down at his crumpled bags, at the small mound of clothes, the scattered blankets, and waited to feel relief and satisfaction.

All she felt was lonely.

She closed her eyes for a moment, listening to the sounds of the barn and her own heavy breathing, and then she laughed bitterly to herself and went down the ladder. Conor's things were scattered over the dirt floor: a few shirts and a pair of pants, a razor and a leather strop. A bottle of bay rum lay broken, the scent reminded her so forcibly of him that Sari caught her breath. She bent down, gathering up the things in a pile, shoving them back into the saddlebags. Her fingers brushed something hard—a small leather folder—and she frowned and pulled it loose. Slowly, feeling a dread she didn't want to feel, she opened the portfolio.

It was a photograph, a portrait of a man. His face was thin and angular, and his sparse hair flew out around his head in defiance of gravity. There was a small smile on his face, as if he were trying very hard to be serious, but the laughter in his eyes belied any illusion of sobriety. He was clad in black, with a small white collar. A priest's collar.

Sari stared at the picture. It was Conor's father, Sean Roarke, and when she looked at that kindly face, those laughing eyes, she felt a wave of sadness, a crushing regret that he was dead, that his life had been taken in an act as meaningless as her uncle's death.

And she felt a sorrow for Conor that over-shadowed her anger. She remembered asking Conor questions about his past, remembered the sweep of pain in his eyes when he mentioned his childhood. What had he said then? *"You don't miss what you never had."*

But that had been a lie. He *had* missed things. Conor had no home, no family—nothing but the street, nothing but hunger and privation. She remembered how he'd told her his story, the steady, unemotional way he'd talked about his prostitute mother and the orphanage. So cold, so untouched.

And then she remembered the softness that had come over his face when he spoke of Sean Roarke. She'd seen something of the child he'd been then— a lonely child, lost and starving, too ill to steal, too alone to turn to anyone for help. Had he looked into other people's windows, as she had, wishing he belonged to the families that laughed and talked inside? Wishing the love shining from their eyes was shining on him?

The image was too real, too affecting. Sari swallowed back the tears welling in her throat. She knew what it felt like to be that alone, to lock up your heart and guard the key so zealously, you forgot to take it out now and again. She had never had to steal or starve, but there was a different kind of starvation, and until her parents had died, and she'd gone to live with her aunt and uncle, she'd known that deprivation. But then her life had changed.

Just as Conor's must have.

Sari started; the realization flooded over her. She knew what it felt like to be alone and then be wrapped in love so strong, you couldn't believe your good fortune. Hadn't she had that with Aunt Bernice and *Onkle*? She knew—too well she knew—how Conor must have felt when Sean Roarke took him in and gave him food for his body and his soul. The priest had given Conor his gentleness, had given him honor. Had given him love. Just as Charles and Bernice had done for her.

And now, at last, she understood Conor's need for revenge. When someone you loved was gone, and it was so stupid, so meaningless . . . Sometimes all that was left was anger. It was a way of grieving, a way of never saying good-bye. As long as she held on to that anger, a part of Charles was still with her. The need for vengeance was only another name for it.

They were just alike, she and Conor. Both grabbing on to things so tightly, they couldn't let them go. Both letting anger take over because they were afraid of grief, of the permanence of letting go. Both terrified of being alone again.

And in spite of that, both alone—

The sound of wheels crunching on the icy ground

startled her. For a moment she thought he was back, but then she heard a soft shout, a high-pitched "Yoo hoo! Sari! Charles! Are you home?"

It was Miriam. Sari brushed the tears from the corners of her eyes and shoved the framed photograph back into the saddlebags. She pushed them out of the way, beneath the ladder, and hurried out of the barn.

She met Miriam coming across the yard. Her friend held a large, bulging box, hastily tied together with string. Her cheeks and her nose were rosy from the cold. Behind her, John was climbing down from the buckboard.

"You *are* here!" Miriam rushed. Her skirts flapped around her legs; loose hair flew into her face as she hurried over. "I thought you'd be staying in town for a day or so after the dance, but Audra Landers said you all came rushing on home."

Sari smiled weakly. "Yes. Well . . . we should have stayed."

"Of course you should have. It's too long a drive to make so late at night."

"Miriam—"

"And so cold. Why, a blizzard could have come right up and swallowed you all." She handed the box to Sari. "Audra sent this on over. She says she's sorry she didn't have it done before the dance."

"Miri—"

John Graham came striding up, rubbing his gloved hands together. "Where's Conor?"

Sari shifted the box to her hip. "He's gone," she said shortly.

"Gone?" Miriam frowned. "Into town, you mean?"

"I don't know," Sari said slowly. She took a deep breath. "We—we had an . . . accident here."

Miriam went very still. John frowned. "An accident?" he asked carefully.

"*Onkle* is dead," Sari said. The words came out short and harsh and much too real.

The aftermath of her words was silence. Miriam paled; John stared at her in shock.

"Dead?" Miriam gasped finally. "But . . . but I just saw him. At the dance. He was smiling, and laughing."

"It was yesterday," Sari said. "He was . . . cleaning his gun and . . . it went off." She swallowed at the heaviness of the lie and looked down at her feet. "We buried him this morning."

John swallowed. "Oh, good Lord."

"You aren't joking, are you?"

Sari shook her head. "I wish I were."

"Oh, my God. Oh, God." Miriam began to cry. She turned her face into John's chest. Her husband's expression was bleak, his eyes pooled with unshed tears. He wrapped his arms around his wife, holding her close, and the gesture sent a shaft of pain deep inside Sari; she felt a loneliness that seemed as big as the sky, as far-reaching as the plains.

"I am so sorry," John said. "I—I don't know what to say. He was a good man."

"Oh, yes." Miriam sobbed. "He was a wonderful man."

Sari motioned to the grave in the distance, the

mound of rocks. "He's over there. If you'd like to pay your respects to him."

John nodded. Sari led them over to the grave, lifting leaden feet over rocks and hard hillocks of grass, nearly stumbling in the force of the wind. She hated looking at it, hated seeing that mound of stone and dirt and knowing her uncle's body was beneath it, that she would never look into his face again or hear the affection in his voice when he called her *Liebling.* She hated feeling that helpless, furious anger.

But this time, as the three of them stood on the edge of the grave and Sari heard John's muttered prayer and the soft whisper of Miriam's hymn, the anger was gone. The rocks were just rocks. The ground was simply ground.

And her uncle wasn't really there at all.

"I wonder," she said softly, "if there really is a heaven."

Miriam squeezed her hand. "If there is, Sari," she said kindly, "then Charles is there. He's in the arms of those who love him."

"In the arms of those who love him." Not here. Not in this cold, unforgiving ground with the lonely wind howling all around. She hoped he was with Bernice. Heaven wouldn't matter to him without her. Not the downy clouds nor golden light nor harps nor angel wings. Her uncle would have been happy in hell if Bernice was waiting for him there.

Sari liked the thought. It made things better somehow, more bearable.

She turned to her friends. "Do you suppose . . . would you mind . . . ?"

"Of course we'll stay," Miriam said impulsively. "As long as you'd like us to."

"I'll admit I'd like the company for a few hours or so. Can I get the two of you some coffee?"

"I'll get *you* some coffee," Miriam said, hugging her fiercely, crushing the box Sari held on her hip. "Oh . . . the box."

Sari glanced down at it. She'd forgotten she even held it. "Audra probably sent it out for *Onkle*," she said. "You know how the two of them liked each other."

John smiled sadly. "Charles used to say that Landers's café had the best cherry pie in the country."

Sari returned his smile. "He used to say that about mine too."

She led them into the soddy. She set the box on the table. It felt good to have them there, as if there was life in the tiny house again, and the warmth and friendship she felt from the two of them filled her heart.

Miriam hung her coat and hurried to the stove. She poured coffee for each of them, and then she began lifting pans from their hooks on the wall.

"What are you doing?" Sari asked.

"Making you some dinner, of course," Miriam replied. "Now you just sit down and relax with John. And open up that box."

Sari sat at the table. She pulled the box toward her. The knots of the string were tight, and she fumbled with them until John drew out his knife and slit them neatly. Sari pushed the string aside and carefully lifted the lid off the box.

It was the silk Conor had bought her. It glistened in the lamplight, the dark green stripes looked deep and rich, and the gold threads woven through the cloth glinted in the weak sunlight slanting through the window. At first she thought it was just the cloth, and it confused her, because the cloth was in her trunk upstairs. But then she noticed the fine stitching, the edge of a seam. A dress. It had been made into a dress.

She gasped and lifted it from the box. It felt smooth and cool, but the delicate silk caught on her roughened hands.

"Oh my," Miriam said breathlessly. "Oh, my Lord. It's beautiful."

She was right, it *was* beautiful. Sari stared at it, stunned both by its elaborateness and by the fact that she recognized it. Not the dress itself but the pattern. It was the same one she'd worn to that dance in Tamaqua, the dance where she'd met Conor for the first time, but it was adorned with touches she had not been able to afford then. The short sleeves were puffed and off the shoulder, trimmed in the same lace that edged the simple neckline. Silk flowers decorated each sleeve, with thin dark ribbons dangling from them. The polonaise skirt was decorated in lace, drawn up by a large green silk bow at the hip. It was beautiful. It was extravagant.

And it was from Conor.

He was the only one who could have known.

Sari's heart stopped, her breath caught in her throat. She'd hidden the silk away because she couldn't look at it without seeing the guilt on his face when he bought it, without wishing that the words he'd said were true. *"Something pretty. A frippery."* She'd thought the words were lies then, but now she wondered if they were. Now she wondered if it had really been guilt she'd seen, or if it had been something else. Regret perhaps.

She thought of the other things in her trunk, things he would have looked at, touched. The Christmas ornaments she'd been too busy to pull out, the soft mohair scarf—a rare gift from her mother—the red rose Conor had given her back in Tamaqua, when she was falling in love with him. She remembered the way he'd handed it to her, with a mock bow and teasing words. And then he'd kissed her so softly, so tenderly. . . .

She wondered if he'd laughed when he saw she'd saved it, and then realized with a start that he wouldn't have. That he wasn't like that. She knew it deep inside her, in the heart that had known him well for a long time.

In the heart that still loved him.

She let the dress fall to her lap and looked at Miriam. Her friend smiled, and in her eyes was a reassurance that warmed Sari to her very core.

"He'll be back," Miriam said. "Don't worry, Sari. He'll come back for you."

Outside came the sound of hoofbeats. John got to his feet.

"Two men," he said briefly, looking out the window. He grabbed the rifle leaning by the door, the same one Charles had held only two days before. "Looks like we've got company, ladies."

CHAPTER 24

"NOW, WHO COULD THAT BE?" MIRIAM peered past her husband. "I don't recognize them, do you, John?"

He shook his head. "Strangers," he said tersely.

Sari's heart raced. Two men. *Mollies.* The word rushed into her mind. Timmy Boyd's face wavered before her. Michael was shot. They could have left him behind. They could be coming for her. . . .

She rose from her chair, edging past Miriam, pushing past John. "It's all right," she said, though her heart was in her throat. "Please, John. Put the rifle down. It's all right."

He hesitated only a moment before he lowered the gun and stood back. "Are you sure, Sari?" he asked in a low voice. "Do you know these men?"

They weren't close enough for her to tell, but Sari nodded, afraid that if she didn't, John would try to protect her, remembering what had happened when *Onkle* tried.

"Wait here," she said, going out the door. "Please just wait here."

Sari tried to ignore the rapid beating of her heart. She waited as they came closer, and she felt a rush of relief when she realized it wasn't Timmy. It wasn't Sean.

But that relief was short-lived. There were other sleepers she didn't know, men in other towns. . . .

Slowly she walked up to the men, waiting while they dismounted.

"Are ye Sari Travers?" one of them asked.

Sari lifted her chin. "Who wants to know?"

"It's Mizz Travers, Roberts." The other man spoke quickly, coming forward. He lifted his hat, sweeping it from his head and bringing his face out of shadow. "Ma'am, I'm Peter Devlin. I believe we've met before."

She squinted at him. He looked vaguely familiar, with his badly cut gray-black hair and a round face that showed signs of dissolution. "Have we? I don't remember."

"In Pennsylvania."

Her panic came racing back. "You'll have to forgive me. I don't remember all . . . of Michael's . . . friends."

The other man laughed and threw an amused glance at an obviously disgruntled Peter Devlin. "Aye, lass, an' there's no reason to remember us, either. We're no Molly Maguires." He pushed back his hat to reveal a lined face and twinkling eyes set deep above a hawklike nose. "I'm Paddy Roberts, from the Pinkerton agency in Chicago. Mr. Devlin, here, he's been workin' in Denver."

Pinkerton men. Sari felt relief tinged with wariness. "Pinkerton men," she said slowly. "What do you want with me?"

"We're looking for Roarke," Devlin said roughly. "Is he here?"

She shook her head. "No."

Devlin looked surprised. "But I assumed he'd be here."

"Well, he's not." Sari motioned toward the house. "Now, if you'll excuse me, I have company—"

Devlin pressed forward. "Mrs. Travers, it's important that we know where he is. It's imperative that we find him."

"You're asking the wrong person," Sari said. "He left several hours ago. I don't know where he went."

"Then do ye . . ." The other man, the Irishman, paused. He flashed a look at Devlin and then he continued. "Do ye know where yer brother might be, then?"

Sari snorted. "In hell, perhaps," she said.

"Mrs. Travers—"

Sari matched Peter Devlin's gaze. "I don't know where my brother is, Mr. Devlin."

"Ye've got no reason to help us, lass, that's for sure."

Sari turned her gaze to the Irishman, suddenly feeling pity for him and his obvious discomfort. "I've got no reason not to help you," she said. "My brother and I are . . . estranged. He was here two days ago, but now he's gone. I would be surprised if I ever saw him again.''

"And Conor?''

"He left this morning. I don't know where he went. Into Woodrow maybe. It's the closest town.''

Paddy Roberts inclined his head. ''Thank ye, Mrs. Travers. You've been a great help to us.''

Sari gave him a weak smile. ''I haven't been any help at all, Mr. Roberts,'' she said. ''But I—I would like you to do one thing for me, if you would.''

Peter Devlin nodded. ''Of course. Whatever we can.''

Sari took a deep breath. She looked past them, into the long and far-reaching plains. ''When you find Conor Roarke, would you . . . would you ask him to come back? There's . . . something . . . I have to tell him.''

Paddy Roberts raised a brow. ''Aye, lass,'' he said kindly. ''We'll make sure he knows that.''

Sari smiled her thanks. She started to turn away.

''Wait, lass.'' Roberts touched her shoulder gently. ''If there's anything we can do . . .''

''There's nothing else, Mr. Roberts,'' she assured him. ''Nothing else at all.''

The gelding's breath was ragged, its sides heaving with exertion as Conor urged it to greater effort. He bent low over the horse's back, feeling the smooth, strong muscles lunge, watching its hooves kick up puffs of snow. He was almost there, and he didn't care if Doyle and his cohorts heard him coming. It was finally time for retribution.

Desperation had clouded his thinking when he left the soddy earlier that day, but now his mind was clear with purpose. He'd gone directly into Woodrow, had asked questions until he had the right answers. Doyle had left a clear trail—a path laid for Conor's benefit, he was sure. The Molly knew as well as he did that the time had come to bring the battle to a close. One of them would die today. Conor didn't intend for it to be him.

The snow had begun to fall a few hours ago, and now it was coming down steadily and hard, freezing Conor's face and hands, stinging his eyes. It didn't matter that he could barely see; he knew where Doyle was. He knew also that Doyle was waiting for him there. During Conor's quick visit to the general store, Clancy had nervously informed Conor that Michael had left a message.

"He's waitin' for you at a place near Kiowa Creek," Clancy had mumbled. "He says it's time for a meeting. Just the two of you. Remember that, he says to me—just the two of you."

Conor smiled grimly. It wouldn't matter if Doyle was lying and the whole gang met him there. He had waited for this day for a long time, and he had more than the death of his father to punish Doyle for. More than Charles's death to avenge.

The past had held on too long, and unless he got rid of it, he and Sari had no future. He no longer wanted to live in fear—for her or for himself. He wanted a life. A family. He wanted dark-haired little girls with their mother's face, and little boys who would never know the fear and loneliness of living

on the streets trying to survive. But most of all, he
wanted the woman who had haunted his days and
nights since he'd first seen her three years ago, at a
Christmas dance.

Conor closed his eyes briefly, feeling the pounding
of the horse's hooves vibrating through his body, the
ice particles of snow biting into his skin. If he had
to settle down on this godforsaken land and learn
how to be a farmer, he'd do it and be glad. But then
he remembered Sari standing against the sky, staring
out at the prairie while the wind whipped her dark
hair around her waist and he realized God hadn't
forsaken Colorado. In fact heaven was right there,
on the plains Conor had hated so much three months
ago. The plains he was now beginning to love.

He glanced up, slowing the gelding at the ice-
covered banks of Kiowa Creek. According to Clancy,
the soddy was near here—less than half a mile away.
The familiar tension of danger and wariness spread
through him, and Conor pushed aside his duster to
grasp the handle of the Colt. The gun fit easily, in-
timately in his hand. Its weight was reassuring. Tapping his heels against the gelding's sides, he urged
the horse through the thin layer of ice and across the
shallow creek.

The tiny lean-to came into sight within minutes,
its shadow a dark, misty shape through the falling
snow. He smelled the smoke drifting from the makeshift chimney, and Conor reined in his horse, pausing before he led the animal closer, tense with
anticipation and fear. Michael Doyle might be Sari's
brother, but he was a killer, and Conor couldn't af-

ford to forget it. Slowly he dismounted, walking the few feet to the front door of the house.

The door opened before he got to it. Conor stopped, his hand tightening on his gun, his stance ready as Michael Doyle filled the doorway. There was a thick bandage around his upper arm, but no sling. Behind him Conor heard voices, saw movement. Timmy and Sean. Michael wasn't alone after all, and Conor cursed under his breath.

"Well, well," Doyle said with a smile. He drew deeply on the cigar between his teeth before he tossed it into the snow. "So you've come to get me, Jamie. I've been waiting for you."

"It's not Jamie anymore, Doyle. You know that. And I thought you said to come alone."

Michael's smile widened. "Well, now, laddie, they won't leave me be. Nothing I could do about it."

"I thought you were a man of your word."

Michael's face darkened. "There comes a time when the only honor a man has is to take care of his enemies—any way he can." He spat into the snow. "And it's a fine thing for you to talk about honor, after what you did to the men you called friends, what you did to my sister. There're no words for a man like you, Roarke. No curse strong enough."

"You called me a Molly once," Conor reminded him. "Think that's enough to get me into hell?"

Behind Michael, Timmy cursed and stepped to the door. The gun in his hand gleamed in the snowlight.

Michael pushed him back. "It's my fight, Tim," he said angrily. "*My* fight." He stepped from the doorway, and it was then that Conor saw the knife glinting in his hand. "You won't be around long enough to blaspheme them further. I'll see you join them all—in heaven or hell."

Conor had no time to react as Michael lunged. He slammed into Conor, and the breath whooshed from Conor's lungs, his fingers loosened. The revolver slipped from his grasp, falling beyond his reach, disappearing in a puff of snow. Michael was on top of him in an instant, slamming him into the ground.

"I promised them I'd see you pay in blood," Michael sneered, his face inches from Conor's. "And now it's time."

From the corner of his eye Conor saw the knife poised above him. He reacted with pure instinct, reflex born of years of practice. Conor thrust forward, smashing his knee into Michael's groin, his fist into Michael's wounded arm. The man snarled in pain, rolling sideways while the knife fell harmlessly into the snow.

Conor scrambled away. "You bastard," he rasped. "What did you expect? You'll die, just like they all did. Like my father, and your uncle. Tell me something, Doyle, did you feel anything when you put a bullet through him? Your own uncle?"

Michael staggered to his feet. His expression darkened. "You don't know anything about it."

"What must it feel like, to know you're going to die with that on your conscience?"

Michael scowled. "If I die, you'll be going with me." He fell to one knee, pulling something from the snow. The gun. It flashed in the light as Doyle lifted it. *Christ, his own gun.* Time slowed; Conor dove to the ground, but he couldn't move fast enough. The explosion crashed through the air, the noise bursting in his brain. Conor twisted sideways, but it was too late. The bullet slammed into his shoulder. The impact sent him sprawling to the snow, the pain brought tears to his eyes.

He struggled to his feet, staggering back as Michael came relentlessly forward. Conor felt the warm, wet heat of blood, the burning, searing pain. The world tilted before him, and he fought it, forcing himself to face Michael, to concentrate. But there was no sound suddenly; Conor couldn't hear anything—not his own choking gasps nor the rush of blood through his veins. He couldn't even hear the wind. He couldn't hear, his body was numb, and he had the quick, unwelcome thought that he was dying. Ah, hell, he was dying, and he never had the chance to tell her what he really wanted, would never be able to tell her about the future he had planned—

"Time to die, my friend," Michael gasped, his face twisted as he moved closer. His finger tightened on the trigger. "Time to die."

Not dying. Not yet. Conor nodded toward the gun. "Try it," he taunted. He couldn't run, there was no way to escape. His vision blurred—there was a haze over everything. He tried to focus, watching Michael warily. "Pull the trigger, Michael, if that's what you want. Go ahead, kill me—I'm half there already."

It was all the urging Michael needed. He aimed the gun, his finger tensed on the trigger—

Conor dove. He aimed for Michael's knees, skidded across the snow into the bigger man's body. Pain exploded in his shoulder, taking his breath away. Michael gasped and went down, the gun flying through the air, skidding across the snow.

From the corner of his eye Conor saw the others—Timmy and Sean—bursting from the cabin. He had moments, if that. Timmy was waving that blasted rifle. Just moments. Conor's head was spinning, his shoulder was going numb. It took nearly all his strength to roll away from Michael's grasp, but he did it. He did it and lunged across the snow for the gun, wrapping his hand around the hilt. He was belly-down in the ice and looking up just as Timmy Boyd yelled out his curses.

Conor aimed instinctively, pulled the trigger almost before he knew it. He heard the crack of gunfire, saw the smoke, and then Timmy's face crumpled before him, just crumpled in an expression of surprise and pain, and Conor saw the blood spurt from his chest as he went down, dead before he hit the snow.

"You bastard—" Sean O'Mallory skidded to a stop. "You've killed him."

"And I'll . . . kill you . . . too." The pain in Conor's shoulder was blinding. He fought the urge to close his eyes, to give in to it.

Sean smiled meanly. He lifted his rifle, trained it on Conor. "Let's see who's the quicker shot, laddie, shall we?"

"No!" Michael screamed.

Conor pulled the trigger. Sean dropped the rifle,

his expression confused, and then he pitched forward, falling onto Timmy's body with a sickening thud. Conor rolled to his side. Blood was dripping from his shoulder, forming dark red-brown ice where it hit the snow. He looked up to see Michael squatting by the bodies, his face distorted by anger and pain. He looked at Conor, his eyes dark with hatred as he reached into Timmy Doyle's belt and pulled out a knife.

"You going to shoot me, Roarke?" he asked. "Or will you fight like a man?"

Conor laughed. The motion sent pain radiating into his chest. "I doubt you'd be saying that if you were the one holding the gun." He tightened his hand around the hilt, got slowly to his feet. The ground wavered before him; he staggered as it seemed to tilt beneath his feet.

Michael laughed. His white teeth flashed in the darkness of his beard. He rose slowly, twisting the knife in his hand, never taking his gaze from Conor. "I've killed lesser men than you," he said quietly.

"And better ones too," Conor said steadily. He blinked, trying to right the crazy spinning of the snow before his eyes. He motioned with the gun. "Give it up, Michael. You can't win this time."

Michael lifted a brow. "Can't I?"

The earth lurched beneath Conor's feet. He staggered, trying to regain his balance, but it was too late. Michael attacked. Conor heard a scream—his own—and the gun went flying. He saw the knife— a flash of reflection, a sharp light—coming toward him. Reflexively he jerked, bringing his knee up into Michael's chest. He heard Michael's whoosh of breath, saw him fall back.

It was the opportunity Conor needed. He lunged up, twisting around, groaning with the effort it took. Michael fell to the ground, and Conor was on top of him in a moment, bringing his boot down on Michael's arm, grinding his foot into the flesh. Bones cracked, splintered. Michael's scream of pain pierced the air. The knife fell from his nerveless fingers.

Frantically Conor reached for it. He couldn't feel the handle when his fingers gripped it, was surprised when he drew it from the snow. He looked at Michael, was stunned by the degree of hatred he saw in the man's eyes.

"Kill me, then," Doyle gasped. "Kill me, like you did the others." He laughed—the obscene sound rang in Conor's ears. "Twenty of us for one preacher. Which is the better deal?" His laughter split the air, the high, tinny sound was almost painful. "Which is the better deal?"

Conor stopped. *"The better deal."* One for twenty. And it would just keep going. Over and over, never stopping until everyone was dead. Never stopping.

Sean Roarke would never have wanted it this way, and now Conor knew why.

Conor backed away, clutching the knife in his fist. He stumbled away from Michael's convulsing body, feeling sick at heart and tired. And hurt. God, he hurt. "You're not worth killing, Doyle," he said softly. "You're not worth one tenth of him, and I won't dirty my hands with you."

He turned away, and as he did so, he heard hoof-beats, muffled in the snow. Two men were riding in at a fast pace. Conor recognized Peter Devlin instantly and felt a rush of relief so intense, it made him dizzy. He staggered, nearly falling to his knees.

Then everything seemed to happen in the same moment. Conor heard the cocking of a gun, Michael's scream: "You coward, Roarke! You were always a coward! Well, you won't run this time. Not this time!" From his horse Devlin reached for his rifle, and Conor twisted around in time to see Michael aiming the revolver that had been lost in the snow, laughing as he pointed it at Conor, his white teeth flashing. Conor threw himself to the ground—too late. The gun fired; he heard the rush of the bullet, waited to feel the pain.

And instead saw Michael Doyle lurch back, clutching his chest. The revolver fell from his hand. He collapsed onto the snow and laid there, unmoving.

Then there was no sound but the wind.

Clumsily, painfully, Conor got to his feet.

"You all right, Roarke?" Devlin's voice was eerily muffled by the wind and snow. He lowered his rifle.

"I'm fine," Conor said, and then wondered if Devlin even heard the quiet words.

He saw Devlin's nod. Saw the other man urge his horse across the snow, past Conor, to Michael's still body. Conor brushed the snow from his coat and dropped the knife he still held, watched it fall into the snow. It disappeared from sight. Disappeared as thoroughly as his hatred had done. Conor stumbled to his horse. Awkwardly he mounted; the pain of the motion nauseated him.

"He's dead!" The man called back. Conor looked over his shoulder to see him leaning over Michael. "Good work, Devlin!"

Good work.

Conor's shoulders sagged; he urged the gelding forward. It was over, he thought, falling over the animal's neck. He could go home. Sari was waiting.

Blackness engulfed him.

CHAPTER 25

THE SNOW WAS COMING DOWN FASTER
now. Sari stared out the soddy window, staring at
the near twilight. John and Miriam had left over an
hour ago, and she had urged them to go, telling them
she wanted to be alone.

But she had not imagined this kind of alone.

The house was so quiet—even the howl of the
wind didn't ease the stillness of it, and the snow muffled every other outside noise. She had put the coffee
on to boil simply because she wanted the sound to
keep her company, but she had long since ceased to
hear it. The silence inside her was too loud.

The snow swirled around the window, creating
shifting shadows, soft light. She stared out at it. Her
uncle had once told her that no two snowflakes were
alike, and she wondered if that was true, wished
there was someone here to ask. In her mind she
imagined it. Imagined turning to someone—a man—
who sat in the rocker by the stove. Imagined asking

the question *"Did you know every snowflake is different?"* and having him smile and rise and take her hand. *"Let's test that theory, shall we?"*

The scene was so real it made her smile and then her smile faded just as quickly when she realized she was here, and she was alone, and there was no man sitting by the fire. There would never be a man sitting by the fire.

This was what made women mad, she thought. Listening for voices in the wind. Hearing them.

Sari turned from the window. The gown, the cream silk, lay spread across a chair, its stripes and gold thread glittering in the lamplight. On the table beside it lay a book, its place marked with a piece of buffalo grass. Marked at *Christabel,* she knew, and the words came into her mind, sharp and poignant with meaning. *"They parted—ne'er to meet again! But never either found another to free the hollow heart from paining—"*

The memory came back to her, flooding over her with painful intensity. Conor, bent over the book, his raspy voice never faltering as he read the words, his low whispers caressing, his glances full of meaning and promise. Conor, smiling at something her uncle said, throwing her such a beguiling grin, she couldn't help but smile in response.

The thought hurt her heart. She wondered if she'd ever see that beguiling grin again. There were so many mistakes between them, so many lies. She had accused Conor of being unable to love, unable to trust, but she herself was just as guilty of that. She had not trusted him with her own heart. She had not loved him enough to be honest with him.

Sari looked again at the cream silk, and she wanted to cry for her own stupidity, her own blindness. For her willingness to sacrifice everything for a brother who cared for nothing and no one. She had lost everything because of it. Her uncle, her lover.

Her brother too.

The thought made her feel tight and sad. Because she couldn't grieve over losing Michael—at least not the Michael of today. But for the little boy she'd loved, the boy who had cared for her once, loved her once—yes, she could grieve for him, she *would* grieve for him. That little boy had been dead to her for a long time. He'd been killed in the mines with their father, buried with their mother. The Michael Doyle who existed now was not the brother she had known. She had just never said good-bye.

But she was saying good-bye now. She had come to Colorado to heal, and it was time now to do that. It was time to put all the past hurts behind her, to go forward without anger. To farm this land the way Charles would have wanted it farmed. To live her life without fear.

And without love too. Unless . . .

Sari looked back at the window, at the growing darkness, and wondered where Conor was, wondered if the Pinkerton men had found him, and if they'd given him her message. *"Ask him to come back. There's something I have to tell him."*

Something, yes. So many things. She wanted to

apologize, she wanted to tell him she understood. She wanted to start over, and she hoped—she prayed—he could forget her last words. They had been said in anger and in grief, and always . . .

Always she had loved him.

Sari closed her eyes, wishing.

It was then she heard the tap on the door. It was soft, muted in the sound of the snow. Sari opened her eyes, staring out the window. There were no shadows outside, nothing but the snow and the falling darkness, and she wondered if she was imagining it, if maybe she wanted so badly to hear a knock that she'd made it happen.

Then she heard it again.

Her hands were trembling. Sari swallowed and got to her feet. She grabbed the rifle leaning by the door and put it to her shoulder, and then she opened the door, yanking it so that it wobbled on its torn hinges, facing down whatever enemy was out there in the snow.

"Conor. Not another gun," he said.

She lowered the rifle. Conor, leaning against the doorjamb, looking exhausted and hurting. But alive. Alive and back. Just as he'd promised. She wanted to laugh with the intensity of her relief.

He inclined his head toward the field. "Devlin and Roberts are in the barn. I told them they could sleep there. I hope you don't mind."

She shook her head. "I don't mind."

"They found me at Kiowa Creek. Your brother . . ." He took a deep breath. "He's dead,

Sari." When she opened her mouth to speak, he quieted her with a shake of his head. "I didn't shoot him," he said. "I—you were right. You were right about everything. I'm no judge. I'm no executioner. Michael can make his excuses to God—when he gets there. But I wasn't the one to send him. He was . . . he was going to kill me. Devlin rode up. . . ."

She closed her eyes briefly. "It was just a matter of time," she whispered.

"I don't want him to come between us," he said. "Not anymore."

"No."

"I don't want any more secrets."

She smiled. "No more secrets."

"I want . . ." He took a deep breath. "I want to love you, Sari. If that means I have to stay on these plains and learn to be a farmer, then I'll do it. I'll do whatever it takes. Just tell me you love me. Tell me that and I'll walk through hell to be with you."

She held out her arms. "I love you," she said.

He stumbled to her. She felt the warm stickiness of blood at his shoulder, the heat of his body. But mostly she felt the way his arms tightened around her as if she were his anchor, his lifeline. The way he squeezed her with all the strength he had and then groaned with the pain of it.

"I love you," he said quietly in her ear.

They stood there while the snow came down around them, and Sari tasted it on her lips, felt it on her cheeks and her eyelashes, saw it melting in his hair, and she looked up at all that whiteness and closed her eyes because of the pain of it. The pain of so much joy.

"Do you know," she said, "that no two snow-flakes are the same?"

The loneliness was gone. Forever, she thought, and smiled into the snow.

Let best-selling, award-winning author **Virginia Henley** capture your heart...

☐ 17161-X	The Raven and the Rose	$5.50
☐ 20144-6	The Hawk and the Dove	$5.99
☐ 20429-1	The Falcon and the Flower	$5.99
☐ 20624-3	The Dragon and the Jewel	$5.50
☐ 20623-5	The Pirate and the Pagan	$5.50
☐ 20625-1	Tempted	$4.99
☐ 21135-2	Seduced	$5.99
☐ 21700-8	Enticed	$5.99
☐ 21703-2	Desired	$5.99
☐ 21706-7	Enslaved	$6.50

Dell

At your local bookstore or use this handy page for ordering:

**DELL READERS SERVICE, DEPT. DHR
2451 S. Wolf Rd., Des Plaines, IL . 60018**

Please send me the above title(s). I am enclosing $ _____
(Please add $2.50 per order to cover shipping and handling.) Send
check or money order—no cash or C.O.D.s please.

Ms./Mrs./Mr._____

Address_____

City/State _____ Zip_____

DHR-9/95

Prices and availability subject to change without notice. Please allow four to six
weeks for delivery.